Madame Lune

D1325082

Kathleen Curtin

Published by Open Books

Copyright © 2015 by Kathleen Curtin

Original image "Hollowness" Copyright © Tatiana Susla

Learn more about the artist at be.net/mon-artifice

ISBN: 0692434100
ISBN-13: 978-0692434109

1

"Get away from me!"

Karen gripped her bag as a pair of grubby hands tried to jerk it out of her grasp. Her own voice, coming from the bottom of her stomach and going from a wail to a growl, sounded strange to her ears. She had turned into a fierce creature and would fight for her bag, full of junk or not.

But the thief wasn't letting go. Although caught red-handed, he'd latched onto it like a bull terrier.

A train burst into the station and Karen yelled even louder, yanking the bag harder. This time the urchin fled—without the bag.

She stood panting, completely disorientated; it had all taken place so quickly, leaving her stunned. Though shaken, she hurried along the train platform as she took a handkerchief from her bag to wipe her mouth.

What was wrong with people? Somebody could have asked if she were okay, or made a move to help. But few had even seemed to notice the incident, and those that had, had simply ignored it. And if they hadn't, then it had just been to stare. The residue of anger took her up the steps two by two, and out of the Metro tunnel.

Karen thought: I don't want anything else to come leaping at me, but at least I held on to my stuff.

Her humor hadn't been great, but now it was foul. It had started the evening before on finding a strange note in the letter box. The French words had translated as: "YOU ARE COLLUDING WITH THE DEVIL." They had been printed with a black marker on white paper; the matching white envelope had been without a name. Deciding that it was a bad joke and not worth mentioning to anybody, she had torn it up and dumped it in the bin. It had, nonetheless, left an unpleasant feeling and had been difficult to totally wipe out of her mind; her sleep had been invaded by nasty dreams. Fortunately, her boyfriend, Olivier, was away on a business trip, saving her the trouble of checking to see if he'd grown devilish features. A very early rise and nine hours spent in a noisy, open-plan office had sent her mood plummeting further. And bustling home on the Tramway and Metro had done nothing to ease her nerves.

She hesitated outside Place Blanche Station—do the shopping now or go back to the apartment first? Home was a more attractive option; the supermarket would be too crowded with long queues of edgy people. Clasping her bag, vice-like, she scanned the area before dodging all obstacles criss-crossing the tree-lined pedestrian strip that split Boulevard de Clichy. It was a cluttered zone, like sharing the space with a miniature fair ground. There were homemade sweet confectioners, claw vending machines, and other glittering stands to attract young and old. A group of tourists that were trying to get on board the little train that would carry them to the foot of Sacre Coeur basilica swallowed her up.

She didn't dawdle and waded into the busy space; she was accustomed to battling waves of people swarming all over touristy Paris. The ninth and eighteenth quarters had a good dose of everything: multi-race, multi-religion, caviar-gauche, and Bourgeois-right. There were transvestites, homosexuals, heterosexuals, not to mention prostitutes and drug dealers mixed in with clubs, music shops, cafes, and bistros. A good sprinkling of cinemas, peep shows and tacky sex shops had also been thrown into the stew, making that stretch from Clichy to Pigalle the most raucous and noisiest section. Whatever one sought, this area had it. It was grimy and shabby, like an out-of-date, cheeky postcard; a vulgar mélange, favorably situated between the majestic Sacre Coeur basilica and the elegant Opera Garnier district.

She nodded begrudgingly at the Moulin Rouge, "Old windmill, don't think that you're above it all; you might be steeped in the past, but you're looking frayed too."

Karen stomped up Rue Lepic but felt the need to look over her shoulder several times and put her hand to her inside coat pocket to reassure that her credit cards, phone and most important possessions were there. Great, now she was paranoid.

Despite her ill humor, Rue Lepic enticed and refreshed with its traditional array of dairies, green grocers, cheese and fish mongers, fruit stores, bakers, flower stalls, and news kiosks. The street was like a snake curling and meandering up and up. It was also home to artists and ordinary blow-ins like herself. While she hadn't met other Irish people living on the street, the popular Irish pubs waved her country's flag proudly for all to see.

"*Pardon...*" An old woman in a long grey coat brushed past her.

Karen realized that she had been holding up the entire footpath by standing stupidly in the middle. Now that her temper had calmed somewhat, appreciation of her victory began to take effect. She'd fought off a pickpocket; no, it had been an aggressive thief; child or not, he had been openly and brazenly trying to take her bag. She felt her pockets again; everything was there, but it was still difficult to shed the idea that something was missing.

Ah, home territory; this part of the street was hers. Many of the faces were familiar, and if Karen didn't quite know them by first name, she had labelled all of them after her own fashion: Monsieur Flower-pot; Monsieur Newsstand; Monsieur and Madame Baker; Madame Dairy; and Madame Dry, of the dry cleaner's shop.

"Attention!"

"Shit!" Karen jumped out of the way, just in the nick of time to avoid a crash with the wheels of Madame Trottinette's elected vehicle of transportation.

Madame Trottinette, otherwise known as Madame Lu, was a tiny Vietnamese woman that wove her way around the streets on a skate scooter. As concierges and guardians were fewer or no longer always dedicated to one building, women such as Madame Lu had managed to fill in the gaps. She washed down court yards, entrances and hallways; put the bins out for collection, and undertook a host of other tasks. Karen was very impressed by her industrious nature. Madame Lu also made a speciality out of relieving shopkeepers for lunchtime or coffee break, and often did that for Madame Dry. Come rain, hail or snow, that plucky woman was out there, beavering away and grabbing every opportunity the district had to offer.

Karen saluted Monsieur Abu, the bin man, standing inside the open door of the drycleaner's. The tall, imposing Tunisian was rarely out of the neighborhood. When done with emptying the bins in the morning with the Municipal rubbish collection team, he too would hang around doing odd jobs or stand in to relieve traders. Monsieur Abu also helped out Madame Dry. Karen often wondered what Madame Dry could be doing to need so many breaks in the day; she'd used her cleaning services many times, and while the work was professional, the woman herself was aloof and unfriendly.

It wasn't all sweetness and honey between Monsieur Abu and Madame Lu. Madame Lu often complained that the collection team deliberately forgot to empty a bin. On several occasions, Karen had seen her race down the street, bin in tow, galloping after Monsieur Abu's truck, hollering blistering curses.

Karen pulled out her phone on the first buzz: "Hi Jane, got your message. Are you serious about wanting to see a fortune teller? You are! I see... No, Olivier is away. Where are you? Okay, okay, just let me pop home, off load my office stuff and I'll meet you at our café in, let's say half an hour?"

Karen's spirits rose. It was nice having her best friend living on the same street. She could look forward to a coffee or a hot chocolate and an opportunity to gripe about the terrible day. Having a boyfriend who worked late and travelled a lot on business suited her just fine, too. Lately, however, Olivier had been hinting at making things more permanent. The thought of marriage petrified her; so Karen pushed it to the back of her mind and told herself that she wasn't going to think about it.

The stairs smelled of fresh wax, inviting her to slow down. She didn't want to slip and break a leg. Still, she didn't delay, except to drop her work bag in the entrance of the flat, close the shutters and switch on the hall lamp. A door was opened and shut noisily downstairs. Karen knew what that meant; the old lady, Chantal Moreau, from two floors below, would have left a small bag of rubbish on her landing to be taken to the courtyard bins. It was something Karen had one day offered to do as unfortunately their building didn't have a lift.

"You are a lovely girl." Chantal had smiled gratefully.

"It's no trouble; I pass your door going up and down, so don't hesitate to use me."

"Such a charming girl, and such a pity about the other one."

"Sorry?" The woman sometimes said odd things.

Chantal had moved on, "In the past we had a concierge, but all that has changed."

"I know," Karen had commiserated, "but the company responsible for cleaning the main parts of the building do send someone."

"Yes, but they often send somebody different, so we have strangers coming in non-stop." Chantal had drawn closer to her, "*And things have gone missing.*"

"What sort of things?"

"Some ornaments—the pair of dancing girls."

"You mean somebody got into your apartment and took those lovely Degas replicas?"

"The ornaments are gone. It could have been one of those cleaners; or maybe Monsieur Abu, he goes everywhere."

"Monsieur Abu only goes to places where he has been given the keys. Madame Lu also does jobs for you, doesn't she?"

"No...yes, sometimes." Chantal didn't seem sure. "You can't trust anybody; there are dangerous people around. They'd kill you for your last coin."

Karen had been somewhat taken aback by Chantal's underhanded accusation of Monsieur Abu's ethics but hadn't commented further.

She felt sorry for Chantal. Her husband, Guillaume, had suffered a stroke some years before, and although he'd recovered his ability to walk, his speech remained badly affected. Things frequently went missing in Chantal's place and she'd blame any member of the population considered to be outsiders. In the end, her husband's forgetfulness was often the cause.

Karen sent a text to her friend: *On my way.*

She skipped down the stairs, picked up Chantal's rubbish and disposed of it.

"*Bon soir*, Karen," the voices of Eric and Frederic, her first floor neighbors, chorused from the entrance.

"Hi, guys."

Eric flashed a brochure in front of her: "This is it, our first promotion for the salon."

"Wow, so you're ready to open then." She put a hand through her long, straight blond hair. "I'm sure I'll be one of your first customers."

"Of course you will!" said Eric.

"And we'll be delighted to give you the hundred percent full organic treatment," added Frederic.

"You must be very excited about the opening."

Frederic frowned at the mail box.

"What's the matter?" Karen asked.

"Junkmail."

"People dump everything and anything into those boxes."

Frederic grimaced and crumpled some papers: "Yeah, stupid publicity."

Eric looked close to tears.

Karen slipped away; it clearly wasn't their lucky day.

Jane was dressed casually in a pair of jeans that showed off her wonderful figure and a colorful top. She came across more cosmopolitan than American. They did 'la bise,' and although chilly, decided to stay on the terrace to catch the last of the daylight. Café Lepic was central and convenient and had become their regular lounging place. It was noisy and busy, popular with locals and tourists alike. The gurgling Espresso machine and clatter of crockery made for a permanent background sound.

They saluted Philippe, one of the café's regular waiters, and called for two Espressos. He shook out his tea towel to wipe the table, then relayed their order to the bar with a loud shout and sped off. Philippe was always in a hurry and hassled, whether he had one table or twenty to serve. His traditional black and white uniform sagged, and even on a good day sported a stain or two.

Monsieur Flower-pot hailed them from his stand and they waved back.

"Hell, I don't feel like working this evening." Jane alighted on a wicker chair. "I'm tired of bar work."

"Tony doesn't pay you half well enough. I know you think he's a hunk, but that man's got some gall."

"There are worse, and he *is* a hunk."

"You're too good for him, and you've got nothing in common."

"He's American, and I'm American."

"Running a fake Irish bar called Fintan Corner; I mean—"

"I know, I know; the spelling. He blames it on a French sign maker. But you must admit that Irish pubs are good business." Jane put forward a well-rehearsed defense of Tony. He was the owner and the one taking the risks, while she was just a bar tender; and they did occasionally have Irish barmen.

Karen yawned, "So you are going to a fortune teller find out about you and Tony?"

"Not really. Although I still think it might be destiny calling; imagine finding that slip of paper in my coat pocket: 'Madame Lune, Medium/Voyant. I wasn't looking for it, wasn't even thinking about a fortune teller, or anything of the sort."

"You probably put that there a long time ago and forgot about it. Those fliers are everywhere. What kills me is that these people pretend to be able to do everything, when in fact they are just quacks whose main aim is to take your fortune."

Jane told her that her only experience with fortune tellers had been at a party when a woman had whispered something to her that nobody could have known. Somebody had told her later that the woman was a medium.

"I usually do things on intuition." Jane turned to face her, "I've had few flashes like that in my life, but each time I've heeded them, they have saved my life."

"Saved your life?" There was something unsettling about how the words had been spoken.

Jane nodded but didn't seem willing to explain.

Karen didn't press to know more. Who was she to tell others what or what not to do? Jane's first love was art, and she asked for nothing more than to set up her easel in some part of the city and sketch for hours and hours. That was her heaven. Lately, she'd started experimenting with designing and making jewelry. Working in a bar at night freed her day and gave her scope to live her dream. One could only admire such dedication.

Yet Jane was still a mystery to her in many ways. They had only known each other for a few months, but they had become best friends immediately. It was just one of those things; you didn't need to know everything about someone to appreciate them. Karen sincerely felt that they would be friends for life. Jane was adventurous whereas she'd always been a homebody and had shown no sign of having itchy feet. Taking the decision to come to Paris had been something of a surprise to everyone. While it had seemed like going against nature, all children had to get out from under their parents' wings and prove that they could do something. French had been her best subject in school, and that along with a solid business degree had opened doors. Who could turn down an offer to go to Paris? The only problem was that she'd absolutely no ambitions to work in a global company and scrape her way around the bottom rung of the ladder; no, that hadn't been a major motivation. Then Olivier had come along at a time when she'd been struggling on all fronts and had been seriously considering returning to Ireland. Everything had moved quickly after that...

"Karen? Karen?" Jane was butting into her thoughts.

"What?"

"You've gone off into your own world again. I've never met anyone with a knack of day dreaming quite like you."

"I'm sorry; it's a skill I've perfected at the office."

"Only at the office?"

Karen blushed.

"Just pulling your leg. Olivier is very—"

"Safe? Is that what you want to say?"

"No, he's more complicated than you give him credit for."

"He's ten years older; that makes a difference."

"Oh, it does. Secret is the word I was looking for—that's what Olivier is..."

Karen raised her brows in puzzlement, but her friend was already foraging in her bag. Jane fished out a small plastic sachet and offered it to her. It was a beautiful pair of earrings made from crystal fragments.

Karen held them up to allow the sunlight to illuminate the crystal. "I'll wear them and treasure them; in fact, I'll put them on right now."

She studied her face in the café mirror and grinned back at Jane: "I really do love them." Part of the street reflected back at her, "You could paint Rue Lepic using that mirror perspective. Monsieur Newsstand looks less grumpy through the glass."

"I'm glad you like the earrings," Jane said. "I've started to design many more. It's not Monsieur Newsstand's depressing face I see though; it's the wonderful colors from Monsieur Flower-pot's stand. Look at how they bounce off the crystal." Jane's face lit up, "That gives me an idea; don't move, I want to sketch something." Her pencil and pad were already on the table.

Karen obliged. Jane was irresistible like that; it was great seeing her creative mind at work. They had often discussed the possibility of opening a business together; with Jane's creativity and her own business background, it wasn't out of the question.

The lights came on. Karen glanced at the sky; they would just have to accept that the days were getting shorter and the next season galloping in. Sensing eyes on them, she looked around and then checked that her bag was at her feet. A thought came to her: she searched her jacket pockets. "Damn it, of course; Mum's postcards."

"What on earth are you talking about?"

"Oh, a pickpocket tried to steal my bag earlier. He didn't get it, but I think an envelope must have fallen out of my pocket during the struggle."

"Was it important?"

"It had a letter and samples of postcards that Mum and Dad have designed to promote their B&B in Ballybunion. I'd planned to show them to you and had tucked the envelope in there."

"Like you said, it probably just fell out."

Karen looked behind her convinced that someone had tapped her on the shoulder, but nobody was there.

"What now? You wouldn't do well sitting for a portrait."

"Sorry, it was nothing, just a shoulder twinge," Karen turned her attention back to the street but dusk was falling and visibility was poorer. What was wrong with her? Why did she feel like someone was watching them? That was plain silly; the pickpocket incident had put her on edge—that was all.

2

I stand in the darkness of the room and watch the street as the day turns to night. I have been watching for a long time, upright for hours until my limbs are deadened and my entire body is without feeling. One group of businesses shuts down for the evening and another opens its doors. A new set of characters arrives and the most ancient trade of all becomes more visible. Every day, layers of life interweave. The whores and pimps are so well painted into the background that the eye takes them for granted—you see them and you don't. In summer, amongst the mass of tourists, they mingle well, but when winter comes and the street is barer they peck the pavements like hungry pigeons searching for crumbs; they dare more, hustle more and show more. Alongside them, sometimes through them, addicts and abusers are drawn to the sellers of foul chemicals and substances that erode the mind. I do not understand them. Why make yourself sick until you can no longer function—until you die? The dealer is easier to understand than the user, just as the pimps and the whores are. I even understand Pierre and know what his enjoyment is. One does not forget what a fruity glass of wine can bring; but a second glass strips and erodes what is most important to me. It interferes with my senses—the skills of survival. It would have been better had I been born an animal; I am an animal—almost.

Pierre is satisfying himself at the café. It is too late to change a man whose mind is numb from years of smoking and drinking rich Bordeaux. His eyes are drawn to the street corner. That whore is older than the others and weathered by years of service. He will take his pleasure there as often before and cannot be blamed for that; I have certainly never sought to restrain him. He will spend all that we have, and tomorrow I will have to earn again. Pierre holds little interest for me, and yet, he is difficult to shake off. Have I really tried very hard? It is not my desire to be cruel, for I have seen his lifeline fading.

America goes down the street. Jane Moore is a simple immigrant resident and not part of the game. Though carrying many bruises from life, she has hopes and dreams but for now must bide her time as a bar tender. My fear is that it no longer matters what America does, for she may never fulfil her dreams.

Jane will come here soon. I rarely receive people anymore but will make an exception. It is because of the other eyes that are watching. The words come to me like a bad dream and will not go away. They are telling me that America is living out her last days. Tonight I am confused: it is not like me; it is her life, not mine. It is not my business. I have never concerned myself with anybody else's business. There is an explanation and it lies in those postcards in my hand. It is not the written words, but what the pictures show. Those cliffs and that sea speak to me. I press the cardboard to my face and can almost the smell the seaweed and taste the salt and iodine. Jane's friend has forced her way into my life, awakening a sensation that has been long dormant. Something deep inside stirs and compels me, and I fear it will carry me on a journey that will cost me dearly.

The wallet is empty and the cupboards are bare. Damn Pierre, he has blown it all, and not just at a café terrace or on a whore; he has also taken money for his son, Dimitri. I should have known—he cannot say no to him. I would have given Pierre's son something, but not that much. Dimitri is not my responsibility, he is not mine. When I came into Pierre's life, his son was in the hands of his alcoholic mother. By the time the boy was a teenager, he was following in her footsteps. It is not all Pierre's fault; he did his best by him. However, Pierre is weak, has always been so; he has never been able to stand his ground and will cushion Dimitri to the end. I have passed that boy many times; crossed his haunts around the city, found him drunk and begging. He never tried to talk to me, and I have never had a conversation with him. His mother died on the streets and Dimitri will die in the same way. I curse Pierre once more, then swallow my words; I am not his provider, nor his doormat, but will have to go out again, for we have not made enough to see us through the week. Still, I forgive him, because many years ago he was good to me and provided the essentials when I was unable to do so. Pierre took me in and accepted me when nobody else would have. It is for that reason I forgive him for all his deceit and lies. I do not know if he has ever understood my silence. I do know that he understood my words when it was important not to pry. There is that between us. So, I leave him to his whore and he knows my limits. That whore has been trading for years and takes no risks; I trust her, rather than Pierre.

If there is more in me, I have never shown it to Pierre. However, those seaside pictures have made me remember what I wanted to forget. They take me back to the child racing across the sand, running from the breaking waves. The child is no longer there; in her place stands an old woman who cannot run fast enough from the tide of memories that are sweeping in and flooding her mind.

The tourist train goes merrily up the hill; the passengers shout out, HURRAY! Their joy cannot lift the shadow that I see. It grows darker and darker and is cast by a creature that thrives in darkness. There is a monster out there watching those girls as they walk Rue Lepic or sit on the café terrace. He has chosen America to be his sacrifice, but they are bound and intertwined and my fear is that she who brings the sea, the Irish girl, will have to fall too. I am chilled to the bone as never before.

The weather has turned; the autumn wind is howling through the cracks and keyholes. The flat is draughty because it is not insulated. The rain lashes down as I lay on the bed and think about having to go out in a few hours. Sleep does not answer to my commands. The blankets over me are warm, but I am touched by neither warmth nor comfort. The elements rage outside and the sleeping hour has passed. I am coming down with something, maybe the flu, but I must not give in yet. I have to get up soon and try to find the rent money. It is important to stay one step ahead. How much longer will this body be able to run? The child is before me again, racing away from the incoming tide; her little legs carry her as quickly as they can. If she stands still, the water will catch her, swell and swirl, and eventually take her under. Would it be so bad? It might be a relief—giving in—giving up. What difference would it make to anybody? It is not for now, it is not the time; I have to stay one step ahead of the tide.

It is morning, my morning, it is four o' clock. My body is hot with a burning temperature. I push my heavy legs onto the floor, Move, old woman, move! My limbs obey slowly; a weary set of bones shake and ache so much that it pains me to shower. I make some coffee and let the liquid enter my system. My throat is dry and it hurts to swallow.

The rain has stopped. Would that I could stay at my window today, but Pierre has left me with no choice. He has had a good night and knows not to come home for several days. I will say nothing, I never do.

I have many words but they are all in my head. Speaking is not my strength, listening is. I have listened all my life; it is one of my main sources of knowledge. There is a fear of words in me because I do not master them. My own words when expressed are not pretty; my tongue does not sculpt the sounds well—they are alien, hostile sounds out of control. Once they have touched my tongue, they splinter off and recite something unrecognizable, even to me.

I return to base, dissatisfied; my pickings have not been enough and I will have to scour my own district to make up what we need for the week. Everything has come alive. An accordion sounds from Place du Tertre, the artists' plaza. The player is not French and is bluffing his way through the tune. Nobody is bothered; Paris is supposed to sound of accordion music.

Even the young mount the steps with difficulty to Sacre Coeur basilica. Age is telling on me. I do not often think about that and rarely count the calendar years, but today no pretence is required to embrace the body of an elderly woman. My clothes are not fashionable, just ordinary; the aim is not to stand out in any way, one must never stand out. Ordinary people go unnoticed.

The basilica is before me, aloof and haughty. Some people call it majestic; I do not know if it is. The scent of incense and candles draws me inside, along with scores of visitors, cameras and accents—a collage of different countries. Silence is called for and for the most part respected. It is easy to follow the shuffling invasion of this sacred monument. I make my way to a pew and kneel, bowing my head in prayer. It is wise to stay on my knees for a while before sitting up and staring straight ahead to the main altar, yet ever watchful of the movements of people in the aisles. *Watch, old woman; watch until you find what you are looking for; wait for the sign.* The sign comes instinctively from a lifetime of experience. I fix my eye on it, slip out of the row of seats and synchronize my entrance back into the crowd.

By the time the crowd takes me to the main door, a day's work has been done. It is the moment to drift outside with the impatient tourists. I walk back down the steps, dally in the artists' plaza to observe the posturing and posing of artists and subjects, and witness money being spent on air.

A bench awaits me. It is not good to do what I have done, or to go against what your body is telling you. I will sit for a while and try to recover enough energy to walk again. The flu must run its cycle. It is not the flu that concerns me; there is another sickness in my stomach—an intense nausea. It is not caused by a fever, but because I have seen his shadow again and have watched him watching. I have tried to ignore it and cannot. It is impossible to rid myself of it, no more than a fox can forget the presence of the hunter. I see him, though he does not see me; I am not what the monster is looking for or looking at.

I make her understand that she is to leave the money in the bowl on the table.

She does as I bid, though is puzzled when I do not check it.

Her coming here is my doing, a force pushing against my will; she is the one I was drawn to see first and to lure here. It is my own fault for putting Madame Lune's number in her purse. Following my usual routine I did not answer the telephone personally, but listened to her message then got Pierre to ring back to arrange the appointment.

The light is sombre and hides the starkness of the flat. I have tried to create the best conditions to work in. The pieces of furniture are of cheap wood, cast-offs, but have been uplifted with richly colored cushions, covers and quilts. The effect is of deep purple, blues and sweet Fuchsia. Everything is set up and in its rightful place, exactly where it should be. You have to give people what they expect; do not disappoint. I have draped heavy crimson curtains around the séance room and placed a crystal ball at the center of the table. Beside it is a silk purse containing Tarot cards. There is some essence burning in a lamp and angel music playing softly in the background. I am dressed in a long black dress, softened by a mauve shawl, and have adorned myself with cheap jewelry. My head is covered with a veil; it is a glittery dark grey and camouflages the essentials. She must not know me, they must never know me. My disguises are many; they are my protection and security. Because speaking is not my talent, the words I use have been put down on large cards; they are neither natural nor spontaneous. Pierre, who understands my impaired speech, has always written down what I want. There is a piece of chalk and slate nearby for any sketch I may add during the reading. My approach captivates the naïve and the needy. By staying within the lines that have been rehearsed and learned by heart, I succeed in making them believe. I am not in my skin, but in that of another. Although it is not comfortable, it is efficient.

In the early years when I told fortunes more often, I prepared meticulously in advance for each client and never received more than one or two a day. Now it is a year. I would memorize a system whereby Pierre organized the cards according to a sequence; from the mysterious and dramatic images on the Tarots to the words and handwritten sentences on other cards, and my own drawings. Pierre would sit in the next room in case his services were required. Today, I will work without him.

I point Jane to where I want her to sit.

She is impressed and obeys.

Even the most skeptical are wary of the future. They

are unsure: Maybe this fortune teller has a special gift; perhaps she can tell them something... Unfortunately, I see too much and know too much of what is not my business; I have the knowledge of the watcher. This session must not last longer than twenty minutes; she will be shown some things and will leave. Jane will go and will be given back her money; one cannot accept the money of someone who has been condemned. I will not have blood on my hands; the blood is there anyway because I cannot tell her the truth.

I will communicate basic things to her. It used to surprise me how people reacted to such information; it no longer does. She is a beautiful girl and bubbling with life. I see what can be seen in many—a yen for something that I have never understood; a longing for a place, a home; seeking to be someone, to be considered. It is easy to recognize those emotions, but not to feel them. I must have known them a long time ago, I surely must; but now they are far away and difficult to trace.

It is Madame Lune's moment; she draws the series of love cards and puts together what is so evident, so obvious to a watcher. There is light in Jane Moore's eyes; an aspiration and a flame that I have never had. Madame Lune does not explain what is most important—that she is lying because the truly vital information never escapes her. How can you tell someone that they will leave it all behind? It is not for Madame Lune to tell her that. This medium has not seen it in the stars, or in the cards—and the crystal ball is just the way to light up a globe. Yet, I have seen the hunter and where his eyes go and know his quarry.

I look at her and turn tormented thoughts in my head. Your name is Jane Moore, I call you America; you have a beauty inside that does not deserve to die. With your past, you should have been bitter, angry and wretched; you are none of those things. Can it be that you were meant to die young? Will you be another innocent victim of his madness? Can someone walk away from what they know? "God," if there is a God, "take me away from this and lift the burden from me. My brain is lacking; it has neither the intelligence nor the cleverness to counter him. Do not put that on my plate. Quiet, old woman—who are you talking to? Forget God, there is nobody who can hear you. Your life is not bound to hers or to that of her Irish friend."

"Hush," the words are repeated silently in my head; "you owe nothing to anybody except to follow your own path to the end. You must keep going because there is nothing to go back to." And suddenly it is clearer to me; it is because I could have been like he who stands and watches—a dark shadow of a monster with feral instincts; nothing more than a rodent.

Jane Moore does not understand when I return the money to her and does not want to accept it. I push it into her hand, it is my only escape. It is better to have nothing to do with her or her life or what will end her life. It makes me maladroit and inept; but she does not notice and only remembers that I have filled her mind with the treasures life has to offer her. I wish Madame Lune had not drawn her. It is too late for regrets; I opened my door because something forced my hand. The hurt and wounds of her past are so visible on her face, but Jane has the instinct of survival. She is a creature who has learned to crawl, to beg, and to fight her way. I have a certain respect for her. "Go away, Jane Moore; go back to America." I hurry her through the door and shake my head when she offers the money once again.

Jane is gone and I stand alone at the window. She takes out her phone and is talking to her friend; to the girl who brought the smell of the sea to my street. It is not just any sea, it is my sea. My eyes go farther, to where the shadows cluster, to where the monster watches. May the eyes that stare from the other side of the street be blighted! The monster is always watching—he sees it all and knows everyone. When night is truly there, he sneaks out again and slinks by, following a trail. I do not know where he goes, but I must find out what draws him into the night. I have rarely been afraid of anyone or anything in my life. Death has not been something to agonize over; it will be and I will accept it when it comes, when it is time. Yet I am afraid of him...

A shaft of gloom distracts me. His shadow is moving, and it burns through me. I do not like that kind of fear. If only I could run; but try as I might, there is no escape. There is no choice—I have to know where he goes.

3

Karen heard the key in the door and automatically contracted.

"Hello!" Olivier dropped his bags with a thud and beamed broadly. "It's great to be home; what an exhausting trip."

She turned her face for his kiss, her skin grated by his stubble and her nose catching the slightly garlicky smell of his breath. She couldn't help her feelings of resentment. It wasn't right to feel that way, but perhaps it was better to admit it, at least to herself. He would want to go to Chez Gerard's for dinner, and she wasn't up to going there, or anywhere else.

"Let's eat right away, I'm hungry." He kissed her again, this time taking her full on the lips.

"Are you that hungry?" Karen hoped he would notice the reluctance behind her question.

He didn't: "I'm ravenous."

She had put on three kilos after they'd moved in together and had struggled to lose them, succeeding mainly because Olivier was away on business trips so often. When living by herself, there hadn't been dinners, not real dinners. With Olivier, meals and meal times were important, and no meal was complete without baguette, meat and cheese.

Chez Gerard was a simple bistro that served solidly French food from the Auvergne. Olivier was eating too fast, again. She hated it when he did that. To make it worse, he didn't always close his mouth when chewing his food. Olivier de Belleville—it was a fine Bourgeois name, and until meeting Olivier her belief was that such families raised their children with better table manners. Karen tried to tune out, but didn't succeed. Olivier was in great form; they were going to have a long weekend together, for the first time in ages. She should be looking forward to it, but in fact she was not. What was wrong with her? When had this 'I'm fed up with our life together' feeling tiptoed up on her? She'd been very content with Olivier—or maybe dependent upon him, it was better not to analyse. A few months back, his habits hadn't irritated her at all. 'Make an effort,' she told herself.

"So, did you manage to sign that IT contract?"

"Oh yes, but it was a hard nut to crack, so many details to hammer out. Let me tell you..." Olivier swirled a mouthful of wine before letting it slip noisily down his throat.

Karen tried to ignore his wine stained teeth, the day's growth on his cheeks and chin, the wrinkles on his shirt after a full day's travel. Overlooking his questionable manners and poor grooming seemed to have become quite a habit, and she also seemed to be growing more and more adept at pretending to give her attention even as her thoughts were miles away. With Oliver, it was easy to do. She simply launched a question, then fifteen or twenty minutes later, she launched another. He talked, not to her but to himself. Her thoughts strayed during his monologues. Olivier didn't seem to notice, and that suited her fine.

Olivier's natural, earthy characteristics had at first attracted her, but she had begun to wonder if there wasn't just a bit too much primitive to him. It was difficult not to be revolted, or at least put off, by the food churning around inside his mouth—it was like looking through the window of a washing machine. 'You're just being bitchy,' she admonished herself. 'You're having an off day, that's all.'

She was still not used to being referred to as 'Olivier and Karen', or 'Karen and Olivier' for that matter. That sort of identification did not wholly appeal. She was only twenty-six, and if Olivier had his way, she would soon be marrying him and probably having lots of children. They'd only been living together for six months and already it felt like they were an old married couple, like Chantal and Guillaume. Olivier, with his penchant for good food and fine wine, might in fact turn out to be a second Guillaume. His dining habits and his smoking might eventually lead to a stroke, and then she'd be looking after him for life. The thought gave her panic attacks.

She tried to bring her wayward self into line, but it was no use. Olivier talked IT, and her mind wandered.

It would probably be better to take a leaf from Jane's book, she thought. Her friend kept her independence and remained true to her nature: the result was a free and easy spirit. There was just something so carefree about the way Jane handled Parisian life. Okay, the late night pub job wasn't all that convenient, nor was her rented *chambre de bonne* a comfortable number (those little rooms had served as servants' quarters in the past, and still did, though these days they were more often than not rented as rooms for students and au-pairs, and the best of them had minimum facilities: washbasin and a shared toilet in the corridor; showers were rare) but Jane worked around such deficiencies with plastic basins and tubs. Jane never complained; she just knuckled down to living there. She said the room had wonderful light in which to do her art work. Jane had the admirable quality of being able to look at the bright side of everything. Karen tried to do the same and began ticking off Olivier's positive points: he was generous and never counted his money; she often had to fight with him to stop him from buying things for her. And here he was doing it again, taking out his credit card to pay for the meal.

"I'll pay, Olivier."

"No, let me."

"It's my turn..." It felt important to her to hang onto that shred of self-respect. His generosity sometimes made her feel mean. This time he gave in, but in compensation he wrapped his big arm around her shoulders. That gesture used to make her feel protected, but lately it felt smothering.

Karen sat on the bed in pyjamas listening to Olivier's gawky movements in the shower. He never sang, only hummed. And from the sounds coming from within, it seemed that he was forever bumping knees or elbows against the walls. A moment later he lumbered out of the bathroom and caught her eye. He wasn't very tall but had broad shoulders. A mat of dark hair defined his pale chest. His square jaw seemed always to be at work; however it was his brown eyes doing that weird twist of showing the whites—a tick he displayed of which he was neither aware nor in control—that stayed with her. Her continuing appraisal rested finally on his engorged shank. Why count imperfections when someone so well-endowed was about to ravish her?

Yet, Karen braced herself to respond to his love making. The last few times had not been good. The change seemed to have come after she had moved in with him. It was gradual at first: little things that resulted in him being less sensitive to her needs. It was almost as if he didn't feel he had to make an effort anymore. However, more recently, Karen sometimes thought she was with a stranger, as if the man beside her were possessed by somebody else.

Olivier made it in two strides to the bed. "We won't need that," a few brusque gestures made short work of her pyjama top, "or those," her pyjama bottoms were dragged off even less skilfully.

Before she could react or try to set the tempo, Olivier had pounced on her, his heavily muscled legs pinning and caging her. It was impossible to move; she had a moment of panic verging on claustrophobia and wanted to escape. She pushed against his shoulders. "Olivier..."

"Shush," he dismissed her efforts, shifting his weight and digging his hands into her flesh.

Karen cried out, "Ouch, stop, that hurts."

Her plea was cut short as he emitted a low growl and rose over her.

Karen tried a second time to redirect him, but Olivier was oblivious. Once again the whites of his eyes startled her. She wriggled desperately for room—

He laughed, "Want to play games, do you?" It sounded like a sinister threat. He pushed her back onto the mattress more brutally.

"It's not a game," She caught his wrist, making another effort to slow things down.

Olivier brushed her hand off impatiently and used his strength to lock her firmly in place. He was immune to her words or touch.

Her arms dropped helplessly to her side and her breathing stopped. Panic returned—this time overwhelming and paralyzing her. She tried to speak but the words stuck in her throat. Her eyes focused only on his open mouth, sweat covered face and white eyeballs. Her ears heard only his grunts and muttered obscenities while he sought his own satisfaction. There was pain and numbness and nothingness. Suddenly he shouted out something unintelligible and crashed completely on top of her. For several seconds he remained pasted to her and then rolled off, still panting loudly. After a few wordless minutes, he yawned, turned over and tugged at the blankets. Soon his snoring filled the otherwise silent bedroom.

It had all taken place in an instant. Stunned by what had happened, Karen lay there mute. The entire act had left her humiliated and confused. She wanted to leave and never return, but she didn't have the courage to move. What had happened tonight was the worst...ever. He hadn't even kissed her, or called her name. She didn't want to put words on the act—was afraid to try.

She heard shouts coming up from the street—a couple of drunks arguing. A car door banged and the siren of an ambulance sounded from farther off. She wiped away a tear and drifted off to an uneasy sleep.

Was that incessant ringing and banging in her dreams? No, it was at the door. Karen shoved her foot against Olivier. He did not wake. She shoved harder: "Hey, somebody's at the door."

He looked at the time: "It's eight o'clock on a Saturday morning, too early to have visitors."

Karen got out of bed, bitter and angry. At one time during the night he had reached out for her, but she had moved away and kept to the edge of the mattress. Her thoughts had turned and turned, but the conclusion was the same: Olivier was all wrong for her. She would talk to him frankly about his behavior and tell him that they couldn't go on like that. She walked to the chair for her dressing gown and noticed the large black bruises all over her. She tightened the robe around her waist.

"Please, please!" somebody shouted.

"Alright, alright, coming..." Karen looked through the spy hole. Chantal—what the hell? She opened the door: "Chantal, what's the matter?"

Behind her, Olivier thumped across the floorboards, looking for something to wear.

Chantal was breathless. "Somebody threw a stone through our window."

"A stone? Is the window broken?"

"Come with me, I'll show you," Chantal urged. "I always leave the bathroom window open; it sailed right through."

"I'm going downstairs," Karen called over her shoulder to Olivier.

"I'll be right with you, just getting my shoes."

Karen followed Chantal inside her apartment, "Hello, Guillaume." It was hard to think of anything else to say to the emotionless man sitting on an armchair by the window. He looked like a wax figure and sounded like a robot as he mumbled some reply.

"There!" Chantal pointed to floor: "There it is!"

It was not a stone, but a rock. Obviously, it was no accident. "Did you call the police?"

"Yes, no, I can't remember. But look! This was wrapped around the stone." Chantal held out a piece of paper.

"You shouldn't put finger prints on that, Chantal." Her advice came too late, the old lady had clearly been holding it all along.

Karen read the message, translating the French words as 'GET OUT OF HERE!' "Whatever do they mean by that?"

Chantal flapped her arms: "I don't know, I don't know."

Olivier bustled in and said, "The police have arrived. Eric and Frederic called them. Somebody threw a rock through their window."

Chantal wrung her hands: "No, not another."

Olivier scratched his head and Karen handed him the note. He read it, grimly, and said, "It's better to let the police deal with this."

"There are bad people on the streets at night." Chantal stared at Olivier with unfriendly eyes. "Bad people in this building and on the street."

"Who are you talking about?" Karen looked from Chantal to Olivier, surprised to see a flush on his face.

"Bad people," Chantal rambled on.

"Let's go downstairs." Olivier turned abruptly and left.

For a moment Karen had thought that Chantal was going to accuse Olivier of the deed, but concluded that she was not in her right senses. They went down to the next floor where Eric and Frederic were in the midst of a long explanation to two gendarmes.

Karen saw the stone on the floor and a piece of paper next to it. Its hateful message was without ambiguity: it had a cross painted in red and next to it was scrawled the words 'GET OUT—UNNATURAL BASTARDS!'

"I don't know why someone would do that," Jane said, disgusted. "That's just sick."

"Well, they did." Karen eyed with some suspicion Monsieur Abu going up the street and Madame Lu going down the street; maybe they'd had an argument and had started firing rocks. They could have been in the courtyard scratching at each other over bins. "The police said that it was probably vandals, and if nothing else happens, then we should forget about it."

"I'm sure they have had other letters but were too upset to report it."

Karen clanked her glass on the table and told Jane about the note she had once received.

"What! Did you inform the police?"

Karen shook her head: "I haven't even told Olivier. I'm beginning to think now that it might have been meant for Eric or Frederic."

"It's just some spiteful person, and maybe you are right to ignore it. I think they are trying to put it behind them, otherwise they wouldn't be organizing this get together."

Jane was referring to Eric and Frederic's invitation for a drink at their apartment to combine celebrating Neighbor's

Day with the opening of their organic hairdressing salon. They both had agreed that it was a courageous way to forget the ugly business about the stones.

"Hello there!" came a loud greeting.

"I think he's cute," Karen returned Monsieur Flowerpot's wave; it helped to restore her form.

"I guess so."

"Not cute enough for you. I know, I know, you don't like his cold smile and pale eyes."

Jane dropped her tone to a whisper: "I haven't spoken about the medium, but Madame Lune was amazing; she told me so many things that were true."

"They always do; they are very good at reading what they see in front of them. We give a lot of information away with our body language, our clothes, our expression, all of that... There's really nothing remarkable about it. You call her a medium, but I think fortune-teller is a more appropriate term."

"I want to learn how to do that. I've heard that, potentially, we all have the gift."

"Jane, since I've known you, you've had several part-time jobs. Do you have time for another?"

Jane was too buoyed with enthusiasm to be discouraged. "This is different: this isn't a job; this would be a *vocation*."

"She took your money; that hardly suggests a vocation," Karen said, trying to make her friend acknowledge common sense.

"That's the crazy thing about it: Madame Lune insisted that I take back the money. What do you think about that?"

"That's probably to impress you, to get you to come again and to bring more clients. It's a tactic to get you hooked. You know how people are; we get a sample of something, and then before we know it, we're addicted."

Jane tasted her hot chocolate, savoring it. "You're too cynical. But I do intend to go back, partly because of feeling guilty about not paying for her service. And sure, I guess if I can bring you along with me, I will."

"Not me... I won't be consulting a fortune-teller." Let it go, Karen thought. Jane's eyes were glowing with hope. Why spoil her fun just because she was grumpy?

Jane bent closer: "I'm going to meet someone."

"Really?" This time Karen totally failed to keep her cynicism hidden.

"There is a man that I already know who likes me a lot..."

"And you think that it's Tony, don't you?"

"I do see him every day."

"Every night, you mean."

"For work; but—"

"Okay, okay..."

"Maybe I can't convince you, but Madame Lune is the real deal. There were so many other things she said that were so true."

"Maybe for you..." Karen drank her wine rather too quickly.

"You're not going to dampen my newfound zeal. You're just bored with things these days. I'm going to find out about this tarot thing; and guess what? You'll be my first client! I'll do it for free, of course. Anyway, you absolutely must go see this woman."

Karen ordered another glass of wine. Olivier had gone to Marseilles on business and she was over indulging, enjoying much too much having the place all to herself.

Karen bounced up the stairs, bolstered by the two glasses of wine she'd drunk with Jane. "Bonsoir, Chantal," she called to her neighbor.

"Bonsoir, Karen."

"Do you want me to take that?" Chantal was making her way down the stairs, step by careful step, while gripping the plastic rubbish bag in her hand.

"You are so kind." Chantal touched her cheek lightly,

"Such a nice neighbor."

The woman seemed frailer than usual. Karen remembered Chantal telling her how they'd lost their son to cancer, and how her thankless nieces and nephews, whose birthdays she always remembered, never visited. The story reminded Karen of her own family. She had great parents, but had been taking them for granted lately. They had all been bereft after the passing of her grandfather; he'd been such an important presence in their lives. She should call them more often, rather than wait for them to do it. Her mother would scold her, but then forgive her so easily. Perhaps that was why helping Chantal Moreau alleviated her conscience. Still, her parents were much younger than Chantal and didn't really need her help. Back in Ballybunion, everyone talked about Tom and Shelia Moroney. Not only did they run a successful B&B and a farm, but her father also turned his hand to renovation work, and her mother was involved in every charity and organization for the good of the community. They were super parents, super neighbors, super citizens— super people—full stop. Perhaps that was why she and her brothers too, Eamon and Gerard, had felt the need to move away from home. They had to leave the shade to capture some light for themselves. They had even chosen different continents, Eamon in America, Gerard in South Africa; although recently both of her brothers had been hinting at returning to Ireland.

Karen had been thinking a lot of her grandfather; she'd come to appreciate him in his later years and had loved listening to his stories. Now her relationship with her parents was even more vital. Her mind was made up to spend quality time with all her family next Christmas. Besides, she missed them.

It wasn't good to worry and fret about things, but something about Chantal seemed to put her in that frame of mind. Karen slammed the lid on the bin and shivered— better get back into the warmth of the apartment and snuggle up. She looked forward to a lazy night in—those moments alone were heaven. Should she be thinking like that? Olivier would be away for a few days and she would have time to really think about their relationship—the good, the not so good, and the downright ugly! But it wasn't really his fault. Or was it? Her intention of talking to him about their relationship, firm at first then put off again and again, hadn't materialized. He'd been working late, gone early each morning and now away on business. Actually, it had been a relief to put off dealing with it... 'You're just a coward Karen Moroney, that's what you are.'

She couldn't help wondering about Jane's family; but it was obviously something her friend was not inclined to talk about. Jane had been in France a number of years, and although the American still came out in her, many traits had been neutralized, especially her accent. It was as if part of her past had been wiped out, making space for something new. She had mentioned once that one of her grandparents had been French, which had made it easier to get her residency and work permit sorted out.

Karen took a tissue out of her pocket. I should have done a minor spring cleaning while in the courtyard, she mused. Over the kitchen bin she shook out her coat pockets. How do things accumulate like that? There was a collection of used tissues, a few centimes, a paper clip and a receipt. No, that was not a receipt. What was it? Karen read the weathered and soiled piece of paper: 'Madame Lune: Medium/Voyant.' How did that get there? She thought about throwing it away then hesitated, changed her mind and put it back inside her pocket.

Jane dropped in at Karen's apartment before going on to Eric and Frederic's get together. "I'm reading!" she announced.

"You don't say..."

"You don't understand; can't you see it? Can't you just feel it?"

"See what? Feel what?"

"My second sight! I'm learning how to see into people's past, present and future by studying the Tarot."

"You're already sharp at sizing people up."

"There's a lot more to it than that."

"So when do you plan to start your new business?"

"Maybe I can generate some interest tonight."

"It's a party, Jane, not a séance."

"Don't worry, I'm not going to embarrass anyone, but we could just let it out casually about my skills, while not actually trolling for business."

Karen gave in: "Why not? What harm will it do?"

* * * *

Eric and Frederic were upbeat and made every effort to welcome people to their apartment. Frederic was older, closer to forty, and kept his black hair tightly cropped. His muscled arms sported several tattoos. Eric was around thirty and of a slighter build, his brown hair styled in a James Dean look. Frederic favored casual outfits, and was usually in jeans and black tops and shirts, while Eric switched from colorful jeans to serious suits depending on the occasion. This evening it was denim and white shirts for both.

"We had been searching a long time to find the right space for our salon, and at a fair price, too," Fredric explained. "We had the idea ever since Eric had to stop working because of his allergies to chemical products."

Chantal seemed interested: "Is it really organic?"

"One hundred percent," Eric puffed. "It's the only hundred percent organic salon in Paris—no, in France!"

"Where will it be located?" Chantal squinted through bespectacled eyes.

"The perfect place! It is situated on Rue Douai, just behind the supermarket." Eric gave her a brochure.

"And we are super excited!" Frederic said.

"You should be," Jane clapped, "it is sure to succeed with Eric's flair and your business acumen."

Frederic blossomed under the compliments. "And it was confirmed when Jane picked it up in the cards," he revealed.

"Is that a fact?" Karen looked open-mouthed at Jane.

"Yes," Eric said; "she has a superb talent. So where is Olivier?"

"He sends his apology; he had a business trip."

"Is that so?" Frederic exchanged looks with Eric.

Chantal tugged on Eric's arm: "If you will excuse me, old folks don't have the stamina of young people. Thank you for inviting me, but I must go now to take care of Guillaume."

"Bye, darling..." Eric kissed the back of her hand.

"Bye, Chantal." Frederic kissed her on the cheek and opened the door gallantly.

"Such a sweet woman," Eric said. "She gave us a nice bouquet of flowers last week."

"It was too generous," Frederic agreed.

The doorbell buzzed.

"Excuse me," Frederic said as he moved to the door. "Oh, Madame Lu, you are very welcome, come right in."

The doorbell rang again thirty seconds later, "Hello, Monsieur Abu, you are welcome too."

Now that should add a few sparks to this sedate party, Karen thought.

4

The door slams—Pierre is there looking at me. I know what that look means; he wants me to make breakfast for him, at least make the coffee. No words pass between us. It was not always that way; Pierre is a talker, loves to talk. That is why he goes out; the silence in here frightens him. I should throw him out, for he is useless and faithless. I will never do that—cannot, for I remember the past and see myself very well. I will make his coffee and put bread on the table. He is a thread; there are very few left to hang on to; but the date is on his face these past months, it is printed more and more clearly. He sits at the table and begins to eat slowly and ponderously. I leave him and go outside.

In the building or on the streets, I transform easily, but can also be myself. When shopping or living the other part of my day to day life, I am an old woman, or Pierre's companion, and nobody could care less. It is easy to play myself.

The energy and vigor of the mornings used to lift me. The footpath is damp, but it has not rained. The streets have been washed and hosed down. Here and there, buckets of disinfected water have been dashed in front of doorways. Somebody is brushing and scrubbing. It reassures people—wash it all, murk, dirt and dust—then set out your displays of flowers, fruit and roasting meat. Everything seems fresher; the sounds are sharper and crisper. It is an impression; it is always like that, an impression.

People, people, and people: some are in a good place, living good lives. The waiter would have liked to have been so much more and dreams of owning his own bar in the Côte d'Azur. He stamps his feet and trips around the tables, trying to forget that he owns nothing. He has never tried to make that dream come true. Dream on...

The newspaper seller breaks the cords and rolls out the papers and magazines. He does not use a pair of scissors, but rather his hands, to rip the binding that holds the bundles together. He has big, strong hands and fingers blackened with ink. Those are not easy hands.

Close by are the sprigs and sprays, petals and leaves. The flower seller is busy snipping the stems and adding new bouquets to his stands. They are nice, perhaps, but dying. There is cruelty everywhere. Why do we need to take what is already well and put it where we know it will die? He goes for a coffee and gets Monsieur Abu to stand in for him.

Monsieur Abu is a tough and fiery man who knows how to defend what is his. The little Vietnamese woman would do well to remember that, but instead she will provoke him, a match to his kindle box. The drycleaner's shop is sleepy, it is always sleepy. The façade looks innocent, yet its owner is clever, too clever.

I think of America and of the things I said to her; Jane Moore has branded herself on my brain. You are a fake, Madame Lune; you gave her a message and she understood another.

I want to convince myself that everything is normal and that it is just another ordinary day. It is not; it is one day less for all of us and destiny draws nearer for Jane Moore. I damn the eyes that make me see too much, and damn the ears that make me hear too much. I curse the mother who tied my tongue and dimmed my brain, and the grandmother who did not explain. I do that, but there is no venom, for one cannot accuse someone who is clueless.

I sit on a bench and continue to watch. That's all I will do today—sit and watch. My fingertips are numb; the feeling is not there and my hands would make mistakes; there are too many emotions stirring inside me. I hope that tomorrow will be a better day for all.

I wake without a clock. Habit tells me when to get up; it is not even three. It is drizzling outside and I take my rain coat and pack several strong plastic bags in a caddy, then brace myself for the outdoors. It appears that few people are moving at this hour. That is just appearance, many are on the march. The day will start with scavenging. It is not a joy to do it. There are other ways and means and I am better at those, but food must be put on the table. A lot of ground can be covered in a short while—I am fast, though not as fast as before. The supermarket dumps are rich in waste; there are laws that decree they can no longer put out their leftovers as before. Fortunately, adherence to the law is loose.

A full caddy is the sign to stop. I have picked up several hard baguettes and soggy, but acceptable fruit. It is a lucky dip; there is even a bottle of oil. I have trawled and rooted out what we may never use: spongy drooping salad and out-of-date packaged sandwiches.

That is enough: Hurry old woman—hurry back to the flat.

Pierre snores.

There is no time to waste. I break a piece of baguette, dip it in the oil and chew on it, wrap a crust in paper and put it in my pocket. The hardest part of the day's work is before me. Rent day is coming and the pressure is greater.

I hate running from the in-coming tide; it can force me to make a slip-up.

I put what Pierre will eat on the table. His snores rock the flat and send me back outside. I sense the change immediately: bad vibes in the air. It grows stronger and stronger. The monster is on the move this morning...preparing. Yes, there is something bad and unpleasant rising up from Rue Lepic. The darkness around him is worse; I have seen it in the church, his blackening stare following Jane Moore when she paints there. Is that hate? Is that what it is? Is that madness or some form of it? When madness and hate come together, they make deadly friends. There is a sort of hate between Monsieur Abu and Madame Lu. There is hate and even poison there, but there is no madness. Yet, danger scrapes at their doors. I know they turn bad tricks, but it is not my business. It is those other eyes that truly bother me, because for as long as I can remember, I've never experienced that darkness.

My way of working is not like others of my kind. This job cannot be done in the way of a chancer who may succeed once or twice when luck is on his side, but sooner or later gets caught. It has to be done with care and precision, and one must sometimes go far from his own street. I will buy my Metro ticket and be like every other person, every other woman...an ordinary woman.

I take the lines to Gare St. Lazare, a large, brave structure, sprawling like a giant over several streets, but there is something warm in its brick. Sculptures built from lifelike suitcases and clocks in the front squares are suitable monuments to life's purpose and meaning. Inside, I am met by the immediacy and the excitement of the long distance traveller and the daily suburban commuter traversing the tiled halls and corridors. Some parts have been renovated, but the marbled walls and floors will not wear so well with time. Better the old bricks and stones.

I stand in front of the departure timetable for the

regional trains—the panel does its domino spin, displaying platforms and changes. I don't know what it says, but from endless announcements understand that the trains are going to places like Le Havre, Cherbourg, Trouville-Deauville, and Dieppe.

Travelling puts doubt in the minds of even the most experienced. Some are very early, others last minute, while the rest are waiting or inquiring—and there are lots of watchers and movers like me. People can be careful or careless. There are those who are well organized; a bag, a folder or holder for everything, and a pocket to put it in. Some are so careful that they will open and close their bag ten times to check and reassure themselves that everything is there and in the right place. Dangerous—dangerous; it is like showing the treasure map over and over again. A few have it all worked out, almost. Sometimes, the most organized are more interesting; everything has been scrupulously thought out. However, it just takes an unexpected occurrence to make them vulnerable; the slightest thing can throw them off their stride. Others are so careless that they deserve what is coming to them.

First, one must strip the area like a painting, then put it back together and set it in motion as one would with a film. There is the background and the foreground, the fixtures—permanent and temporary—slow moving and fast moving. The main café space is well situated. A quick coffee makes me one of the crowd. The minutes tick by. My eyes are not as good as they used to be, and my senses are now dulled and my gestures stiffer and frailer. The tide is catching up with me.

A man in jeans and leather jacket is not in a hurry. He is standing with folded arms, looking up at the timetable. Silly man, behaving as if he were at home. His wallet is thick in his back pocket. Why would he be so imprudent? I wonder, would he listen if somebody went up to him and told him how unwise it was to do that? Would he heed the warning, or would he shrug and carry on?

Railway stations are pleasing places, they do me good. I owe myself a little ride and to feel young again, like a child at the fair ground. Why not take a short ride to St. Cloud? A ticket costs a few euros, but it costs nothing to get into line, punch the card and pick my carriage. The suburban route is comfortable compared to taking the Metro. A window seat suits me today. I button my coat, close my eyes and sleep a little. My day is not over yet, but the tide is farther away; the rent will be paid and there will be enough to get by in case of an emergency.

The stations are familiar to me: St. Lazare, Montparnasse, Gare de Lyon, Gare du Nord, Gare de L'est, and Australitz. St. Lazare and Montparnasse stations have always been my favorite because they link me to the north and the west; the Channel and the Atlantic; cows and fields. I think of the Atlantic Ocean because that is where my roots are. It makes me laugh, for I know that is impossible, but Normandy and Brittany feel closer to where I came from. In whimsical extravaganzas, my illusions carry me back there, visiting like an old tourist. Nobody would know me; I would smell the grass and taste the rain. I am rarely given to fantasy, it is risky to do that; my life is in the present, it has always been. Yet in my dreams, it comes to me, the little cottage by the sea. The child is there, sitting on the cliffs, lost in the cries and squeals of sea birds. Waves crash off the rocks, the spray flying so high that it showers the gliding birds, and the foam softens the glassy bed. The child watches the sea as I have watched the waves of people on the streets of Paris. We merge with the tide, waiting for the change, until my grandmother's face appears. She calls to me and I go willingly and gently. We meet at that moment, that split second when the tide turns.

It is too early for crowds on Boulevard Haussmann, but on Saturday afternoons women swing handbags that bulge with personal effects near the department stores; shoppers are warier and yet less aware. It is a peculiar change in people that I have noticed in my years here; we carry too many useless things. The gadgets we cling to are our downfall, yet we will not live without them. We need to know what our hands can do by themselves before we fill them. Misusing a hand is like removing an eye, an ear, or an arm. It is a fact that people carry more credit cards and less cash.

Some days, my wish is to be a tourist, with them and among them. How lovely to sit on the Opera steps and watch, or to sit in Notre Dame square and muse. It would be no trial to join the queues outside the large Louvre Pyramid and pay my respects to its fine artists. One could go to Musée d'Orsay and bow before Van Gogh. What would it be like to have free time to wander the Tuilleries gardens, or to applaud Monet's Lilies in the Orangerie, or to exclaim out loud at the shimmering Eiffel Tower? It is a luxury I cannot afford. It is possible to look like a tourist, but it is impossible to see it like one, for Paris is more than a few stars on a canvas, and a lot more than fountains and illuminated districts.

One day, while doing the rounds in Versailles Gardens, weary from lifting and thieving, I took the notion to become a lady and to be at one with the ghosts. It was my own chimera, for there are no such things. All at once, the past was there, coming through a foggy vapor as a different century cloaked and layered the palace. There were many gardeners who were not of our time; one could touch the cobwebs and tendrils on the manicured shrubs and trees. It was a world where smells and odors were much stronger. There were sounds of horses and carriages thundering all around—so much noise! We are quieter today. It was surely my tired eyes that had conjured such images, or my mind that had created them; but it seemed so real.

The noise grew louder—there were lords and ladies

and nobility. Their suits, dresses and ornamentation were amazing. Could all of that have been? There must have been three hundred carriages and three hundred more; they kept coming and coming. The stench of horse dung and sweat permeated the air. There were thousands of maids, foot soldiers and grooms. And still they kept coming and coming.

And I could also see the tourists of today, some with guides, others with guide books, and others with nothing but their eyes wide with wonder. Oh tourists and scholars, you do not know, you cannot know. Many of you have read a lot, and some of you are historians. I have never read books, but have instead stolen into groups as guides have led them from place to place. That is how I learn; I saturate myself with the words and explanations of others. And if what those guides speak of is what is actually in the history books, then it is nothing like what I experienced. The people in my vision were different. We know them only as we know the other creatures on this earth; we recognize them but have no idea.

It was difficult to bear the smells of that Versailles— sweat, sweat and more sweat; my nose could not take it. How delicate we have become. The air was heavy with smoke; it rose thickly from the chimneys of the palace. I found those unfamiliar faces to be clever; they were pulling horses, carrying guns, or parasols, silk bags and snuff boxes. It struck me again...how we like to carry things. Is that what distinguishes us as humans, carrying things? Is that why the God we invented, or who invented us, put us on this planet?

That day in Versailles, I was overcome with hysterical laughter. People nearby thought me crazy, and I must be crazy because only a crazy person could have seen what I saw. Can anyone tell me what we might have become if instead of developing our back bone and hands, we had developed long teeth? Are we the superior species? Surely, it should be the birds, with claws as dexterous as fingers and the ability to soar and fly, that should be kings and queens. Maybe they are and we are simply not aware of it. What do I know? If man were so superior, why is he capable of evil? Animals are not evil.

Still, I am glad to have experienced what I did at Versailles. It is improbable that it was real; I must have made it up, for people that lived and died in the past have no part in the here and now. They have nothing to do with me, or I with them. I would rather be mad than to say all that is on my mind. Madness would allow me to escape the evil on my street and to have no responsibility for it. I have asked myself over and over if he is evil...is he? He is more than that. His eyes are filled with demons, his hands engrained with the blood and suffering of his victims. He has chosen Jane Moore, and I am the only one who knows it.

5

Karen lost count of the number of times Jane had brought up Tony's name in conversation. Fintan Corner, one day to be Fintan's Corner, was exactly that—a corner, a very tight corner. You angled yourself when you entered; if you went there after seven in the evening, you didn't expect to sit. It attracted drinkers and wasters. Karen was convinced that Jane's good nature and personality gave the corner something extra; it helped bring in a better quality clientele, making it more than the kip that it was. She had style and aplomb, and managed drunks with great skill.

Jane was determined to see only the good in Tony, and Karen did not want to hurt her.

"Sorry, Jane, I'm crossing the line; you're right—it's not any of my business. At least, get Tony to pin the apostrophe on; no self-respecting Irish man would let that go; I'm uncomfortable drinking inside with that mistake over my head."

"Next summer; he's promised to redo it next summer."

"You are the class there, Jane, you know that."

"You put me too high. He pays me well enough; it's a practical solution, the job covers the bills and allows me to concentrate on my art during the day. It could be worse."

"I know, but we're combining forces as soon as possible and getting that crystal jewelry business going."

"I'm all for it." Jane reached for her bag. "So, are you ready?"

"For what?"

"To hear about your future." Jane cleared Karen's coffee table. "That's why I'm here, remember. Now, get serious."

"Hang on for Eric and Frederic; for some reason, once they knew you were doing a reading with me, they decided it was opportune to drop in and say hello."

Karen couldn't really bring herself to 'ooh,' and 'aah', nevertheless, Jane was a good actress and would give people value for money.

With her new psychic vision, Jane channelled in on Eric and Frederic: "Something is troubling you, isn't it? You aren't here by accident."

"Am—" Frederic hesitated.

"Don't tell me," Jane raised her hand, "I see another envelope; there is hate around it, I feel it."

Eric looked at Jane in amazement.

"That's it," Frederic confirmed, "we've once again received, not one, but several hate notes in our mailbox."

"And they carry the same message as those on the stone through your window, and previous notes," Jane affirmed.

"That appears to be it," Eric said.

Karen picked up a card and dropped it back on the table, "Have you informed the police this time?"

"They're only letters," Frederic shrugged, "although they are unpleasant, they are not openly threatening."

"Not openly threatening, my eye," Karen said.

Eric examined the cards closely. "How did you pick that up, was it a vibe?"

"Yes," Jane nodded, "that's exactly it; it's hard to

explain, but since I began doing the cards, I've started to have feelings, insights."

Karen looked sideways at Jane. Maybe people did pick up vibes, but since the guys had already gotten letters, it was evidently a good guess.

A door banged. "Hello, folks." Olivier, armed with a bulky computer case, bustled in and looked around, quizzically.

"I've got to get to the pub." Jane tidied the cards and stood.

"We've got to go, too," Frederic said.

Eric was on his feet.

"Bye," they all said in unison.

The door slammed after them.

"Why did they all dash off like that?" Olivier dropped his bag on an armchair. "Is that the effect I have on people? Are they afraid?"

Karen made light of it. "They'd been here awhile; it was time to go." She knew that it wasn't everybody leaving at once that bothered Olivier—it was the cold glances that Eric and Frederic had once again cast in his direction; he could tell that they really did not like him.

Olivier looked at his watch.

"Going out again?"

"Yeah, I just came back to change. I have to meet someone about the new project I'm working on. It's in Lemans, so I'll be staying overnight."

Karen breathed a sigh.

Olivier shuffled some papers in his bag, "I was wondering if it's safe for Jane to walk home in the early hours?"

His concern surprised Karen, "It's about a twenty-minute walk; I have the impression that she likes to go home on foot to get the bar out of her system."

"But it isn't safe; these streets can get rough at night. Does Jane have a choice? Does Tony pay for a taxi if she needs it?"

"You must be joking; he'd charge her to drink the slop buckets under the beer taps. You've never spoken about that before—is there some reason?"

"It's just that the last time I was coming home in the small hours I noticed that there are a lot of shady characters around at that time ."

"When was that?"

"That time my flight was delayed when returning from a business trip to Shanghai."

Karen was troubled; when Olivier digressed beyond the world of business to mention things like that, it usually was to say something important. It might be good to ring Jane and ask her to text if she needed someone to accompany her home. 'Don't go there,' Karen told herself; 'Jane has been doing this for months, and if you start checking up on her, you'll make her nervous.'

"What is it, Jane?"

"He likes you."

"Who?"

"Monsieur Flower-pot."

"Oh, really," Didn't Jane realize that it was she who was attracting his attention?

"Selling flowers is a hard job. When I'm getting home from Fintan's, his van is already gone to Rungis market. He has to buy his stuff, get back here, prepare the flowers, and set up his stand."

"It is exhausting thinking about it; and then he's on his feet for the rest of the day. What's his real name again?"

"Laurent...Lebois, if I remember. I think your idea works great."

"My idea?"

"Yes, calling the different people on the street by their trade: Madame Baker and Monsieur Dairy."

Karen laughed. "Yes, like a children's story book. Speaking of getting home from Fintan's, you must finish very late if Monsieur Flower-pot is already gone?"

"Yes."

"Ever think of taking a taxi?"

"Not really... Tony drove me last night. Why?"

"No reason." Karen saw a change on Jane's face. "You and Tony—has something happened?"

"No, not really—he just asked me out on a date. No harm in that, is there? Anyway, I'll see what Madame Lune has to say."

"Again?" Karen thought the visits had been abandoned.

"It's only the second time—and don't forget, you promised to go too. Think of it as a link with our future business, consider it research."

"I don't recall promising to go, and I don't see how Madame Lune could be a link to market research."

"She might have useful advice to give on that and other areas of your life."

"Huh."

"Look, I might have made mistakes in my life, but I have some idea where I'm going—you don't. You don't like your work, and you're very iffy about Olivier."

"What?"

"Don't act shocked." Jane raised a palm: "It's easy to see that when Olivier's travelling for work, you're a different person. When he's back, you're uptight."

"Now, listen here..." Jane had a point.

Jane patted her hand, "Sorry, I'm making assumptions, and it's not my place to do so. However, I do see us in business together, and very soon."

"You mean you have a vision?"

"Oh yes..."

It was easy to be suspicious of fortune-tellers; there was just something unnerving about someone focusing on your most private traits and yearnings. The woman had refused to see them together, insisting on separate sessions. Jane had gone in first and left with a cheeky grin on her face; evidently she was satisfied.

Madame Lune's flat wasn't what Karen had expected. It was a bare bones affair, cold and sombre. Dressed in long dark robes, her face covered by a gray veil, Madame Lune led Karen to a small room—the *voyance* room. This looked like the real thing. There were red silk drapes hanging from the ceiling and colorful cushions tossed here and there; the low lighting made everything somewhat obscure.

Madame Lune beckoned her inside.

The room smelled sweet and the soft music relaxed her. Karen had a peculiar feeling, as if she somehow knew the medium, and had known her for a long time. Of course that was impossible, though their paths might have crossed on the street.

The medium held a large white card before her; it asked if she had come for a general reading or wished to ask something specific.

"General," she answered. What an odd way of conducting the session. Yet she had to acknowledge that it was intriguing and more effective than if words had been spoken.

Madame Lune put a bowl on a side table and Karen understood that a payment of fifty euros was expected. It killed her to throw money away like that; it took a lot of the mystery out of things, brought her down to earth and fed her suspicions. No genuine medium should soil the reading with money. If they really had a gift, they should treat it as sacred, like religious people.

Madame Lune shook her finger and laid her hands flat on the table. She mumbled something—raised her eyes and looked at Karen as if studying her aura. Her head tilted, giving the impression of listening to something otherwise inaudible. She then placed a blue silk bag between them.

Madame Lune revealed a second white card with instructions: shuffle the deck, cut it in three, select one bundle, and from that bundle pick seven cards.

Karen did as ordered, shuffling the deck awkwardly;

these cards were larger than normal playing cards and the backs were decorated with a full yellow moon against a black background.

The selection looked disappointing; the cards didn't speak to her or look particularly interesting:

FOUR OF CRESENTS
EIGHT OF SPHERES
THE TOWER
THE CHARIOT
THE MAKER OF STAVES
THE SIX OF WEAPONS
GIVER OF CRESENTS

Madame Lune seemed to find them interesting though, and took each one in her hand to study it before replacing it on the spread. She began to carefully lay out a series of white cards. Each had a message: YOU HAVE LOST YOUR WAY IN LIFE; YOU ARE WITHOUT AIM IN YOUR JOB; YOU ARE WITHOUT SATISFACTION IN YOUR RELAIONSHIP...

Taking a slate and chalk from a drawer, Madame Lune first sketched a matchstick man and woman, before crossing the figures out with a large X.

Bah, Karen thought, nothing amazing about that; her words were pure cliché. Madame Lune had obviously picked up a lot from her body language and demeanour. Jane had also probably let things out about her. The woman's manner of communicating seemed detached, rehearsed, and unnatural. It was likely that whatever cards had been drawn, Madame Lune would have presented the same message.

The medium held up a large card and her eyes penetrated through her: YOU ARE SURROUNDED BY DARKNESS.

"What?"

YOUR FRIEND IS IN MORTAL DANGER.

This message was accompanied by an image of a woman slumped over a tomb stone.

That jolted Karen. "Don't say things like that about Jane," she cautioned the medium.

Madame Lune held up the card again: YOUR FRIEND IS IN MORTAL DANGER.

Karen decided to play along; after all, Jane hadn't looked worried when leaving. "Did you tell Jane that?"

Madame Lune shook her head and held up once more the image of the dead woman. Karen looked at it closely and saw that in detail it was quite terrifying. Her hands had been chopped off and there was blood streaming from her neck.

Suddenly, Madame Lune turned the card and Karen drew back. On the reverse side, the same woman was staring wide-eyed in horror; her mouth was open and the rest of her body mutilated.

Panic rose in Karen. She didn't believe Madame Lune and didn't want to be impressed by her. Why would the medium tell her about Jane being in mortal danger and show her such things?

"You cannot terrify people with images like that. What do you mean exactly?"

Madame Lune stood.

"I can't leave now," Karen protested. "Please, you can't just spin that tale and send me off on my merry way. Tell me more."

Madame Lune flicked her hand.

"Do you want me to make another appointment, give you another fifty euros? Is that it?"

The medium took the fifty euros from the bowl, walked to the door and laid the note on the outside banister.

Karen went out onto the landing and tried in the brighter light to see the woman more clearly, but Madame Lune's clothes and veil covered all. The door closed firmly in her face.

She switched on her phone and was shocked to see her hand shaking. "Jane, yes, I've finished my reading; just going back to the flat. Can you meet me there?"

Karen prepared the coffee and turned things over and over in her mind: What to do? Dismiss it all as crack pot stuff?

Jane burst in the door. "What did the medium tell you? Good, isn't she?"

"The woman doesn't open her mouth; it's disconcerting."

"But interesting..."

"I have yet to decide. What did she tell you?"

"She reaffirmed that the man who would change my life was under my nose. Naturally, I thought of Tony. But when I mentioned him, she wouldn't confirm or deny it, just insisted on the word nose, and something to do with *smelling* him."

"Smelling him? What sort of nonsense is that?"

"I don't know; body smell, I suppose. We all have a scent, but we've lost our sense of smell."

"How does Tony smell?"

Jane shrugged. "Bar smells...cigarettes."

"Were you told anything else?"

"Madame Lune indicated that he was from the countryside and showed me a picture of a field with wild flowers."

"That doesn't sound very profound to me."

"It depends on how you take it."

"Did she come up with something about your job?"

"The card said I would enter a partnership with another person."

"The pub? With Tony?"

"No, silly; she probably meant you and me, and our plans to start a venture."

"Was there more?"

"No," Jane shook her head far too quickly, "just small details, a few very personal things from my past. What happened with you? What were you told?"

Karen informed Jane about everything except the 'mortal danger.'

Jane winced. "Change your job and boyfriend? That's all?"

"That about sums it up."

"Well, that doesn't have to mean that you and Olivier should split; it could just be changing your point of view on some things."

"When did you get to be so wise?"

"I told you, I'm learning the cards."

"You have to be careful about drawing people to your room. You could get weirdoes, you know," Karen warned.

"Like the two of us," Jane laughed.

Karen tried to laugh, but it came out all wrong. Everything was wrong. Madame Lune had not only been strange, but downright scary.

6

My bags are heavy, this time with real shopping. Pierre will be back soon; he always senses when the cupboards have been stocked.

He is not a fool, but is not that clever either. We are well matched, for I have lived my life stupidly at times. Sometimes, we are both no better than animals; we eat and sleep, eat and sleep. Oh, to sleep and never wake up—that would be fine. Crying has never been for me, yet I think I have cried once or twice in my sleep. Crying in your sleep does not count; you are not aware of it. The last time, it was because of a dream in which the taunts of children followed me around the schoolyard. On waking, my face was wet; I knew I had cried. But my face is dry now, and my eyes are drier.

Everything has to be put away: coffee, meat, vegetables, butter and pasta. There is one bottle of wine to please Pierre; when he returns I will be playing host to him.

Pierre does not know what to say to me anymore. At the beginning, he expected that I follow him as a stray dog might follow its master. He never asked me about my past or home, just played his accordion and did his street magic. The sound of the music and allure of illusion drew me. I was useful as an assistant to his tricks. The street entertainer talked of his dreams and hopes, but already he had responsibility—he had Dimitri, and I was carrying a child, from another. His accordion and magic tricks rustled up barely enough to get by. Little by little, we added my skills. Our in-takings increased and Pierre talked more and more of his dreams, for a while. I have never had life dreams or a desire for what others might wish to have: a house, beautiful clothes, or a career. I do not know such dreams. They have something to do with believing in the future—without them we are dry and cry no real tears. For a dream gives hope; that is the dew on the morning grass; that is what you thirst for and what makes your eyes bright. When you dream, it also brings disappointment and pain. That is the rain, when your face is wet with tears. That is the gamble of life. So you must spin a new dream and fly again; keep spinning and you will keep living. I have never been able to do that and have preferred to stay in my flat land; a land so featureless that one cannot see a horizon. The sun never rises or sets there. Pierre spun dreams for both of us, though I never really believed them.

When tired of busking, Pierre would do some magic with knives. He had a coat with dozens of secret pockets. Each pocket held a dagger with a blade as sharp as a lance, enough to slice a limb in two. The same pockets also held fake magnetic daggers. Once upon a time, he was good at magic, had it down to a fine art. I would stand with my back against a special target board while he would launch his daggers. There was never any danger. He would switch knives so quickly that the street audience were duped. In later years, he lost his appetite for magic and abandoned the act, preferring our accordion game. He played to distract while his partner picked and plucked.

With time, the shine and glitter dulled, dazzling itself out. I looked at the tarnished goods and stayed. I had my baby and called him Patrick. For a time, Patrick gave a new dimension to my flat land. But my baby slipped away, and with him the last ember of a dream. Flat land is okay; there are worse places to be.

In my recollections of childhood, I am turning the pages of the cardboard dolls that are waiting to be cut out, to be dressed and played with. They looked better on the pages than when neatly cut and standing on their own. Once taken out of their slots, you saw what they really were—cut-out dolls without dimension. At least on the page, they were pictures and didn't have the pretence to be more. I prefer to be without dreams or dimension, rather than to pretend. That would not have been a good world for Patrick, and I would have wanted him to have more, much more. I did not have to choose.

Patrick, I was afraid for you, my baby; but I would have tried. I covered you in hugs and kisses and reached inside myself to give you all the affection possible. Pierre was not your father and never tried to be; still he was good to you for the short time you were with us.

I thought that one day my baby would grow into a child and then become an adult. It requires no intelligence to know that. However, it was not to be. With all my vision and insight, I could neither predict nor change fate.

I tried to be a good mother, but was not able to protect Patrick from all. I think of my own mother and tell myself that maybe my baby escaped the worst. Nobody could be prepared for that sort of mother. Somebody once said to my grandmother that her grandchild had been cheated. The child never felt cheated; there was no anger or bitterness. As the child grew, there was shame and embarrassment. There were no words for it then, there are no words for it now. It might have been easier to go through life as a fool; a fool cannot understand. An animal understands better than a fool. An animal will suffer physical pain; it has needs, has to eat and survive, but it does not have wishes and feelings. If one's mother is a

good mother or a bad mother, but normal, then there is
something to fight with or against. If one's mother is a
fool, what can they do? They can build nothing with her
because they feel nothing. Does that make them a bad
person?

The Irish girl, Karen, did not like it when I told her of
the mortal danger to her American friend—she did not
like it at all, but she was told the truth. I am a watcher: I
watch the streets and see the pieces like parts of a puzzle
scattered on the floor. Rue Lepic is closing in on all of us.

Watching has taken over my days and nights. The monster
does not sleep either; tormented souls cannot rest.

I am filled with doubts. It was a grave error to have
encouraged those girls even once. It was a waste of time,
because it is not the right way to inform them. It is too late
now; Karen Moroney has started to believe me, at least
part of her does. What can she do with the warning?
Somewhere inside me is a voice, and it speaks clearly, 'You
must act: it is your task, and not that of Karen Moroney.'

I cannot ignore him; I'm being pulled into his story as he
steps into theirs. The monster has not seen me because his
view is colored. He sees the color of the rose, sees that it is
pink or yellow or purple, and all that is gray escapes his
eye. He knows there are other duller colors there
somewhere, but they are not under his lens.

Jane Moore sketches in the square; that is her talent.
However, she is playing a dangerous game and risks
attracting trouble. Pretending to be a medium is risky; it
gives you importance in people's lives. By staying
anonymous, you cannot be important and you avoid the
temptation of power. When people know or believe you
are clairvoyant, they revere you and want to be around
you. Power is a heady lotion. You must do fortune telling
for one or two reasons. First, you do it for the money,
because you are a fake and you simply need to live. That is

acceptable and you will never lose sight of danger. Or secondly, you are genuinely gifted, thus you only intervene because it is really important to do so. However, if you are gifted, as Jane Moore might be, and you decide you can make money out of your gift, then your problems begin. I did it for money, but soon realized I had more. I do not call it a gift; I call it 'sight.' Knowing that, I stopped doing it on a regular basis. My greatest talent is moving my quicksilver fingers.

Let Jane Moore amuse herself—it will not be for long—but she must not bring him inside her door. Today, she paints though, and Rue Lepic is her study. He has been sketched into her pictures many times. It has happened consciously and by accident; her chalks and crayons take on a life of their own when they meet the page.

He walks near her and enters the café. What is on his mind? His movements are very controlled yet nobody really notices that unless they have studied him for as long as I have. He is ordinary, so very ordinary; but not for any price would I accept to enter his world or to glimpse his thoughts, not even for a second. Nobody could live with themselves afterwards. Oh, Jane Moore, watch out. Karen Moroney, watch out for your friend. Is it already too late? If I were to tell them all, would it change their minds, would they believe me? Telling Karen Moroney what I did might even have been too much. It could just push her friend into his path.

There are footsteps on the stairs. Pierre is returning. When I compare him to what I see on the streets, a little affection returns in my heart for him. It is a relief to appreciate his brand of normality with all his human failings. He is no saint, but cannot compete with the evil outside my window. That knowledge makes me lighter, almost.

Pierre stands at the doorway and lets me kiss him on the cheek. He puts his hand to where my lips touched. He has craved it, has been looking for warmth. I have been unable to give him any, except to allow him rare instants, like now. If I had been different, perhaps he too would have been happier and not felt the cold so much. I will never forget your kindness, Pierre, never. Though it is sometimes hard not to despise you for your lack of backbone or willingness to be more. It is reasonable to detest the coward who runs off to the whore at the corner. Courage failed you; it would have taken courage to have left me. You do not really need me, but think you do. The responsibility for my emotional lack is my own, but I cannot take on responsibility for your failings, Pierre. If there was anything to forgive, I would do it; if your life needed saving, I would do it. But no one can stop you from marching to the end as quickly as you do; nobody can make you change your way of living.

I will prepare a nice meal for you. You lift your head—another surprise. I seldom cook. Yes, I put food on the table; that is different, that is not the same as cooking. You go to the bathroom to wash and shave; you are as easy to lead as a lame puppy. Why reproach you for that? At our age we should leave all that behind. But I think of what I watched on the street and believe that I can love you a little tonight. I am able to give some warmth to the man who has been my companion for so long.

So we eat and share a moment of companionship. I do not want to think that there is another reason for doing this; I hope and even pray that there is not more to my actions. My prayers are of my own making and do not include God. God is not the first person I pray to. It is strange to think that one would play the fortune-teller and not know the first thing about fortune or luck, that one would act the clairvoyant and medium and yet truly believe that death ends all, that I would see ghosts in Versailles and not be convinced. Yet, if death ends all, would it not have been wiser to leave those girls alone when one can do nothing for either of them? Where is the proof that would convince them and condemn him? How can I live in the contradiction of my deeds?

Pierre licks the sauce from his fork. His fingers are long and slender, the only part of his body that reflects how he was as a young man. Young Pierre was light and nimble with a boyish face and a roguish grin; gypsy dark eyes and tanned skin. It used to make him angry to be mistaken for a gypsy and he would explain that his looks were typical of the south and the Spanish in his blood. Today his body is puffed and swollen and carries a paunch that owes as much to idleness as to age. His face is weathered and wrinkled. He has never been to the place where I was born and grew up, never walked the grass there or stood on the cliffs, and will never do so.

He is waiting: this will be a different evening, this will not be the gauche fumbling of rutting animals. 'But that is how it always finishes, Pierre—we are what we are.' He puts the cork back on the bottle. The gesture is clear; no more wine in case it would displease me. He does not want to miss out on a flicker of fire that might melt through the ice and bring some warmth into his day. His whore cannot do that; she can do many things for him, but his woman can do more. He has a hunger that only I can satisfy. There is something about me that he needs, even with my shrivelled skin and dead eyes. My body is arid; there isn't a drop of youth left in me.

He sips a glass of water. I rise from the table, look at him, then go to the bathroom to make my body ready; it is an effort, but it's for Pierre. I do not close the door and though my back is to him, know that he is standing behind me.

I feel his hands on my waist. My eyes close making it easier to pretend that we are twenty again. I do not want to be twenty again or to go back to those times, but want to feel it for a moment. It is his night. I turn and make each movement count. My mouth trails across his face, the tip of the tongue feeling each prickle on his grizzled skin. My arms draw him closer and I slowly undress him. He groans and his head falls on my shoulder.

We move to the bedroom, to the shadows, where the brush strokes of the evening sun smooth out the lines and add a pink glow to our skins. We are indeed young again. There is anticipation in his eyes as he fondles my breasts while not noticing the sagging emptiness. I give him everything my being allows; it may never happen again, but Pierre will remember this night.

His sex swells and hardens in my hand, but he is out of control and cannot hold it for long. I see him try and know that it is not in his power, so I take pity and do not delay the torture. My legs coil around him and animal instinct takes over. Pierre clings to my hips and jolts inside; he manages a few strokes at a ragged rhythm and then it all comes quickly, too quickly, squirting out of him, into me and on me. He convulses with mumbles of satisfaction and I know that he has not been able to do it this way, even badly, for a long time. Age, wine and cigarettes have sapped his energy.

I take him in my arms to give him warmth, for that is what he wants—not to wake up to the cold gray dawn alone. He kisses me on the shoulder and nestles his head there. Pierre does not have the right words to express his needs, nor does he read enough to be able to understand what they might be; he is uneducated. Still, he has read more than I have and that is no credit to him. We lie with his breathing uneven and my ears tuned to his heavy gasps. I feel the stickiness on my thighs, but stay with him. He snuggles close again, his head on my breast, a baby returning to his mother. He is at peace.

I run my fingers through his hair; he has kept all of it, no longer black, but silky gray. His head moves aside, but not before my hand touches his cheek. My finger tips are damp—tears (they are his tears) flowing down his cheek. Unconsciously, something in him already knows. In my mind, I say, 'Goodbye, Pierre, goodbye. I will never give you this again; time has run out for both of us; you will not make it to next year. Yet, I insist, I do not believe in fortune telling, and I do not believe in God. 'I do not love you, Pierre, I am sorry, but I do not love you. What I can tell you is that I have understood you and have given more to you than to anybody else except Patrick. For Patrick, despite his short life, I sacrificed and suffered. You have had the best of what was left, Pierre, but it cannot be called love, for this old woman knows nothing of love.'

Dawn is breaking and Pierre looks for me. I let him find me. He takes my hand, and I hold his until his grip loosens and he goes into a heavy sleep. I get up; he does not stir and will sleep for several more hours. My body smells of him. I go noiselessly to the bathroom, walking without taking real steps, air under my feet. The water flows and eases my stiffness, and the last of Pierre's seed drains away. Just as silently, I dress.

There is a new purpose to this morning, it is clearer in my mind. I have not done many good acts in my life and have rarely been touched by emotion. This will be an exception. I am wearing the colors to be as invisible as possible—my habitual gray. The bench is empty; Pierre will walk past and not recognize me, will not even remember that someone was sitting there. They will all go past: frowns, heavy legs and leaden hearts, walking somewhere. There will be happy souls too, eyes bright and the sun in their sights. The Irish girl, Karen, comes along. She is in the wrong life and does not know how to get out but may make it in the end and do better than what is her life today. Karen is a lot more than I was at her age; she has the grassy fields of home and the Atlantic waves to live for, the solid foundation of a mother and father, and a family. All that will keep her feet on the ground. She can go home any time; look back and feel complete. There is a place that Karen came from and will always be from.

Karen Moroney was born out of love. I cast aside my own memories; when you are born of a violent act, that is your home, that is where you have come from. When the first tremors, vibrations, and sounds are not normal, you are warned. When the blurred vision clears and the eyes of the baby focus and look into the eyes of a fool, they already know too much.

It is Sunday and some shops close at one o'clock. The monster has been here all morning and is free to leave his post. He walks casually and I follow at a distance. We go up the hill. He looks around him once or twice; the hunter is aroused. Could somebody be following him? I take a parallel street because I know now his destination and want to get there before him. It is necessary to quicken my pace and gain ground by taking every shortcut.

I arrive at the cemetery gates and descend the steps into the granite hollow; it is crowded with homes for the dead. I pass through the tombs and graves—ornate mausoleums to deserted forgotten crypts. A cat sits by a tombstone and stares; my intuition tells me to wait by that monument. I press my body to it and make myself invisible once again. I can be stiller than stillness, for hours if needed. If the monster looks, his eyes will see a gray tombstone. There are several more cats sitting or wandering here and there, birds chirp loudly, rodents and insects are everywhere, and the city background noise is dimmed. There is nobody but the creatures and me. It is not the season to visit, too cold except for the bravest. It is an easy cemetery to hide in; the staff and security are few and the grounds are often untended. A fit individual could steal in at night simply by dropping down from the street above or jumping from the blue steel bridge that crosses over.

He enters as noiselessly as I did. The spot has already been selected, but he does not go there immediately and first turns around the graves, finally stopping near me. The cat has fled. The monster is very near but does not see me. With gloved hands, he removes something wrapped in plastic from his inside jacket pocket and disappears inside a mausoleum outside my line of vision. There is the scraping sound of a trowel on gravel and the crinkling of plastic; he is digging a shallow hole and will place the plastic bag there then cover it over, paying attention to every detail. That is his way.

He steps back outside and takes something else from his pocket. It is a camera. He moves it slowly, filming and muttering. Suddenly, he swings it around and I freeze. They say cameras pick up things that the eye might not; ghosts can be captured on film. I am not a ghost, I am invisible. When he replays that scene, I hope that nothing shows of me. The risk is mine, perhaps one too many but based on the odds that he will not replay that scene until after the deed is done. The moment of pleasure is viewing the deed afterwards, replaying it again and again. The camera goes back into his pocket, but his head turns several times before leaving; checking north, south, east, and west. I do not move; it is not over: he has doubt, an uncertain feeling of not being alone.

I did well to stay in my place for he returns, hurrying back to the mausoleum while his eyes scour the place. He frowns; something is wrong. Of course it is! I am here. The sky has clouded over and rain begins to fall. It will turn into a downpour. He is reluctant to leave and keeps circling the graves and tombs before coming to a standstill, this time in front of me. We are almost facing each other for several minutes. Finally, he turns and walks back through the gates. I will not move yet, not until I'm certain that he is really gone.

I leave Montmartre cemetery with a bitter load on my stomach. The rain has gone through my coat and is soaking my clothes. I will pay the price but prefer to keep walking outside, making aimless rings and eventually returning to the flat. Pierre has gone out and will be back today or maybe tomorrow. It is of no importance. Counting the hours and measuring time as others do is not for me. It has always been clear: you are born and you die. I have not cared much about estimating how long we have between. However, for once I need to measure time, for the monster that stood in the cemetery is operating on his particular clock.

'Take off your clothes, old woman that you are, your body is shivering and trembling.' I boil some water, cover my head with a cloth and hold my face over the steam.

I let the steam do its work then lie down upon the bed. Sleep comes unwillingly, and when it does, it is not a peaceful sleep; there are many dreams, bad dreams. A fever has taken over that will make me lose time; my body sweats it out, hour after hour, until it is defeated.

My limbs are jelly, but I am vertical. I go to the window to watch. There is America walking past the flower stand. Jane Moore is indeed a beautiful woman; she wants to come back for a third reading—that would make too many. Jane has to leave prediction and fortune telling behind her, and I must refuse to see her again, because it will not serve my purpose or hers. I am wracked with misgivings. How is one supposed to help, to even try to turn the hands of the clock? The decision to act is not mine; it is beyond me, but I must do something. If that is the case, then solitude will be my best friend, even more than it is today. I have to take his path; it sickens me, but what else am I to do? I have to become him and walk in his shadow.

7

"Oh, la-la!"

Karen braked her descent downstairs and just about avoided bumping into her neighbor who was hovering on the landing, a bundle of letters in her hand.

"The young..." Chantal adjusted her glasses, looking confused.

"I'm sorry," Karen tried to make amends, "you're very early. Are you posting those?"

"Yes, I'm early because I want them to go in the first post."

"Do you want me to drop them into the letter box for you?"

"That's nice of you, dear; it will spare me going out in the cold."

"It's no bother; I'm on my way to work." Karen took the bundle, "My, that's a lot of letters."

Chantal looked sad. "I find it's the best way to keep in touch with family and friends; sometimes, it's the only way. After getting a letter, there is a chance that they will ring. It reminds them that we are still here."

"That's a good idea." 'Not very clever,' Karen sifted

through the letters quickly.

"They're all outside Paris, dear, except for the top two."

"Consider it done," Karen said as she hurried off.

Her work wasn't really hard and certainly not mentally taxing. It might be described as monotonous. People were sometimes nervous and customers occasionally insulting over the phone, but she usually got over those things quickly. A typical day would consist of making up excuses as to why deliveries weren't on time, lying politely, pretending, and telling half-truths.

The words 'mortal danger' suddenly came back to her. It had shocked her at the moment, but since returning to her routine, the words had lost some of their effect; they were, after all, only words.

Fortunately, Karen's day was even busier than expected and there was little time to ponder over the threats of a fortune-teller. By the time she'd found herself once more squashed inside a crowded carriage during the evening rush-hour, her mind was numbed. The Parisian expression '*Metro, Boulot, Dodo*," was quite apt. People's lives were reduced to 'Commuting, Working, Sleeping.' That certainly had been her life lately: underground trains, offices and bed. Ah bed! And it was nice to cuddle up on the sofa in front of the television. But that wouldn't be the case tonight; they were going out this evening.

Olivier had asked her to go with him to an important cocktail party. God, she hated those occasions, making trivial conversation with strangers, people who didn't care anyway. Duty was duty, and it would be done for his career.

Karen greeted Monsieur Martin at the News kiosk, her eye falling on a magazine displayed upon a rack. The title spoke to her loud and clear: How To Start Your Own Company.

"Cold, isn't it?" she tried to engage the cranky newspaper seller.

Monsieur Martin's grumpy acknowledgement told her

he wasn't having any of it; there would be no friendly half-smile from him this evening. On looking through the magazine, she brightened up. Long winded bureaucracy and red tape sent her running; but how to start your own company seemed to be explained very simply in the magazine article.

Karen was now running late and accelerated, but stopped abruptly at a window covered in posters: it was an evening for revelations. That place had been empty since she'd moved to Montmartre, but now, for some reason, it jumped out at her like destiny. The future premises for her partnership with Jane was staring her in the face. But it would surely be expensive; nothing was that easy. Shouldn't they research the business idea more comprehensively? They might not need premises at all, but it would be nice to have a small space to display crystals, even if most of the business was done online. Could they make a living out of that? Maybe, if they picked their own rocks on trips to the mountains. Whatever else, Jane's talent was certain. Her friend could concentrate on the jewelry and they could add the feel good factor by explaining how crystals channelled energy. They would need to do lots of promotion and marketing, but that was her forté.

...Not a soul on the street—it was calm, deadly calm. Someone out there, somebody dangerous—Jane was in mortal danger...

Karen woke up perspiring. She was generally a sound sleeper and wasn't used to nasty dreams. Olivier was splayed all over the bed. The cocktail party had finished by half past nine, but he had gone with his office team to continue the party at a night club. She had been happy to separate, having consumed enough champagne for one evening. The idea of having the bed all to herself for a while had also appealed; but the hope of avoiding his advances appealed more. What time had he straggled in?

The sound of the shower running had woken her for a few seconds.

She pushed at him for more space, opened one eye and caught the digits flashing on the face of the clock: it was just after three. If she didn't get back to sleep immediately, it would be catastrophic. It was the end of the month, the sales department would be crazy trying to process orders, and everybody would be shouting. Pressure, pressure, and more pressure. Karen pushed at Olivier again and won two millimeters. But now the toilet was calling; damn that third champagne. Getting up would mean Olivier taking over the entire bed, again. The toilet won. She grumbled her way out from under the blankets and padded off to the bathroom. The place was a mess, which was Olivier's doing. He couldn't seem to put things back where they belonged. The spattered toothpaste on the mirror bore his oafish signature. He'd dumped his clothes in the laundry basket, and they stank of smoke and other stale smells. Olivier was supposed to have kicked the habit.

Karen paused at the living room window. The street was poorly lit but there was movement in one of the apartments at the other side; somebody else was up and looking out. It was Madame Lune's window. She rubbed at the goose bumps on her arms. Home came into her mind; I should call next weekend to see that everyone is okay. The thought made her feel better.

Oh no, the clock. Morning already? Karen just wanted sleep but willed herself to stand. Slow, stiff movements made her think of old age; this was how an old woman must feel. She wondered about Madame Lune's age. The medium had seemed a fit woman, probably near sixty. What was her real personality like? She let the shower hammer her body, hoping to revitalize herself.

Olivier waddled heavily across the floor boards and avoided her eyes. "Good morning," he said.

"Morning."

Had they nothing more to say to each other? She thought about his background and his family. Meeting the De Belleville's the first time had been a strain. It had seemed obvious to her that she wasn't what they'd had in mind for their only son. 'Our boy could do a lot better' was printed plainly upon their foreheads each time she sat painfully through a Sunday lunch in Versailles town.

'Let it go, Karen, let it go. Come on, go through the motions: coffee, toast, and more coffee. Maybe she was depressed and hence the lethargy. No one in her family was like that; her mother literally bounded out of bed every morning and her father right after her, and her brothers were models of contentment. Perhaps she wasn't cut out for life as a couple. 'Mortal danger, yes; it is I, not Jane, who is in mortal danger...of going insane!'

What was that perfume? His cologne...it was on the tip of her tongue to say, 'I don't like it.' She mentally slapped herself, put more toast on the table for him and poured coffee, only just managing to avoid scalding his hand.

Olivier leaned over and kissed her stiffly, "Thanks for making breakfast, darling."

"You're welcome." She could hear him chewing bread, swallowing coffee; she could practically see the roof of his mouth. Who else made those sorts of noises when they ate? 'Come on, Karen, you're not being fair.' He was looking at her, something like neediness in his eyes and talking with his mouth full of food.

She focused on his words: 'I should do it now...just tell him that I can't go on like this. Why is that so hard?'

"Olivier," she interrupted him.

"Yes?"

"Are you happy?"

Olivier was momentarily taken aback then burst out laughing. "I love your sense of humor," he said. "Of course I'm happy."

He rose from the table. The next sound that Karen heard was the rotating of his electric tooth brush; a few minutes later, the toilet flushed. He came out of the bathroom and collected his office materials. "I'll be going now; don't forget we are expected in Versailles this weekend."

"Olivier—"

The door closed.

Karen had only five minutes to herself, but it was enough to allow her to brood. The thought of suffering through another heavy Sunday lunch with his family in Versailles was too much.

She put the cups on the sink, drew back the brown curtains fully and opened the shutters. Something seemed to shift inside Madame Lune's window. Was it possible that Madame Lune had been standing there all night? Is that what the medium did? Spend her days—and her nights—watching people and collecting information that might help her to tell fortunes?

Karen put on her coat, grabbed her phone and bag. Oh, there was a message; how had she missed it? Jane must have sent it last night.

It was a simple text: 'Call me.'

It was too early to call now; Jane would still be asleep. Karen decided to text her: 'Just saw your message—do you still want me to call?' Jane hadn't said it was urgent, so it was probably nothing that couldn't wait.

It was tense at the office: people were stressed out and unhappy customers populated the phone line with snarly complaints. Goods had been stolen from a truck, defective products needed replacements, they weren't going to make the turnover forecast, but of course they did. They always did. Karen performed her work automatically and without real concern. Distracted, she wondered if there was some way of getting out of Versailles. Going there would just give the impression that everything was alright.

And why hadn't Jane answered her return text? She

took a breather to call her friend, but there was no answer.

Several coffee pauses and unanswered messages later, Karen phoned Fintan's.

"Hi, Tony, I'm a bit worried, Jane isn't answering her phone."

He told her calmly that Jane was in hospital.

"What! What happened?"

Karen managed to get the details but would have strangled Tony if she'd been standing near him. He seemed more annoyed that he would have to get someone to stand in for Jane than concerned for her condition. She hung up before finding herself saying something regrettable and rang Olivier only to be informed by some assistant that Monsieur De Belleville was in the middle of a meeting and could not be disturbed.

It wasn't possible to get off early from work, but a text stating 'I'm okay' from Jane calmed her...a little.

Poor Jane must have sent her that first message because she'd been in trouble. It was terrible to imagine her sitting in the Emergency Room by herself in the early hours of the morning.

Karen rushed up the eight flights to the *chambre de bonne*. On crutches, Jane opened the door.

"Jane," Karen almost wept, "you shouldn't be walking. What happened?"

"I don't know."

"What do you mean, you don't know?"

"Oh, I know the succession of events, but don't know how I could have been so stupid. It was such a silly accident."

"Tell me."

"I finished helping Tony to close for the night; you know how it is, Tony was cleaning up and I stayed on to help him. He'd just told me that he'd have to cancel our dinner date. It was supposed to be for tomorrow evening, but he had to change plans because of family issues. Then, a few minutes later, he came on to me, and was heavy about it, and I got very annoyed."

"What an asshole!"

"I told him in no uncertain terms that I wasn't interested in getting between the sheets. It was mortifying, the whole situation was impossible."

Karen silently applauded Jane.

"So, I was a bit down leaving the pub, and very tired. And that's what caused it. I was crossing Rue Lepic and tripped over uneven pavement. And this is the result!" Jane tried to wiggle her foot.

"That's all?"

"Yes. I hadn't been drinking and was just tired. It was an awkward fall. My ankle turned and something snapped, and then came the pain. That's when I sent you the message; walking the rest of the way home alone seemed impossible."

"And I didn't see your message on time," Karen said mournfully. "You should have called me."

"In hindsight, yes. But at first, I didn't want to wake you. I honestly thought I'd manage to hobble home. I rang Tony, but his phone was off, so I left a message for him, too."

"Did you limp up here, or call an ambulance?"

"It was the strangest thing: somebody came out of nowhere to help me while I was on the street?"

"Who?"

"That's just it...I don't know. It was very dark, and he was wearing a long coat and a hat. He had a scarf wrapped round his mouth, so his face wasn't visible."

"Were you afraid?"

"I was at first. He just stood there for a few seconds without uttering a word. Then he gave me his arm. And when I couldn't walk, he lifted me and carried me as far as my door. When I turned to thank him, he was gone."

"You could have encountered any crank, pimp, druggie, or who-knows-who. You were lucky."

"It was so odd: he appeared in front of me like a ghost and didn't utter a word—not one word."

"You had a close call. Never, never, do that again. If you are in trouble, ring me directly—do you hear me?"

"I hear you, and that's exactly what I would have done if that man hadn't come along."

"So, the man left you at your door, and then you called the ambulance to take you to the hospital?"

"That's right."

Jane swallowed several times and Karen realized that she was on the brink of tears. There she had been chastising and interrogating instead of giving some support. She went to the fridge, opened a bottle of water and filled a glass for her friend.

"Did something else happen?"

Jane took a sip, "Tony disappointed me; he must have gotten my message at some time, but didn't answer. I don't know how I could have been so stupid about him."

"Don't blame yourself."

"You never liked him, and you were right. He's pissed off because I spurned his advance, and more to the point, I won't be able to get back to work for at least two months."

"If I were you, I would never go back again."

"I have made up my mind to quit, but to do it the proper legal way. After my sick leave, I'll go back to work for a short while and then hand in my official resignation."

"Well—alright. You do get a proper payslip every month, don't you?"

"Of course I do. Without it, I couldn't have gotten my work permit. But I'm not sure about my insurance coverage."

"And you have a Vital card, I hope..."

"Yes, I have a medical card."

"Then that means your coverage is okay. I'll help you out if you're short in other ways, don't worry."

"Are you sure? Tony got quite nasty when I asked him

about complementary insurance."

"He's worse than all the names I called him. Don't worry, we'll work something out; that's what friends are for. Now, do you have enough to get by for a few days?"

"I do. Thankfully, I've been putting a little away for a rainy day. And I can do some readings to earn a little extra while I'm room bound."

Karen looked around Jane's room and shook her head slowly. "Don't do that."

"Karen, please—"

"Look, Jane, I've never been in love with this tarot reading business. The room is so confined, it's too risky; and now that you're on crutches, it's even more so. Why don't you come and stay with me?"

Jane took her crutches and stood up straight, "Much as I appreciate the offer, I don't need a minder.

"At least let me do the shopping for you... Just make out your list; it's easy for me to do it."

Karen didn't just go to the supermarket for Jane, but visited the flower stand and explained to Laurent what had happened.

"Laurent picked out a pretty plant. "Give her this one: a beautiful plant for a beautiful lady."

Monsieur Martin wasn't giving away anything for free, but she bought several magazines for Jane anyway.

Karen returned to Jane's room carrying the plant, chocolates and reading material. Doing something made her feel better. Olivier had called back telling her to help Jane in every way possible, and to spare no expense.

"I was thinking," said Jane, placing the plant on her window sill, "this accident may be a blessing in disguise. First, it will give me time to research crystals, how we might tackle setting up our own business, and work on my designs. It will also give me the opportunity to hone in on my clairvoyant skills, and do more readings, and get a real feel for it."

"That's fine; but just be careful not to step on Madame Lune's toes." If Jane wasn't going to be sensible and give up the idea, maybe she would succumb to a different sort of pressure.

"Madame Lune won't mind; I don't think readings are her main source of income. The woman didn't take money from us; she has a real gift and it was no accident that we found her."

Convinced that there was nothing accidental about their encounter with Madame Lune, Karen got ready to argue; but Jane had already taken a tarot deck in her hand and began to go through them one by one.

And for the next minute any kind of conversation was impossible as loud ringing from the basilica's bells deafened them.

Karen was finally able to take her hands from her ears, "What a racket, I hadn't realized how close to Sacre Coeur you are."

"They must be celebrating something."

Or mourning someone, Karen thought. The sound reminded her of the bells that had tolled for her grandfather's funeral. There was something so final about the call of the bells.

8

*T*he monster is less in control today, more agitated and careless. The hoary gasps from his lungs punch the air— cigarette lungs. He is off guard, but that is not a reason for me to let my defenses down. Something has caused it— excitement—Jane Moore's accident threw her right into his path. However, it was not the moment, not how it has been planned. He has chosen a day, a time and a way; the deed must take place then—according to *his* schedule. Yes, he almost lost control; it was a struggle, but he mastered it. Now, his blood pumps faster and his hunger grows.

Darkness is our chaperone. I follow him far from Rue Lepic to the elegant suburb of Neuilly-sur-Seine, to another cemetery. He climbs over the wall; it takes but a few seconds. I used to like graveyards; they brought me peace, but not anymore.

I wait some time before attempting the same climb that makes me feel every year of my life. It is harder because he must not hear a sound or know that someone walks in his steps.

He halts at a tomb and fumbles with the lock. The mausoleum door opens easily; it has been well oiled. He goes inside with assurance; it is not his right, but the monster has taken possession of this one. The light from his lamp is faint behind the narrow vents. The old mausoleums are all the same inside; the ground will be covered with dried out plants and withered flowers.

What is that in his hand? I cannot draw any closer, but it looks like a small iron bar is being used to lift a stone slab. It slides back and he descends into a crypt.

Five minutes, ten minutes, a quarter of an hour... The monster reappears, a smirk upon his face, and stands over the open tomb. He is in ecstasy, delirious, his face contorted. He breaks into a repulsive laugh, then fondles himself, sneers and spills his seed into the grave before finally collapsing on his belly. Revulsion ripples through me; nobody wants to watch such a display. I am too near, so I turn away and retreat behind another tomb.

He comes out looking calmer, locks the door and leaves the grounds. I return to the mausoleum and take a pen and paper from my pocket. I have always carried a pen and paper, even if I have done very little with them. I can draw though; it takes but little talent to copy the engraving on the stone and make a rough map.

By the time it is finished, I am feeling weak. 'Old woman, you are too far past your best years for these night adventures. Listen to your inner voice: you cannot keep up with him; that man is not fresh, but he is fresher than you are. Smoking has given him the lungs of a sixty-year-old, but he is far from that age and would still overpower you. Do things at your own pace, follow your own design.'

At last, the Champs Elysées. My legs are giving up. It is too much to go underground right away, my stomach cannot take it. It is seven in the morning and the avenue is alive; there are a lot of people already on the go for work and pleasure, and others finishing the night.

I eat a croissant and drink some tea, but take little delight in my breakfast. My mind has not left the cemetery;

it is on all I have seen. Traffic thunders up and down; the wide footpaths are being power-washed; people file by—fast steps, slow steps—some old and serious, others young and carefree. I have never been young and carefree.

It was a mistake to try to eat. I barely make it downstairs to the café toilets. The cubicle is small and has just been cleaned. Everything comes up, I vomit my insides out. What does one expect after the grotesque scene in the cemetery? What is to be done with something so loathsome and evil? It is only the beginning; to uncover all, there will be days of following him. I have not the stomach to see more. The boil pours out, reliving his deeds, his awful deeds.

The movement helps me. I walk and walk the streets, meandering northwards. I find a water fountain near Rue Pigalle and wash out my mouth. Rue Lepic is harder to climb today and it takes a great effort to struggle up the stairs. Pierre is there, he came back sometime in the night; he would not have been happy to find a cold bed. I do not go under the blankets beside him, but lie on top and watch the moody sky outside the window. The sun will rise and set and shame me into trailing him once more.

It is after midnight and the monster leaves earlier. 'Where are you going to take me tonight?' I am bound to follow him—wherever he goes, I go too.

We are going into the Metro; the tunnel will bring respite from the bitter wind that is blowing. He is not disguised; there is no reason, not yet. We make a line change and then another.

We get out at Montparnasse; it is not hard to guess the final destination. His form shrinks as he draws his body in; though wearing the same clothes, he is transforming himself inside them. I too can do that; it is the trick of a magician to change who you are before undiscerning eyes. He pulls out a scarf and wraps it around his neck—a cap for his head, glasses on his nose and gloves on those hands. It is done naturally while walking, and his entire body changes. At various points along the street, people have seen a new person.

Montparnasse cemetery is a place for tens of thousands, but the path is familiar to he who slides in like a contortionist. His body has been compressed, his bones are made of rubber. I copy his movements; that trick comes naturally to me. Passing through the bars of a railing is easier than climbing a wall. The monster knows exactly where he is going and needs no map but does not go directly to the tomb of his choice. Instead, he takes various paths to the right and to the left, twisting this way and that. It is safer to hang far behind. I have always been blessed with a good sense of direction, a powerful memory and sharp senses, and they have not abandoned me.

Finally, he stops by a mausoleum. It is ancient. Nobody has been inside it for years and years. He enters. I do not want to watch anymore and prefer to take shelter from the wind that cuts my skin. His nocturnal excursions are taking their toll on me.

An hour passes. My body is ice and the air is as wild as the monster. He is famished for the spoils of the past. He leaves satiated and satisfied.

The mausoleum has been forsaken. The iron-gate is rusted. Anyone can walk inside. I leave the biting wind and for a second it feels warm; then a musky scent grows stronger, drawing me to lift the stone slab covering the casket. I take a sharp instrument from a hidden pocket in my coat and use it as a lever. My gut tightens. It is in semi-decay, a head maybe, just a head. I let the cover drop and flee the tomb. It is not the sight of the body that repulses me, though it is rotting and gruesome. What is worse is the memory that sticks to it. There is horrendous pain, and the cemetery is filled with screams. Everything comes to my eyes and my ears. It is like walking in his shoes, like being him. It is unbearable.

Shush! What is that? Someone is here. Be still...

He suspects something and has come back. I have been careless and lowered my shield. I should have anticipated his return. I did not. Any suspicion that somebody has followed him will make him break his routine, and then we will all be sorry.

Where is he? The unknown makes me nervous. Is he hiding somewhere? My body cramps from head to toe—I am stone. My senses cannot locate him. Time passes and finally it is possible to breathe again. I was mistaken; there is nobody there. My nerves overruled my sense of reason, and that is dangerous.

The monster has taken me all over Paris and its suburbs. All Souls has passed and the memory of his many victims has been stirred. Such memories remind him of his glorious triumphs, even as he prepares for the next one. The need has been building within him for a long time now; for a year, perhaps two, since Jane Moore came to the street. The mountain of martyrs has been chosen; Jane's resting place will be Montmartre cemetery. The tomb has been selected and the tools to be used have been placed; the cask has been unlocked. His evil is inside my head; it is everywhere. What am I to do with this knowledge? It is not like me to change my mind. What good would be served by bringing the girls back? What would I tell them? Maybe if Jane Moore left the street, and if he didn't see her every day, her life would be spared.

We are out of money again; we always seem to need more money.

Pierre is asking me for something. He holds out both hands as he makes his request, something hopeful in his eyes: "You will go on the Metro with me?"

It is like a dying man's request. His accordion sits in the corner; the keys a sickly sallow and the jaded bellows in better shape than either of us. I nod, "Tomorrow, I will go with you."

That is enough to make him happy.

I have never refused to follow his busking escapades; it is not in me to belittle him. He whistles contentedly, puts on his coat and goes out. Pierre pretends to be the provider and I let him believe that. In a certain way he is; we would not be tenants in this apartment without him. It is his find, a lucky stroke in his life to have had friends who got us this far. It is his name on the phone, on the bills, on everything that needs a signature. I am anonymous; yet without me he would never have kept us off the streets. Pierre could never have been a true gypsy, or a roving busker; it was not in his blood. But it is in mine. It would not have taxed me to have taken to the roads forever, going from fair to fair. I think it would not be a bad life. But my companion would not have borne it for long, preferring his street, his café and his pleasures.

Something is tearing inside me; I will have to open the past. Some days I feel the scrubbing soap of my grandmother on my hands; I smell the iodine of the sea-grass and taste the salt on my tongue. Karen Moroney has brought them back to me, has brought what I would rather have forgotten.

I have rarely made decisions that would have brought me back into society, moved me away from the margins and shadowy borders. I did it when I left home, left the salt and the sea behind me, and would have done it for my baby. I will have to do it for her, for them, for Jane Moore and Karen Moroney.

Is that not what you would have done, Grandmother? You must have taken me many times in your arms when I was a baby. You must have had your doubts and scrutinized in fear. Though my memory gives no proof, it would be quite normal to compare the mother and child and harbor doubts. You often defended me, Grandmother, and tried to protect me from the worst, but you were not always around when the other children ganged up, swarming like flies around me, jeering and mocking. I hear them as if it were yesterday. I hear them shouting, "She isn't all there, can't be; it runs in the blood, runs in the family!"

There is no hate in me. How can one hate people who do not understand, could not understand? You cannot hate ignorance; you can only try to shield yourself from it. Hate has never been my driving force, only survival and a wish to be left alone.

I see the child kneeling in the corner of the schoolroom, and I hear the voices: "The child is slow and dumb, holding back the others." They pin a board on the child's back and shout out the word written on it: DUNCE! But the child was not a dunce, yet was not like the others, and understood that one day there would be no choice but to run.

You bring back the memories, Karen Moroney—you and your postcards: the sweet smell of grass, hay-making, the quiet sounds of nature, and the freedom that a child has to race wildly. It tempts me: the little place by the sea, the shriek of seagulls calling over the cliffs—walking along the shore, sand imprinted on the soles of my feet, collecting shells. However, part of the child would not have that again: avoiding people, the shame and the ridicule...standing on the shore and wishing for the tide to come and sweep her out to the infinite sea.

There was a boy who saw who I was. He talked to me, child to child. He did not mock and run, did not look at me with eyes that ridiculed. His name was Padraig. Every time I ran to the sand, that boy was there. He talked about his home, the farm where he lived; he told me about his mother and father and his sisters. I loved to listen to him because he talked to me as an equal. Nobody had talked to me before in that way; they talked at me, about me and around me, but never to me. I helped him discover the shell fish, the birds and the insects. When we played in the fields, I took him to my secret places. The knowledge of nature was in my head, everything my grandmother had told me; I had memorised all. Listening and memorizing was how I learned; it was my book, the only way I could read.

It was simple at that age, when we would run barefoot and never feel the cold. I feel the cold now; it goes into my veins and eats into my bones. Even during hot summers when the heat torments, and the sweat runs down my body, and the dust dries on my skin, I am cold. As cold as the bodies that lie in the cemetery...

Jane has not given up the notion of dabbling in fortune-telling. She must finish with her dabbling and move on. A business that predicts the future has no future. I have no vision of Jane Moore in the future. Does that mean the end? Does that mean her friend will lose her? But recently, it has also taken more of an effort to make out Karen Moroney's face in years to come; it too is fading. Are my warnings driving them into his path?

Karen sits at the café table across the room but does not see me. The disconnected events of her life force their way into my consciousness. The trouble in her building concerns her. It is not my business, but Madame Lune can predict that Karen will soon discover the spiteful person who torments the gay couple...very, very soon. I could tell her that it will be to her own sorrow and that the same spiteful person could enlighten her more about the danger on Rue Lepic; or that her neighbors have eyes and they too can open hers to understand the man who shares her bed. She would like to leave her boyfriend, but does not dare. I could tell her all that; but it is not my place. My rule is only tell people what they need to know; avoid denouncing others, for one should never try to cheat the hand of fate. It is not the task of the medium to make the future.

I have had difficulty looking directly at her. Karen Moroney, you have his eyes. There is so much of him in you; it is hard to imagine that it could be so. The past is relentless as it chases us. I cannot run from it, no more than stay one step ahead of the in-coming tide. The waves rise up and will soon enfold me, until I am no more.

9

Karen put down the book on Tarot cards that Jane had lent her. It was odd stuff. Did people just write this off the top of their heads? Nobody could deny the value of intuition and feelings, but when people started calling themselves clairvoyants and explaining the practice as if it were science, that seemed ridiculous. Besides, dissecting the steps of fortune telling like one would a card trick simply killed the mystery.

Having lost patience with it, Karen put the book away and got ready for lunch. She'd promised to take Jane out of her room to the café. Eric and Frederic were coming along too, and that sounded like a more pleasant way to spend an hour.

"Jingle bells, Jingle bells," Frederic sang.

Karen blocked her ears. "That's the only Christmas song French people know."

"That's not true," Eric retorted, "though we don't have quite the collection of songs and carols that you Anglos have. Hey, isn't Rue Lepic looking lovely? Aren't those lights fabulous?"

Jane stood her crutches in the corner. "And the window displays are very tasteful."

Karen looked out from the terrace. "It is nice; I wish our building were as festive."

Eric tapped his knife and fork together to make a tinkling sound. "Ours isn't a very funny building."

Her ears pricked up. "Well—Chantal does have a crib with a pretty nativity scene," she added cautiously.

"She would," said Frederic.

Karen had heard enough, "Anyway, it won't feel like Christmas until I smell the turkey cooking in my mother's kitchen."

"Going home then?" Frederic surmised.

"Just for a few days."

"Jane?" Eric asked.

"Christmas in Ballybunion with Karen's family. I'm thrilled, really looking forward to it."

"The Moroney family is very excited about Jane's visit," Karen confirmed.

"And perhaps Olivier's visit too?" Frederic didn't try to be subtle.

"No—No, he's spending Christmas with his own family in Versailles. Will you guys be working?"

"Yes, it's our busiest season. Money, money, money!" Frederic pretended to pick bills out of the air.

"We're researching solutions for Afro hair." Eric took a mouthful of salad.

"Can't be done without chemicals," Jane challenged them.

"That's what I heard too," Karen said. "The same goes for color, especially blond. There are limitations to organic."

"We already have the answer for some colors," Eric pointed out. "Admittedly, they are not perfect, but the experts are working on improving them. And we do have one or two things to offer those with Afro." He studied Jane's mane. "There might be some possibilities."

Jane shook her head. "I'm sorry, but you can't turn steel wire into cotton candy. A lady's got to do what a lady's got to do."

"We could try," Eric insisted.

"You're too charming and good looking for your own good," Jane flattered him. "I might be tempted to go to your salon just to be spoiled by you."

"Eric is good at bringing in business." Frederic smiled at his partner.

"I can see that," Jane said. "He'd put wigs on ladybirds and convince bald eagles they needed hair to fly."

Eric bowed in false modesty and fingered Jane's hair. "Where do you usually get it done?"

"Jean Gabriel."

"There are other specialists that cost less," Frederic was quick to point out.

"I don't like specialists...don't like 'black only' salons," Jane said.

Jane had already explained about not feeling at home in specialized, black salons; they were just too clique and too ethnic. Karen understood her point of view and felt exactly the same way about socializing in Irish pubs when abroad.

"Oops—watch out, Philippe!" Jane's warning came too late as the waiter brought her crutches clattering to the ground.

"Pardon, Pardon," he hurried to replace them and darted off to another table.

Jane shook her head and laughed.

Her friend had bounced back from her accident quickly, and while it was awkward getting around on crutches, the fracture wasn't as bad as they'd first thought. Perhaps the broken ankle was the danger that Madame Lune had been talking about, and that would be the end of it.

The living room was designed to impress, but to Karen the style was heavy and sterile. The best feature was the bay windows which welcomed the winter sun. There was no hint of Christmas in the apartment. Unlike the Irish, the French didn't get down to putting up a tree at home until a few days ahead of the big meal, or as they called it, 'le Réveillon de Noël.'

Although it did make her feel like being in a museum full of antiques, objectively there were a lot of valuable pieces in Olivier's family home. Marie-Claude, Madame de Belleville, and her husband, Charles, had inherited some of the furniture; other pieces they had bought with care and restored over the years. The dark polished wooden floor boards were decorated with Oriental carpets, while the white walls and ceilings showed off detailed plaster work.

The furniture was Sun King style; it was all Louis XIV. But the pieces weren't imitation, rather the real thing. Olivier had given her several lectures on the subject. Karen grimaced at her seldom worn skirt; being in such surroundings brought out her more lady-like qualities. The place was made for chic dresses and fancy heels.

She curled her lips politely at Monsieur de Belleville until her jaws ached. The only thing to do was cling to her crystal aperitif glass and incline her head in agreement as he explained why the Scots produced the best whiskey.

"Tell me, mademoiselle, have you been to Scotland?"

"No, I haven't, but the Irish -"

"Yes, yes—the Irish are well known for their drinking." He had a habit of leaning in too closely when he spoke which in turn forced her to step back.

"Ah, I prefer Irish whiskey," Jean-Baptiste, Madame de Belleville's brother, joined them. He had returned from a two year mission in the Ivory Coast as a diplomat at the French Embassy and had a lot to say about many things.

"So you work in Paris?" He bent over her until his face was almost right in hers.

"In the suburbs," she corrected.

"Karen works for TX Satellites," Monsieur de Belleville clarified.

"Is that's right; what do you do exactly?"

"She's a sales assistant," Monsieur de Belleville didn't seem to think that she could make her own replies in French.

"Oh," Jean-Baptiste took a sip of his whiskey.

She might have dressed it up with fancier words: 'I work in logistics' or 'I work in data management' or better still, 'I'm in import-export.' But why bother?

"Do they have a good promotion system there?" Jean-Baptiste looked for the positives.

"Well—am -"

Monsieur de Belleville put his arm around Karen's shoulder, "I think in those global companies where they are always outsourcing, one is lucky to keep his job. Am I right?"

"I suppose," Karen said.

"I see," Jean-Baptiste took another sip. "I do like Ireland, a beautiful country. I love Connemara." Diplomacy was his business after all.

On feeling the back of her legs touch a chair, she could retreat no farther and looked for moral support. However, Olivier had sneaked out on the balcony to smoke with his brother-in- law, Antoine, leaving her to her own devices.

Karen decided that sitting down was probably the only way of getting away from these imposing gentlemen. She lowered herself gingerly and perched on the edge. By modern standards, it should have been difficult to sit on such chairs but in fact she was forced to admit, begrudgingly, that it could be managed. They were very low to the ground and especially comfortable for short-legged people. Our ancestors had clearly been of much smaller stature. It wasn't the ideal place for balancing her glass, and she just managed to save hers from falling, limiting the damage to a few drops on the gold and cream striped upholstery. She spread out her skirt a little to hide the offending spots. On second thoughts, sitting might not have been the brightest of ideas; she was face to face with Madame de Belleville who pinned her with a frown. Karen smiled innocently and focused her attention on the other female members of the family around the coffee table.

Olivier's older sister, Claire, seemed friendlier than her mother. But she was busy fussing over her baby, Albert. Prams, soothers, and baby bottles were not Karen's thing; still any distraction was welcome. Béatrice, the youngest in the family, was much more reserved and apart from stealing glances at her didn't seem willing to engage in long conversations.

Emphasizing the formal 'vous,' Madame de Belleville made polite inquiries about Karen's family.

"You must be very happy to be a grandmother," Karen returned.

"Pardon?"

Shit, obviously not the right thing to say, "You have a beautiful grandchild."

A delighted Claire held up Albert while Madame de Belleville nodded coldly.

Béatrice offered her more pistachios.

Karen grabbed a handful. It was hard to imagine her own parents reacting so indifferently to their first grandchild. Cracking open the shells had suddenly become a challenge to her butter fingers; she rescued a shell that had fallen on the floor. Another whiskey would have been appreciated, but as the other ladies were on fruit juice, shouting out loud for a refill would be the height of bad manners. Defeated, she risked munching a second nut and did the only safe thing—looked around.

Even if it wasn't her taste, Karen couldn't deny that the apartment was chic—everything was gilded, worked, and majestic. The writing desk was a sight to behold with its carved, caned, gilt-wood. The fireplaces were fine pieces, the marble workmanship excellent. And who could fault the chandeliers? There was a lot to admire, not least the awesome mirrors with antique gold-leaf; the slightly tarnished finish was a give-away that they were the genuine article.

"Would you mind?"

Startled, Karen looked up to find Claire pushing a bag into her arms. "Sorry?"

"I need to change Albert." A second bag was handed to her sister. "Come—come into the bedroom across the corridor; there is a bathroom en-suite there."

She sighed and tried to make the most of if. Claire was paying her a compliment by asking her to help with changing the baby.

Claire's mother didn't seem interested and excused herself to go and check up on things in the kitchen.

Karen stood up—the word 'fusil de chasse,' reached her ears. Monsieur de Belleville was telling a very animated story about the wild boars he had killed with his new hunting gun. He then invited the other gentlemen into a side room to see his armory collection.

She made a face at Olivier's back and followed his sisters meekly into the bedroom. In her opinion, Olivier's behavior changed when among his family in Versailles. He filled even more space, his gestures became grander and his voice went up a notch.

Karen quickly understood that little more was expected of her except to admire Claire's nappy changing skills.

She glanced around curiously. "Whose bedroom is this?"

"It was Olivier's." Béatrice stood beside her to watch Claire ooh and ahh over the baby.

"Really, does he still stay here?"

Béatrice snorted, "Not very often, but mother keeps it for him."

Karen looked more closely and realized that it was a boy's rather than a man's room. The book shelves had lots of comics, including several volumes of 'Tintin, Céderic,' and 'Super Boy.' There were building bricks, toy soldiers, a large plastic sword, and other such treasures from his childhood.

"I hate this room," The distain in Béatrice's voice was difficult to ignore.

"There, there," Claire gave an embarrassed laugh and kissed Albert. "You're not going to start sulking about that old story again, are you?"

Béatrice walked out.

"It's nothing," Claire explained to Karen. "When we were children Olivier delighted in teasing his younger sister. One day he gathered all her dolls and sawed them to pieces here. They were ruined. He was very sorry afterwards, but Béatrice has never forgiven him, especially because he didn't get punished—mother spoiled him."

"It was a horrible thing to do."

"Your brothers never teased you?"

"Sometimes—yes."

"All little boys are horrible and break their sisters' dolls. But they grow up."

"Sure they do."

"Albert looks quite like him, doesn't he?" Claire pointed to a portrait on the wall.

Karen walked over to study it. It was Olivier as a boy. He looked so sad. There was something very haunting and ethereal about children's portraits. This one made her uneasy; it was as if the artist had captured something that should never have been revealed. The boy in the portrait seemed lost and forlorn.

"Did he have many friends?"

"A few; we always had lots of cousins around."

Until then, Karen had never felt that Olivier had suffered loneliness growing up in his family. Yet the artist had chosen to paint that aspect in. Olivier had told her that his childhood memories were of endless walks in the Versailles grounds with their nanny. The family had personal relations with the curator of the palace, so they were afforded many private visits to the interior. Karen had been inside Versailles Chateau and gardens as a common tourist and had found it quite tame, preferring her own upbringing on the farm by the sea, which seemed wilder and freer than the immense park and grounds of Versailles.

In the style of all old wealthy families, the house didn't abound with servants. The only other person visible was a discreet Portuguese woman who helped with serving the food. Madame de Belleville had supervised all the cooking, and Karen was made to understand that the menu was decided on with her in mind. Maybe there was a hint in there somewhere for her; the main dish of Chou-croute Garnie was definitely a peasant affair. The French were wonderful cooks; no one doubted that. However, of all the dishes, Karen hated Chou-croute with a passion; it was the closest one could get to bacon and cabbage, but dressed up with a whole series of other tastes and pickled flavors. It was preceded by a starter of Cepes a la Savoyarde. Her knowledge of wild mushrooms had been pretty limited before coming to Paris, but France had taught her a thing or two about them, and Cepes were just the tip of the iceberg.

The Sauternes wine that was being served featured as the main subject right through the meal. Karen took comfort in every glass; at last something decent to keep her going.

Feeling a little dizzy, she was quite happy to sit back and listen. While the men were doing most of the talking, it was clear that the atmosphere was controlled by Madame de Belleville. A smile from her was high praise indeed and she often smiled when Olivier spoke.

Karen fixed her gaze on the face of Monsieur de Belleville seated opposite her. Something about him unnerved her. It was like looking into Olivier's eyes, and it was that expression that had been niggling—one that was all the more evident when studied from this angle—a sly and sneaky look that hadn't struck her so directly before. She didn't like it one bit, especially when his eyes kept resting on her rather ample bosom, and pulled her cardigan firmly closed.

Feeling restless, she picked up one of the knives. The cutlery was made of heavy stainless steel. Each piece was handmade from Laguiole, a famous name in the world of cutlery. Olivier even carried a Laguiole pocket knife which had been a gift from his father; it was distinctive with its sinuous outline and carved ivory handle.

Madame de Belleville's glance reminded her that it was bad manners to fidget.

Like a naughty child, Karen put the knife down and tried to keep up with the conversation as it continued to swing in the direction of cuisine and wines, and never swung back to anything else. They reeled off history, dates and stories about every morsel on the table; but the Château d'Yquem opened in Jean-Baptiste's honor got the greatest adulation. Karen felt like going on her knees and bowing before the bottle.

That was until the cheese board. Without checking her watch, she ascertained that discussion around the Bleu d'Auvergne, Brie de Melun, Fourme de Cantal and Crottin de Chauvignol must have gone on at least one hour. But it meant more wine; Karen had passed the merry stage and was, by now, quite certain that some objects on the table had begun to float by themselves. To help dilute the alcohol effect, she reached across the table for a decanter of water.

"Let me," Olivier had taken it.

"I can do it," he was patronizing her as if she were a child. She took it back from him; but the decanter was heavier than expected and it slipped through her hands, crashing on the table. "Sorry, sorry—I'm terrible sorry."

"It's only water," said Jean-Baptiste.

Claire made a soothing noise and mopped it up as she might do for her baby.

Karen didn't dare look in the direction of Olivier or his mother, but could feel a freeze setting in. From blurry thoughts, she had the brilliant idea that the best way to win back favor was to shine with some clever questions.

"Do—do you hunt a lot Monsieur—Monsieur de Belleville?"

All heads turned towards her.

"Hunting goes back several generations in this family; peasants and hunters are the soul of this country." He moved the bottle of wine away from her.

"I'm against it myself; I—I think it's a very cruel sport—cruel and prim—primitive." Karen was too drunk to notice her slurred words echoing back in the hush; a hush only broken by a giggle from Béatrice—and Olivier's—"For goodness sake, Karen."

What was wrong with them; a good debate was always exciting at the dinner table?

"Where are we, are we home?" Karen pulled herself up in the car seat; god everything was spinning around her.

Olivier hung over the steering wheel in moody silence.

Karen made another effort to drag her body upright in the seat, "Those—those are trees; we're in the wood."

"Yes, I took this way to avoid traffic."

"Good—good thinking. Jesus! What was that—where did all those bodies come from?" She pressed her face to the window; there were strange creatures, stark naked or in nothing but bras and knickers, standing near tree trunks—she must be hallucinating.

"Prostitutes," Olivier said drily, "If you drive through Les Bois de Boulogne at this time of the night, you see prostitutes." He made a sound in his throat.

"Are you laughing at me?"

"Hardly. You're going to have some hangover tomorrow."

"The—the Irish can—can handle their drink."

"Evidently. I hope you remember enough to apologize to my mother."

"Huh."

"You told her that the Tarte Tatin she'd baked paled in comparison with your mother's apple tart."

"Shit," Karen slid back down in the seat, the images of boobs and bottoms, and Monsieur de Belleville's drooling mouth doing the rounds in her head—or was it Olivier's drooling mouth?

"It was nasty of—of you to destroy Béatrice's dolls; that was—was horrid."

Olivier shifted in his seat.

She opened one eye and shut it quickly again. Olivier hadn't been laughing this time; his face had been dark and thunderous.

The car slowed down to a stop.

"What are you doing?" she opened her eyes once more.

"I need to pee," he banged the door.

Karen put a hand to her stomach, already sorely regretting her day in Versailles.

10

Lately, I feel everything around me, every small detail that is not mine to feel. There is an ache when someone hurts—even a stranger. I am touched by their despair, their happiness, their love and joy. In that, at least, I rejoice; it is like being reborn. I never had the freedom of owning such feelings, never knew how it could be. I am a child again, but without the burden of wearing the cloak, or carrying the stone on my back. Should that upset me? Is this something that could have been shaken off before, dealt with earlier in my life? A voice tells me no: you cannot make the sun rise or set earlier, you cannot make the day turn faster.

The bells of the basilica ring out in portent, filling me with dread. That is part of their design and we cannot be indifferent; they are there to summon us to prayer, to ritual, and to lead us in the final march.

The monster stops dead in his tracks. Is he too listening to the bells? Is that why he has stopped? It is a poignant sound; even when resounding for celebratory occasions, it is sad. Pierre's ashen face put fear in me this morning. After breakfast, he returned to the bedroom to lie down, something he has never done before. I was afraid to leave him alone, but his heart sputtered to a start again and the rest of his body seemed to recover.

I have begun to remember things that had been forgotten, things about his family in the south of France. Pierre will one day return to Provence, to his roots. He has no direct family left, except his son Dimitri, and he has been lost for a long time. It is fortunate for Pierre that his family never knew all of his life—his real life. He lived a lie for most of it, but it hurt nobody. In bygone days, Pierre would make visits alone to Provence—he would go home. His family thought their boy was a musician, a proper musician, not a Metro busker. They thought he had moderate success in clubs and bars, and that was success enough for them. When Pierre went south, he spent like a man of comfortable means as I worked harder to make those visits possible. I did not mind. Pierre has nephews and nieces, and would want to find his final resting place in the resting place in the south of France. I will do that for him; there are names and numbers in my memory. It is not my wish, but everything has to be ready.

The music of the bells expires and the monster walks onward, but without my shadow. I have no desire to follow him today. He will go to Montmartre Cemetery and continue setting the place for his ritual. There are things that must be done on my side...to be prepared for the unknown.

I go the hard way up to Sacre Coeur, step by painful step. The toy-like train trundles past, mocking me with its speed, but I have a purpose and never lose sight of that.

At the top, my pockets are heavier with spoils; it has been a lucrative trip. The basilica is my house of respite, a place to kneel and pray. I bless myself—it has always been my way to tell my right hand from my left. I say some prayers; they are not for me, they are for Pierre, for Jane Moore, and for Karen Moroney. It is hopeless; without belief my prayers are empty and hollow.

I inhale powerful incense... Like a genie from a bottle,

my grandmother is there. It is a fond moment—she is standing at the kitchen table and the fire is burning in the old stove. Grandmother is talking—talking is what she was good at. My mother is there, talking too—nonsense, lots of nonsense; it is no wonder I have no words. Still, it is a happy moment; for when I return to it, the child is not old enough to envisage what life might hold. Grandmother is in full throes of getting everything organized for the Christmas feast. The sounds of cooking lull me into a peaceful trance; the ham is bubbling in a pot over the fire and the potatoes are being boiled for the stuffing. She asks me to peel the onions; it is a chore that everybody dislikes, but I want to help. We fry the onions; I love the taste of the juice and put my finger in the pan to lick the drippings...

I would scurry around like a cat, getting all the scraps. Grandmother usually started to cook the turkey early on Christmas morning, and the aroma would entice me out of bed. That moment was more important than my presents, which might be knitted gloves or a scarf. Then there were the books. In the beginning, I told Santa Claus to bring me books with lots of pictures, but later, when I knew it was Grandmother, I would plead with her not to give me any books. They brought only hurt and incomprehension. She would insist that all children wanted books. How could I explain to her that something was wrong? How indeed, when I could not explain it to myself? My mother would laugh foolishly, and Grandmother would look annoyed and send her out to fetch more turf from the shed.

I didn't know then what the word happiness was, but believe I was happy, while still childish enough to be unaware. I rarely return in memory, but Karen Moroney has broken the seal. It is nice to shelter in that warm kitchen of long ago, where the fire dances and the walls whisper and sigh. The stone floor is solid under my feet; I can doze there and hear the tiles settling.

The wooden floor boarding in the bedroom was the

finest. It seemed that way because Grandmother spoke of how respected a carpenter my grandfather was and often pointed out the workmanship that went into making those floors...

My mother knew I only liked the icing on the Christmas cake, and I remember that one time she protected me; it still surprises me that Mother could do and understand that much. There is regret deep inside, something I do not want to feel. It is the same regret one might have about a dog or a cat that has been unfairly locked out in the rain, or whose tail has been accidentally stepped on.

I had stolen behind my grandmother's back—picked a chunky piece of icing from the cake. I already had the makings of a thief in me. My grandmother would slap me if she found out—and find out she would! But I risked it for my fleeting sinful pleasure. It was so obvious when you looked at the cake, but the greedy child did not think about all of that and stole a large piece of icing. My mother came into the kitchen, saw the cake and understood. She took a knife and cut a thick slice from that part of the cake, buttered and ate it.

Grandmother discovered the damaged cake and was angry. Mother took the blame and the cuff across her ear, "Your appetite will be gone and you won't be able to eat supper," Grandmother cuffed her again.

My mother just smiled and did her skit, saying that it was such a lovely cake that she just could not help it...

We were used to her garbled way of speaking, but many people could not understand her. They said that maybe her tongue was stuck to the roof of her mouth. I was not much better and had inherited her crippling handicap. What I remember is that Mother never mentioned me taking the icing, and her action that day saved me a punishment. It was the one moment, perhaps the only moment, when I looked at her with different eyes and kissed her.

I bat those memories from me, like one would the midges on a warm evening. Such memories only serve to distract and weaken my will. By softening me, they will not help against what is to come. I have to stay in the present, that is all that counts. Watch him, see him, and know him.

The monster is on the other side of the street and looking at me, but I cannot be sure. Something trembles inside me: 'Do not be given to fear, do not be afraid; maybe he is looking in your direction, but not at you.' I test him by leaving my bench and walking up the street; his eyes follow me. He takes the risk of leaving his post unattended. Has the monster seen through my disguise? Does he realize that I know? No, I am mistaken. She is there, also in his line of vision. He is not following me but Jane Moore, who is walking ahead of me. I am between them, and invisible to both; an ordinary walker on the street, the person you see and then don't see.

Jane Moore walks the hill that I have just descended. I will have to climb it again because he is following her. It is the first time he has done that. Jane goes very slowly on her crutches and enters the church. She is troubled over something and kneels to pray.

I watch him watching her as she makes her way to the candles and lights one. Jane goes back outside. She takes out her phone and calls someone...her friend, Karen. Karen is not in love with her boyfriend; there is something about him that isn't right. It is hard to accept that we have made a mistake and easier to remain blind. 'Walk out, Karen, and leave him. Leave him now. Not only is he sick, but deceptive and weak, and weak people are dangerous.' But it is not my place to tell you how to live your life. I must follow the monster and cannot allow others' troubles to divert me.

Why her? Why Jane Moore? There is nothing extraordinary in Jane Moore's actions, nor is there something special in her words. Yet there is something for which he thirsts. What does she have that others do not? Is it her youth, her beauty, her joy? Is it random?

It is vital to try to understand and to have a notion of his time. The only way is to return to the cemetery. I choose an hour when he never goes, though lately everything about him has become more unpredictable, leaving his post at odd moments, following impulses.

I retrace his steps to the mausoleum he has chosen in Montmartre. It has a name engraved on it, as well as a date and a short prayer. It means nothing to me. I close my eyes and lose myself in meditation until something strange comes into my body; there will be a price to pay later, when beastly dreams come back to haunt me. I am full of hate, his hate—my body swells with it. It sickens me. And coming from all of that, there is tremendous hurt. It is not that which interests me; that is an old and well-worn road, walked by many. It is not useful to seek to understand everything that cannot be understood, not in this world. I am only interested in knowing the order of his mind, not his feelings. There is a difference. What is the timescale? How long does she have? A day, a week, a month? To know the answer, one must think as he thinks, function as he functions, get inside his skin. I can do it; I have been functioning out of my skin for a long time, all my life.

It is time to return to Rue Lepic, to make my way back to the square, every step a reluctant one. Jane Moore and Karen Moroney are at their favorite café; the waiter frets around them, more brusque in his movements than usual. In a clumsy gesture, he lets crockery fall from his tray and it smashes on the tiles, causing conversations to abate for a second and then resume at a normal rhythm. With a brush and shovel he tries to gather the pieces. That waiter has been helping himself to the bar, and his actions are not steady.

Nothing on Rue Lepic is different; life continues as

usual. Everybody is there, as they should be: the shops and the traders, the grocers, the newspaper and flower-stands. All the smells reach me: croissants, fresh bread, coffee, cheese, fruit and perfume—the odour of people.

The flower seller draws on his cigarette; the smoke whirls around him as he stands in the open air, city air, polluted air. He is overdosed on petrol and fumes. I am as weather beaten as he is.

The newspaper man sees a lot and says little; and his hands grow blacker and blacker. The Vietnamese woman will have it out with her Arab enemy; yes, Madame Lu and Monsieur Abu will come to blows. Under different circumstances, they might have liked each other, but there is only room for one here on this street. I see the drycleaner and a woman more selfish than any other leaning against the door jam. It is a seductive pose and is not wasted.

I walk the Pigalle District with no aim other than to walk. It is as familiar and strange to me as the places of my childhood. Tourists throng the boulevard, music drifts out of bars and clubs. The smell of crepes, caramel coated nuts, homemade sweets, and liquorice seasons the air. Stands hog the central island, along with a merry-go-round and carnival glitter. Christmas is everywhere. Everything will be glazed over with layers of festive tinsel. They are setting up wooden chalets for the Christmas market. Soon there will be new fragrances; the air will reak with richer food, spicy bread, and festive roasts. There will be scented candles, mulled wine, and crowds of browsers looking desperately for gift ideas. It is of no matter to me.

Nearby, vulgar, sluttish posters call from walls, and the whores display their wares inside windows. Others stand in doorways and on corners. A mother pushes a pram into the supermarket. Transvestites parade their confusion; it is not truly theirs—it is ours—for normality does not exist. Evil does, and evil is never on show.

Anger is my new friend. I will need it, because it is

obvious to me that I will be obliged to change myself, to go into the darker corners of his mind. I have only been to the periphery. I have followed, watched and walked his way, but it is not enough. His hate terrifies me. Everything in me resists entering his world. His evil is abhorrent to me, but something is telling me that there is no choice.

I find myself tidying and tidying, throwing away pieces of the past, putting things into boxes. They are not valuable things, they are useless. Collecting has never been my pastime; all this material is Pierre's. I have attached myself to nothing in life and to nobody. The flat is not mine, it is not ours; I never wasted time making it mine.

Night has fallen and catches me unaware. It is not good to lose touch with one's basic senses. I rarely work at night—too much darkness and too many things that are better not to see. I am not the night owl or the prowling cat, but a slow careful creature that prefers the dawn, but I will go back out this evening.

The girls are seated inside the café window. He is close by, watching, never far, often there and then gone. He is listening to every word they say. Jane Moore senses something and looks around. She does not know what it is, but it bothers her, a constant chill that cannot be explained. I try to understand, as often before, and ask myself the same questions. Is it something in her look, her color, her size? Is it her foreignness? Is there something in the way she speaks?

I too am sitting nearby, and nobody notices me. I listen to them speak, and I hear her voice, the tone, timbre, and the rhythm. Is that what drives him into his dementia, her voice? As she speaks, the nerves rise within him, and it is an effort to control his ticks. The monster grows calmer when she stops speaking. Her voice must be torture to him.

Would it change something if she were to speak

differently, alter her accent? No, because it is much more than that, it is in the vibrations carrying emotions from the pit of our stomach through our lungs, from afar. We can disguise ourselves, cover our faces with make-up and put on wigs, but the essence of our being is always there, in the voice. It does not change. In the same way, we can speak with different accents, pitch higher or lower, but even under such a veneer, the real voice is never hidden. The voice carries something we do not control. To him, voices are flat and functional, or voices are persecution. He has one dominant sense, hearing. It is twisted and warped to any other ear but his. A voice can reassure, make us happy and give us hope, but it can also deceive us and let us down. It can be the instrument of pain.

The monster is addicted to her voice but also hates it for stirring his need and suffering. He will only be satisfied when he hears it weep and cry out with agony. He will torture her and savor every second.

It comes to him from the womb, from the cradle. He did not hear words of love or comfort, but words that destroyed him, and yet his parents were normal. There is no excuse. Others have borne worse and turned it to joy. I know now that he is not just a watcher, but a true listener. His ear will catch the slightest sound: a robin perching on a branch, light footsteps on the soft ground. I have walked behind him: have my footsteps already been recorded in his mind? Listening is a gift. He might have been a singer, a musician, or a composer; might have been so much, but he is none of these. Our memories are patchy and selective—his too. He has made up his own memories, his own story, and it is his truth, only his. It is an accident, pure chance that Jane Moore's voice crossed his ear. How many accidents have there been? How many people have by chance fallen into his range?

The gay couple talk a lot; they have trouble, lots of trouble. Karen has her troubles too, but he does not hear their voices, only Jane's. The answer should be simple:

Jane Moore must get out of here, leave the district and better still, leave the city. She can build her life elsewhere; leave the country, if necessary. He is bound to this place, having neither the means nor the ability to migrate. Surely, if I tell the girls, they will understand. My task should be straightforward. It is never that simple. If Jane leaves, then he will go into a rage and will look for her. But he will not find her if she is careful and goes far away. What would he do then, seethe and smoulder until one day another voice accidentally comes his way? His evil must be stopped, forever. How easy it seems and how hard it will be.

But what is that they are saying? She will go with Karen to Ireland for Christmas. Go then, Jane. Go quickly, and stay there. We have gained a little time, just a little.

11

*K*aren didn't know where it had come from. It just popped into her head and then straight out of her mouth. "He has a mistress, hasn't he?"

"What? Who?"

"Your father."

Olivier flushed. "He loves my mother, and I don't ask them questions about their private lives."

"You are part of their private lives, and your sisters too."

"They have been married almost forty years; that's a long time to be in love."

Karen thought: it's also a long time to suffer. "I have no right to put my nose in your family's business, and it's not the biggest scandal in the world..." Be quiet, she cautioned her devilish side, but the voice kept whispering, sowing the idea that Olivier's father probably had had several mistresses. It wasn't a big deal; some husbands did see other women, just as some wives took lovers. Somehow, Madame de Belleville didn't come across as playing the role of lover; she was too good at playing the part of dutiful wife.

"But Olivier, if your father has had mistresses, how does that make you feel? I mean, is it a problem? Have you always known?"

He picked up the T.V magazine and flicked through the pages, "Yes, I've always known, it's one of those things children realize quickly. Me, I have no opinion on the subject; it's not something that has affected my life. I have a good relationship with my father; even if we aren't close, I respect him."

"But it must bother you?" Just tell me how you feel, Olivier, Karen thought, maybe it will help me to see you differently.

He shrugged. "People must live their lives in their own way. There are many reasons why a man would take a mistress." Olivier looked at Karen as if discovering her for the first time. "It happens, you know. It's not our place to judge others."

"You're right; it isn't any of my business."

Olivier threw the magazine on the table and put his arm around her waist. "You would do anything to keep your man, wouldn't you?" He pinched her nipple.

Karen moved away. "No, I would not. Anyway, we aren't married."

Olivier's face darkened.

Before he could say something else, Karen added, "I mean, if I were married to someone and discovered he had a mistress, I would leave him."

"Wouldn't you try to win him back?"

"It's a coward's way to want the best of both worlds. It takes guts to really deal with the situation. If a man isn't happily married, then he should leave his wife and not try to have the best of both worlds, or live a double life. That's the part that bothers me. I couldn't bear that."

"You'd fight for your man, I'm sure of it. All women do. They say they wouldn't, but they don't give up, even if their man strays."

"That's arrogant."

"It's a fact."

She couldn't decide if he was being obstinate or obtuse. Olivier worked with facts: if you're hungry, you eat; if you don't want to do that or go there, then you do something else. That's how he'd convinced her to move in with him. It will cost less, he reasoned, and we can have sex when we want. He'd told her that from the day they'd met, she was the one for him and he knew she would be his wife. Karen had brushed that idea aside and laughed. Olivier had simply said, "We'll see" and again pointed out why living together made more sense. She'd allowed herself to be persuaded.

"I would not fight for someone except if—"

"What?"

"Nothing..." Karen knew that if she really loved someone, her answer might be different.

"I've told you, I want something more permanent."

Olivier raised his hand as Karen started to protest. "I haven't asked you directly yet, because you won't hear of it, but I haven't changed my mind and am not going to. We'll talk about that again soon. I'm off on business a lot this coming month, but after that, we'll deal with it."

"Don't treat our relationship like a piece of business; I'm not sure anymore..."

"Don't get yourself in a state, we'll see about all this later." Olivier pushed her down on the sofa.

"No, Olivier, listen to me! A lot of things are not resolved between us."

Olivier didn't seem to want to talk about it anymore and moved on top of her with determination.

"No."

"No?"

"I don't feel like it."

"Karen, I want you," he repeated.

The tone of his voice chilled her. She looked into his eyes and tried to see what he was thinking but could only see hunger and desire. He tore at her bra and didn't waste time over fineries, pulling everything up over her head.

"Stop," her voice trembled, "this isn't how I want it."

"You want this as much as I do."

"No."

Olivier stopped. "What's the matter with you?"

"I don't want to have sex."

"Why?"

"Not like this." Karen grabbed him by the shoulders: "Lately, you don't consider me or my feelings."

A shadow crossed his face; then tears came into his eyes. "Karen, I'm sorry; I don't mean to go so quickly. I want you so much...it's my love for you."

Karen turned her face away; she didn't want to hear him say that.

"Please, Karen, I need you and don't want to go on like before we met. My life is so much better since you came into it; you are my anchor. I have to make love to you—let me, please. Forgive me for being so clumsy." His eyes held hers and he caressed her face.

Karen despised herself for weakening and feeling sorry for him, for succumbing to his kisses.

"Please, Karen, let me..."

"I have a better idea..." Karen spoke cautiously and guided him onto his back, then slipped down. "Let's do it this way tonight." She reached to take his sex in her hand.

Oliver didn't reply.

Karen was surprised to find his penis wasn't firm; and despite her encouragement didn't swell or harden. "What's the matter?"

"It's okay, Karen, I'm tired; let it go." His voice was clipped and closed.

She didn't dare to look at his face, deciding that silence and hopefully sleep were the best solutions.

When Karen woke up in the middle of the night, she still didn't know her own mind. A part of her wanted to give

Olivier a chance. Another part of her was just frustrated. The little devil sat on her shoulder repeating, 'And what does your lover boy do when he goes on those long trips? Remember: like father, like son. Does he abstain and wait for you? What does he do when temptation comes his way? Why don't you take a little more interest in these things? Listen to him when he speaks and see if he's hiding something?' She slapped at her shoulder as if those pesky thoughts could be flicked off. But the voice continued: 'You have to leave him, because if you don't, soon you will be tied down with children, nothing but a watered down version his mother. Suppose you get pregnant: you've been having a lot of sex. You took the pill, didn't you?'

She had taken it, hadn't she? Of course she had—she'd made a point of not forgetting. Of course the pill doesn't' always work, and you could still get pregnant. Why couldn't she leave him?

A return to sleep came reluctantly.

In the land between sleep and dreams, Olivier's' hands caressed and touched her in the most intimate way. Then there was a strange sensation coming from behind, pushing; "Olivier!"

The movement stilled.

"We haven't ever tried this..." His voice was gruff.

"It hurts!" Karen woke fully and pulled away. "What are you trying to do, sneaking up on me?"

"I'm sorry." His words were flat and emotionless. Then came that pleading Olivier: "I'm making so many mistakes, Karen; getting it all wrong with you. That's why I couldn't do it when you took me in your hand."

"Look, Olivier, I don't—"

"Karen, please don't be angry." His head grovelled against a cheek. "I'll be gentle, I promise. Love you, love you so much..." His mouth roamed the surface of her bottom. "I promise I won't hurt you."

"I'm afraid, Olivier; you are frightening me."

Olivier didn't speak. Instead, he abruptly got out of bed and disappeared into the living room. Karen breathed a sigh of relief; one night on the sofa wouldn't kill him. Then came the feelings of guilt; it was an impossible situation.

Karen slept through the clock and stumbled out of bed in a panic. Damn it, there was no time for breakfast. Where was Olivier? She hurried to the living room, but he was nowhere to be found. Damn it again, Olivier had already gone off to work and would be travelling all week. Maybe it was a good thing; that would give her time to consider leaving him and how to handle it.

"Sit down," Jane ordered.

Karen sat on the edge of her friend's bed. There wasn't anywhere else to sit as Jane had taken the only chair in the tiny room.

"Now listen to me."

It was the first time Karen had heard her friend speak to her in such a firm voice. It was a novelty to obey.

"I'm your friend," Jane began, "and being your friend, I have the licence to say what I wouldn't normally say to someone else. Are you with me?"

"Sure, I mean of course, what's this about, our business venture or—"

"It's about Olivier."

"Olivier?"

"Olivier and you."

"I see." Karen was getting a bad feeling about this. However, Jane didn't raise her voice or shout and simply asked, "Do you love Olivier?"

"Well, I thought I did at the beginning, and then I wasn't sure; and then thought I didn't, and no, I don't."

"Look, I don't want to interfere..."

"Yeah?"

"I thought you knew your own mind. Why did you agree to move in with him?"

"Because he wore me down."

"Really?"

"Okay, because I liked him and thought that was love...and I was weary."

"Weary?"

"Weary of scraping together the rent, and of making ends meet. At my age, it's a bit pathetic to say that, I know."

"You were trying to prove independence from your family. By the way, and sorry for repeating myself, but you have a great family; I've never felt more welcome in my life. For the first time, Christmas was special. I mean that," Jane spoke sincerely.

"I'm glad." Christmas had been special for all her family and it had been because of her friend's presence. Jane had brought that something extra that had made them appreciate what they had. The holiday had been a success and Jane had fallen in love with Ireland. Karen's only regret was not being able to stay longer.

"My family has nothing to do with it. I have to prove to myself that I can make my own way. I was trying to do that, and then met Olivier, and it's like he has a hold over me."

"You're not making sense. I should know, being an expert on irrational relationships."

"Olivier likes sex a lot."

"That's good, isn't it?"

"I suppose."

"Can you explain more?"

Karen didn't want to and was annoyed when her eyes teared up. "Look, the bottom line is that I don't think we're really matched; there is something flat and automatic about him."

Jane leaned forward and scrutinized her for a moment. "I see; then you must leave him. Promise not to bottle things up, and talk to me any time you like."

"I promise."

Seeing Karen's discomfort, Jane changed the subject and told her that Laurent Le Bois, the Flower-Pot man, had offered her flowers. Happy to put the spot light on her friend, Karen reminded Jane that Laurent had a soft spot for her.

Jane reiterated how she hated flowers cut up and hacked into bouquets and preferred real flowers growing in the soil."

"You didn't throw them away, did you?"

"No, I took them to the graveyard and at random laid them near a tomb."

"How macabre! What graveyard?"

"Montmartre, of course, the nearest one. I've started doing some sketches there."

"Whose tomb was it?"

"It was an old, neglected one; it was so faded that I couldn't even read the engraving on the stone. At least the flowers will wither and turn to dust, and maybe from their dust, something will grow."

"Maybe..." Karen felt down all of the sudden. Jane's words were morbid and fatalistic.

12

*H*is face is growing skeletal; it is difficult to keep a vigil day and night. Every human must sleep; a person goes insane if he does not. I have been close to that state. But if one is already insane, what awaits him at the end of that dark tunnel, where neither night nor day exists? If there is a hell, then that is surely it. I am alone today; Pierre did not come back last night. He is with Dimitri, trying to right something and make his own closure. I wish him well, but it will come down to money that will be converted to cheap wine and poured down his son's throat.

Something comes over me: I want to smell wild flowers in my place. Not just any wild flowers, this one is special for me. It is not a rose, though roses are beautiful and sinful. There were some that had taken their freedom and spread wild through the bramble wood near the seaside where I grew up. It is not the primrose, dainty and childlike; it is more shrub than flower. It is the sweet scented woodbine, honeysuckle. Imagining that scent gives me a heady feeling, like a child skipping dizzily in the fields. I imagine harder and the perfume grows stronger. It brings pain at first, but gradually it is bearable. I like it and embrace it.

It is not on Rue Lepic; or anywhere else within the city. If one passed by all the flower shops in Paris, they might find something similar, but it would not be the same. I go to the flower seller and show him the name that Pierre wrote down for me. He was not anticipating such a request. Yet, something else bothers him: this flower seller thinks he should know me, but he cannot place me because my appearance is different today. He is in his mid-forties and has been setting out his flowers for years, since he was eleven or twelve. His parents were not without means. Life could have been easier for him; there were other choices he might have made, other directions he might have taken. But nothing else appealed to him, only the flowers.

He is good with flowers—he has learned a lot—and he is even better with displays. But this flower seller does not have sweet woodbine. He shakes his head and smiles. He knows many that are like it, but when I smell them, they are foreign to my nose. I buy a small plant. He smiles again. No, he has no woodbine, but will look for it. I leave and will not come back. Does he realize that during our exchange, the old woman in front of him has uttered only one word? Woodbine... I walk away and the flower seller has already forgotten me; there is much more on his mind.

I want to smell it again and cannot understand this obsession. My energy must be stored for more important things. It is running out quickly and must be preserved. What difference will that smell make? To find it again would be nothing more than nostalgia. They say that people in desperate situations make strange requests; and mine is to smell once more the sweet woodbine. Maybe it is our instinct to hang on to life, the hunger to survive. If you are thirsty, would you ask for water just minutes before you die? What would it change? Would you sprinkle water on a flower and then rip it from the earth, crush it in your hands and toss it to the wind?

Who can answer those questions? But I want to smell woodbine, and want it badly. It is almost something I would die for. I go to the forests of Boulogne, Vincennes, Saint Germain and Fontainebleau. Surely it is growing in those woods and forests? But to me, they are not woods or forests, they are like cities within cities, streets of trees, they do not feel wild or natural. They don't smell of the Irish rain. It becomes a vexing fixation...peeping over garden gates, asking florists. What they show me does not smell the same.

The monster's stark face is sharpened by high cheek bones and his eyes haunt me. There is so much emptiness there. I pass by him again and again. Each time he falls short of recognizing me; he must never recognize me. As long as I am careful, he will not know it is me. For it is I and not he who is the watcher; he is a listener, and a master of voices.

I learned much from my grandmother, that rough but capable woman. Grandmother knew how to make a lot out of little. Her words have stayed with me and become mine—words of wisdom. Grandmother knew how to raise and kill a chicken, knew how to raise and kill a pig. I hated seeing her do it and would run away. But I know how to use my hands, how to use a knife, and how to defend myself. I will need that skill.

He has started to roam again, and my punishment is to follow him. He places a single flower on a cold stone. Each is a different color and shade: white, pink, red, yellow, orange... Every flower is of a different variety: a rose, a lily, a tulip, a chrysanthemum. That is how he has identified and remembers them. He goes back to pay his perverted respects; it is his mass. If there is a pattern to his visits, it is not clear. Perhaps it is an anniversary or is linked to something that has meaning only for him.

This time it is a sunflower, bright, cheerful, it cannot be missed. He has left it there. I stand over it and an image comes to me... She is black-haired and smiling. The sunflower cannot capture the warmth of her smile or her *joie de vivre*. The young woman is humming to herself, full of hope and optimism. But it is a long time ago, many, many years. It is very cold and she has buttoned up her coat and wrapped a colorful scarf around her neck. Such a pretty face. Marie stamps her new boots on the ground; they were a birthday present. She is so happy.

He is not far away, he follows with soft steps, tracking her, covering the distance so easily. Marie has no doubts about her future; her thoughts are full of romance. An engagement ring sparkles on her finger and the small diamond winks at her. It has been in her suitor's family for years. She is looking forward to a new life and believes herself to be in love. Indeed, she is in love.

In his mind, he is sure of respecting and loving her. It is his kind of love. Bad things do not happen to good people; good people must be preserved and protected. And Marie was good, very good; she raised people's spirits with laughter and sang like a linnet. Her mind was blessed with humility and kindness. He heard the sound of her voice filled with goodness and hungered for that angelic gift, for her blessing. He needed her light to purge the dark corners of his mind. The monster followed in the radiance of her light, and eclipsed it slowly, step by step. Streets were quieter in those days and lighting timid. He was still a fledgling teenager, but strong, very strong and driven by that hunger. The monster followed his angel as the moon guided her way and the stars saluted her. Tears flowed down his face as he drew closer and closer. He would soon have her, and by devouring her, he would feed that hunger.

Marie turns suddenly, alerted by her instincts, but sees nothing and continues, undaunted. Then he overtakes her, this time making himself visible. The moonlight is in her face. Her eyes are opened wide and fear comes into them. She starts to run, but it is too late. There is no escape. He presses his hands around her milk white neck, as his fingers sink tremulously into her skin. He does not let go and Marie struggles in vain, finally losing consciousness. It seems so easy and she is very light. She floats like a fairy to the ground. He has but a few minutes before she will reawaken so he takes her in his arms, his desire fouling the air. He carries her through the cemetery gates. In those days, long ago and not so long ago, people did not believe in locking gates. The monster did not have to be so clever then; there was nobody to mind the gate.

He carries her, as a young groom would his bride, with reverence and growing confidence. Arriving at the chosen tomb, he kicks open the door with his booted foot. Everything has been prepared. Marie never had a chance. He lays her reverently on the slab, covers her with a blanket to keep her warm...and waits.

She comes to and his hand is placed over her mouth to dampen her scream. The monster strikes her once with a heavy blow and puts a knife to her throat. She will do as he commands. He orders her to strip herself bare. In his mind, his angel wants this and is welcoming him. He pushes her down, forcing his body on hers. His beautiful Marie offers herself to him again and again, her screams are not screams of terror, but pleading sobs of welcome. She is giving herself to him, wants to be his sacrifice. Her tears are of joy and ecstasy. He is free. He is liberated. His infinity...

Then he smothers her sounds forever. This time, his fingers remain until he is certain that Marie will never reawaken. He snaps her neck, cracks her arms, and crushes her face with the mallet. She is no use to him anymore.

The monster returns night after night to break her into tiny pieces. He does not try to do it all at once, but is patient and takes his time.

Marie had been so close to home—is still close to

home—and yet she has never been found. And every year, the monster returns on that date. He closes his eyes and relives the exhilaration of those moments, pacifying his dark soul for a short while....

I turn away and try to block it out, but I have witnessed too much and cannot stop the rest from coming. I am inside his mind and forced to see. I want to push out those odious visions, but they will not go. I have relived it and now must live with it. It was the beginning for him, and with it came the need for more and more and more. It is difficult to believe that one can relive somebody else's experience, but that is what has happened. It cannot be denied, not even by someone like me who believes there is no God. My feet give up and I sit on a slab. My whole being is drained and sullied by his deed. My spirit feels dirty because of what it has witnessed. If I am not to become a beast, unfeeling, I must allow myself to feel it all.

The wracking cries of her groom come to me; Michel fears the worst and will cease to live the same day he hears the news. He will wait until the end of his life, but she will never return. Michel blames himself: Why had he not gone to meet Marie? Why did he allow her walk alone? Why did he not come in search sooner? The poor man could not have changed events. He had been working late, trying to make more money; he'd wanted to offer his bride a better future. Oh yes, Michel will one day meet a new love and try to move on, many years onward. But try and try as he will, Michel will never really move on. How can he ever forget Marie, his one and only true love? One day, it will be too much for him, and Michel will take his own life.

The pain and guilt of her friends and loved ones falls upon me—their sense of loss, their incomprehension. Marie is another missing person; for until they find the body, they cannot mourn. Of course the body has never been found.

The knife goes into my gut when her parents appear, bent in old age—the blade turns; it sears and scars. They enter the cemetery where Marie lies but they do not know how close she is. They stand at a different tomb—the one which will be theirs. They kneel there and are as close to her as if they were in the same house. For a long time, they never gave up hope that one day their daughter would be found. They prayed that Marie would walk in the door, prayed that she would be found alive and well. But they know as only parents know that Marie is no longer in the world. Their daughter is still that young happy woman in their eyes, never to grow older. Time as we live it, is over for her. The words of my grandmother come to me: 'Jesus, Mary and Joseph, have mercy on them.'

Marie is near them and they do not know it or cannot hear her. She says, 'Mama, papa, forgive me, I was foolish to walk alone that night. I saw no danger. I was walking to my love's home with a gift for him, a cake made with my own hands. Do not blame yourselves; you were perfect parents, you were wonderful. I had been longing for my wedding day; and the joy of loving and lying by my love's side. I wished to be a mother, to see you as grandparents, and to live a very long life. You were so happy—I wanted to be like you. I no longer wish for that, and just hope for your release; that you would mourn no more. My groom took his own life, but it was not that which freed me. Michel will find peace when you find peace.'

I wonder: do they hear Marie? Does her message enter their hearts? They are old, but they hang on. Is there another world, then, a world where they will join their daughter, capture what they have missed together, or find something greater? Is there a place where Marie's death and the nature of her dying will be wiped out? Can she look from somewhere, some secret sky and see him, see the monster who took her life so brutally? Has she tried to protect others? Is the pain inflicted on her worse than his darkness, darkness that has grown heavier, and that he has carried from that sordid night?

And yet, he would kill and kill again. Her suffering is

over; her hours of pain on this earth are done. Still, her spirit floats around the earth. I look heavenwards: Is that it? Tell me, is there something there, is there hope and forgiveness? Tell me, please: what is only in my mind, and what is real?

I can see what happened to Marie. I retrace her steps. But what happens afterward? Is it just the ravings of an old woman that imagine Marie hovering around her parents? God, if you exist, then hear me out. You allow me to enter Marie's world, but you do not tell me what happens afterward. Where is my mother? Where is my grandmother? What will become of me? The pain and suffering that I have just lived with Marie is real. Like a cloud it hangs over Montmartre cemetery. You permit him the memory of how he raped and killed her; it is his, it is part of him. But what does she have? The curse of living in his memory...

I am between fury and confusion, because I do not understand. Are there no answers? God, you put things like that in my mind, yet you give me no proof that it is not my own fantasies that deceive me. Lunacy, that's what ails me!

Why do I claim madness? I am mad because I had an idiot for a mother. Do I know what sort of mother he had, the man who took her life? Perhaps he had a perfect mother, and a perfect father. And Marie's parents? Average, very ordinary. I should like to have had an ordinary mother.

Still, I measure things by my own standards. That man has had the best, an abundance of love, and yet has done this!

The womb, the family and home is not always an excuse. Sometimes there is no cause, and there is no excuse, as we might understand it. I question whether or not there is another existence, but if I did not believe it on some level of consciousness, then I suppose I would not be here. I will try to do good by her, and by all of them. I may be a social misfit, but the good is in me. It was in him too, but he did not want it and will never find it in this world.

I put my hand to my ear: "Tell me plainly, for I hear nothing that offers comprehensible answers. I sit on her unknown tomb. Marie's remains are here and her life is no more, but she is trapped within the memory of others. From that realm she speaks to me. I cry out, "Marie is dead; there is only pain and suffering. Is that it? Is that what her life is worth? Put the answer in my ear."

But nothing else comes into my ear; not a note, or a tune or a song, not even a whisper.

What am I to do? What does she want from me? I am called upon because I am a watcher, and I am blessed with special sight. I must do what I know to be right, take responsibility, stop running, turn and face it as Marie did.

I catch echoes of her voice in the air. My ears are blistering with sound, and my tears fall. Her laughter is beautiful and lovely. Her happiness makes me happy. "Is that you, Marie? If it is you, then you are not chained to the memories of others, you are free. You suffered here, died in the worst possible way, and yet you are happy. Is that what the gift of forgiveness brings you?"

When we know the happiness of true love, we live forever. I have walked outside of my life for years, lived on streets, in corridors and tunnels, between walls and behind windows. I have watched through glass panes. It is time for me to engage. If I do nothing else, I must do that.

Night has stolen upon me. The moon stares down and Marie's laughter has gone. I am left only with the monster's empty soul.

Sadness has joined my company and it is new for me. I am sad because I was touched by Marie's joy. Something is beginning to crack and break. Dare I walk out of that place that has been so solidly built for me, my fortress from the world?

I leave the cemetery and am back on the street. For a

few seconds, I am in it, but I withdraw to where it is safe in my mind and walk the pavement alone. Distance from all emotion is essential. I will need to be outside myself if I am to follow him and do what is asked of me. Forgiveness is Marie's gift, not mine. Only one thing is sure: I have to bring him down.

13

*K*aren took the bill from between Jane's fingers. "I'm glad you sat me down the other day for that heart to heart talk."

Jane bit her lip. "I don't know about that; it was none of my business. I don't like it when people butt into *my* life—and that's just what I did."

"You were right to do so; I now know what I have to do. It's simply a question of when."

"I'm glad for that...at least, I think I am." Jane made a face.

Karen drained her coffee.

"Are you going somewhere?"

"I'll be right back; I just remembered that Monsieur Martin told me that he might have the Irish Sunday Independent today. He only gets a few copies, if any at all."

"Can't you read it online?"

"I can, but it's not the same. It makes me feel like I'm in Ireland when I have it in my hands."

Jane stretched back in her chair trying to catch the

most of the mid-morning sun through the glass of the enclosed terrace. "Take your time, I'll relax here and read a little of this book that I am forever finishing."

Karen looked down the winding street which, as usual, was bursting with life. Locals and traders were out in force, gossiping, shouting, calling, haggling, and drumming up a busy atmosphere; while curious and delighted tourists made their way slowly toward the basilica. The place was full of sounds, colors and smells. Sunday morning was her favorite time on Rue Lepic; on either side it had become an open street market and merchandise spilled out from little shops onto the footpaths. Chickens were being roasted on skewers; every cut of meat from bird and beast, game or tame, hung from butchers' hooks. The smell of fish on beds of ice challenged the nose, as did the cheeses: Roquefort, Crotin de Chavignol, Beaufort, Brie, Gruyère, Cantal... The charcuteries displayed varieties of cured and preserved hams, smoked salmon, *saucisson* and sausage, and under their glass counters a multitude of salads were ready to be spooned into cartons. There were greens, grated carrot, celery, cucumber, tomato, peppers, taboulé, patés and terrines... There was so much fruit that it looked like thousands of magnified skittles had been shaken onto pavements; rich yellows, greens, purples, oranges, and reds. One could spend hours feasting his eyes in front of the baker and confectioner's shop that displayed macaroons, éclairs, meringues, gourmet cookies, creams and vanilla custards. The perfectly layered and shaped cakes and fruit tarts looked too good to eat. There was every flavor possible: coffee, raspberry, strawberry, apricot, cherry, lemon, and delicacies with a host of quirky names such as Religieuse, Quatre-quart, Paris Brest... The cost in potential weight gain and hard earned money had prevented Karen many times from diving into an 'Opera' with its almond sponge cake, coffee syrup and chocolate glaze. It was really a shame to settle for just sniffing the air as she walked toward the newspaper kiosk.

The spray from Laurent's flower stand caught her eye. Jane didn't appreciate flowers taken out of the wild, but Karen appreciated the displays. The blaze of colors refreshed and invigorated, and Laurent always had a ready smile. Why couldn't Monsieur Martin be more like that? Neither trader was given to great exuberance, but one was welcoming and the other not. They nevertheless shared other common traits, not least being early birds, on the go before anybody else. Laurent had to do his preening and cleaning and dress up his presentations and displays. Monsieur Martin had to organize dozens of newspapers and magazines.

"Bonjour, Monsieur Martin."

He didn't raise his head as he bundled a bunch of flowers in his big hands. She noticed his thick fingers and dirty chipped fingernails. That wasn't just newspaper ink, but basic hygiene. "Nice flowers!" Karen tried again to get his attention.

He laid down the bunch roughly and mumbled something, his scowl never lifting.

Rather than asking, Karen browsed the area for the Independent but couldn't see it.

He tilted his head towards the English papers.

"Those are the English ones. I'm looking for the Irish Independent. You told me you would have it."

Monsieur Martin shrugged and muttered that they hadn't been delivered.

His attitude was beginning to niggle, so Karen shrugged too. "Well, that's all I was looking for, thank you all the same."

She had to wait for the tourist train to make its way past and gave a last glance back at Monsieur Martin. His fierce look took her by surprise; moreover because he wasn't looking at her, but appeared to be scrutinizing Jane, who was stretching like a cat inside the window. What a glare! What was his problem?

Karen practically walked into Monsieur Abu as he

joined Monsieur Martin. He was clearly there to relieve him for a few minutes from duty. It was striking how powerfully built Monsieur Abu was; he clapped his hands in a gesture of beating off the cold of the morning, and squashed himself behind the counter. He picked up the flowers curiously: "That is love."

Monsieur Martin took the bunch of flowers and bundled them under a shelf out of view.

"Ah," Monsieur Abu laughed, "the lady must be special."

"I can't wait to get rid of those!" Jane pointed to her crutches. "I'm going to be mobile very soon. But my convalescence has given me time to think...and I've been thinking that it's time to start getting up at dawn, like Laurent or Monsieur Martin. I've been talking to Laurent more these days, while you're off working, and I've learned a lot. I can make crystal roses or a crystal sunflower...capture flowers in my designs."

"People love that sort of thing."

"There's nothing new or original in that; the difference would be my designs, and I'm working hard on those. Laurent has given me lots of ideas."

"And I'll bet he's asked you out..."

"He's hinted at it, but—"

"But?"

CRASH!

"Shit, what was that?" Jane jumped.

"Only Philippe; I swear, that's the second time this week he's dropped crockery."

The waiter hurried past them with brush and shovel to clean up the mess.

"You've got to love this place..."

"Kansas must have been different."

"Here I'm happy; not there."

It had been said so easily and casually that Karen wondered if Jane had actually said it. "You weren't happy there?"

"No. My life was awful. As a child, you don't think in those terms. You just accept things as they are and get along. Then you try to escape it, and hopefully succeed in leaving it behind. It's so stereotyped that it sounds like a familiar story. Basically, my mother was...is a drug addict, and she drinks, too...whatever she can get her hands on. I didn't know them, but I think her parents, my grandparents, were good people, but very strict. My mother didn't just rebel, she had no morals at all. I guess she was one of those bad seeds and had me along the way. My father didn't hang around long. He was out of our lives very early, and we heard later that he died in a fight. It was a fitting end because he was violent...I won't go into all the details."

"If you don't want to talk about it, I understand." Karen picked at a cardboard coaster.

"I'm okay...I want you to know. My grandparents were already dead when my mother made her way to New York with me as part of her baggage. She went from one pimp to another, one abusive man to another, all to satisfy her addictions. I was taken into foster care by social services at various times in my childhood, which was actually lucky otherwise I would probably be illiterate today."

Karen dropped the coaster pieces onto a saucer. Jane seemed so gentle and mild, without bitterness or anger, even though that had been her start in life. "I'm sorry, it must have been hell for you."

"Paris saved me."

"How?"

"One day, while still a child, there was a drinking party going on in the grotty apartment where we had been staying. I'd snuck into the smallest corner to try to hide— I'd gotten very good at being invisible. I knew when things got really dirty, one of mother's friends would come looking for me..."

"She let them!"

"Not if she was still in her right senses. She saved me from some, not all. I couldn't count on her. Mother was out of it most of the time. If my mother needed a fix, and if I could be sold for it, she would do it. Anyway, this time I managed to stay in hiding, and they were so stoned that they forgot about me. At some point, they decided to go out to some club. I was alone, and I remember crawling out of my hiding place and finding a magazine on the floor. Inside there was a feature on Paris. It was a revelation for me—the pictures were magical, exotic and dreamy—and somewhere else. Paris became my touchstone, my salvation, my dream."

"You decided you would come here at that moment?"

"Yes; Paris would take me away from where I was. My mind was made up, and I began to work toward that dream. I tore out those pages and kept them. I began to plan, and my first step was to run away from my mother, and from everybody she knew."

"Not easy to do."

"No, but I'd run away before. Except this time I had a purpose, and it was on those glossy pages. Paris was in another country, on another continent, another part of the world..."

"Elsewhere..."

"Elsewhere and with another language... But most of all, it was a place where I could have a life. Well, it didn't happen immediately; it took time. In short, after many failed escapades, I ended up on the streets living rough, but that wasn't new. I'd been there before. However, I'd fixed my eye on a star, and it's difficult to explain why, but my luck started to change. People helped me; there were little things, small jobs... I managed to haul myself up inch by inch. I got work at a restaurant, got into nightschool, and did what I could."

Karen ordered another coffee. How easy and comfortable her life had been. Her biggest problem was Olivier, whereas Jane had clawed her way out of the gutters. "You have a lot of courage."

"I had nothing to lose; it was either succeed or end up back in the cage of my past."

Karen wiped a tear. "I think you are well and truly out of that cage."

"Ah, don't cry, Karen. Don't cry for me, I'm alright now." Jane hugged her.

"I'm sorry, it should be me comforting you. Sorry to be so weepy. So when you finally got to Paris, did it live up to your expectations?"

"Talk about crying! I cried a lot. I didn't really feel it when the plane landed, but when the bus finally stopped near the Arc de Triomphe at the top of the Champs Elysées, I wept floods. People didn't know what was wrong with me. I hardly noticed the buildings at first; it was just this emotion which was so overwhelming and telling me that I'd finally made it, that I was finally here. I couldn't speak for days. I just wandered around open-mouthed, thinking, I'm free, I'm free, I'm finally free!"

"Has the dream dimmed?"

"No, no, it's taken another shape. When living in a new place, you necessarily adjust your lens. But I'm even more in love with Paris, and I'm as determined as ever to make a life here."

Strange as it may seem, Jane thought of her childhood as the greatest gift, because when she found happiness, she recognized it. Jane Moore was happy. Maybe one day Jane would meet a man that was right for her; perhaps even have children. But her happiness did not depend on others. Her mother, dead or alive, would never drag her down again. Meeting Karen had the best thing in her life since coming to Paris.

"Me? What did I do?"

"You are my first real friend."

Karen was very touched.

"You accepted me as I was, and that's what counted. I'd never had that before, someone who just wanted to be my friend."

"That's what you are for me, Jane Moore, my friend."

"And soon to be business partner," Jane laughed.

"Ah, yes! Very soon..."

Jane took her hand and squeezed it tightly, "But most of all, friends forever."

"Yes, for life."

A skate scooter flew past them. They shouted out hello to the driver.

Madame Lu waved and was gone.

"Boy," Jane said, "does she get around."

"At the rate that scooter was going, a speeding ticket is in order."

They watched as Madame Lu skidded in front of the newspaper kiosk, where Monsieur Abu was still chatting with Monsieur Martin. She didn't wait for niceties, but jumped off and tore right into an argument. Monsieur Abu had apparently switched the bins: the drycleaner's bin had been put in the wrong yard. To add to her woe, the bin for apartment block # 15 hadn't been done, and two other bins had been left behind. Monsieur Abu seemed to be replying in equally hard terms, telling her that it had been her fault for putting the bins in the wrong place and for putting the others out late.

"Do they ever let up?" Karen shook her head.

"No, a few nights, or should I say mornings, when coming home from the bar, I saw them skulking around."

"Skulking?"

"That's what it seemed like to me. I'd say one of them, or both of them, are up to no good," Jane explained.

"Crime?"

"I don't want to speculate about things like that, but I've been on the streets and know 'up to no good' when I see it. I wonder if one of them is behind that hate mail that Frederic and Eric keep getting?"

"Madame Lu and Monsieur Abu are too busy hating each other. The hate mail is the work of a sneaky coward."

For once Olivier wasn't on Karen's mind. She tried to process everything her friend had told her. Perhaps Madame Lune had picked up on that dark energy in Jane's past. Whatever, her warning had faded with time and the broken ankle.

Monsieur Martin caught her attention, mainly because he was staring once again at Jane. What was up with that guy? She saw Laurent stub out a cigarette, engage a new customer in a conversation and make a sale of two plants. Something prickled at the back of her neck; it was becoming a familiar sensation. Yet, they were sitting peacefully inside a café window, enjoying Rue Lepic on a Sunday morning. An old lady passed by, wheeling a shopping caddy. She was in no hurry. Was she living on their street? Probably... Karen had a vague notion of having seen her before, then again maybe not. A stressed mother with young children went past. The café was bustling and noisy, the clattering of crockery and the steaming coffee percolator whistled cheerfully. Still Monsieur Martin stared. Even when with a customer, he stared.

14

The monster is restless, but today will not be the day; there are still things to do, preparations to be made. I see where he is looking and my eyes are pulled in the same direction. He would prefer to ignore that woman, but cannot. Madame Lu is a lure, a magnet. Silly little woman, do you know what you are doing? I too am forced to follow your movements. That is easy; nothing about you is secret. Duty takes you from place to place, and the destinations are lit up like a Metro board as your bell signals to the world, 'Here I am, this is where I am going, and this is where I am coming from.'

Madame Lu and Monsieur Abu are part of the reason I have always filled my caddy outside this district. If there is anything valuable to lift, they have taken it long before it reaches a bin on the street. They are resourceful people. For her, washing, cleaning and ironing make up the honest part. But there is the other side too, and I'm certainly no example. When Madame Lu stumbles upon an opportunity, she seizes it. The old couple in Karen Moroney's building have been useful to her, especially the woman, Chantal. Chantal Moreau confuses things, and that is her problem, but her deranged comments will drive people to their death.

When you have been killing for twenty-five years or more, without any hint of suspicion from anyone, you take risks. From time to time, he has kept a token, a souvenir, something to remember them by. There are also things that had to be discarded. Sometimes a bundle of bloody rags, or a cloth used to wipe a head, a face, or a pair of strong hands; it might be to clean the moist edge of a sharp knife. Such fripperies have gone unnoticed when thrown into a dustbin full of soggy vegetables or dead leaves and flowers. He has picked the bins not worth searching, or buried his rags and pieces underground. But not always, not a pair of blue shoes wrapped in a dress that had been ripped and torn. That time the monster had become over confident.

Madame Lu found them: Little woman, you found the shoes. There was a dark stain on one of them, but they were made of quality leather. You like blue, so you didn't dye them to change the color. You tried cleaning instead, but the stain remained. Despite that, they were still good, practical shoes. You are a tiny woman, but your feet are not so small; the corns and bunions tire you. It is difficult to find a comfortable pair of shoes with a pretty finish. You have no idea of their age. When you took them they looked new, totally new, but in fact, though new, they were ten years old.

The monster had kept them wrapped in the matching torn, blue dress. It was an exciting memory. She had screamed louder than any girl before, louder and longer. His pleasure had gone on and on. It was the last time he kept something as a souvenir. Now he has his camera, but each picture must eventually be destroyed. In the end, the safest way is to walk from grave to grave in the dead of night to relive the experience.

He was slow to get rid of those shoes, and you, Madame Lu, were quick to find and take them. But they were not on the street, and that was the problem. They were in a bin, ready for dumping. You entered his private territory and found them in his storage area. That was not good, not wise.

Your fate was decided that day your tongue wagged too much. It was a sunny day near the café. You were talking to Chantal Moreau and could not help it; you showed her your new shoes. You were even proud to say that they had been thrown away and that you had retrieved them. The dark stain confused you, as did the torn dress which bore spots of blood. You had a theory and shared it with Madame Moreau, whispering that it had probably belonged to a girlfriend that he had broken up with. Maybe there had been a fight and he had beaten her; perhaps his girlfriend had scratched him. Lovers' fights are often dangerous.

Poor Madame Lu, I do believe that if you had not pointed out your new shoes to Madame Moreau that day, then he would never have noticed. I would not have looked twice either at the shoes or the stain. You whispered your story; but Madame Lu, your whisper is a shout to others. And now the monster has to shut you up. Every time his eyes fall on that blue leather, he digs his hands deep inside his pockets to stop himself from putting them around your throat and strangling you. I cannot save you, Madame Lu, but if you are clever, then it is still possible to save yourself. Unfortunately, I do not think you have that sort of cleverness. I have never thought much about you, neither like nor dislike you, Madame Lu, but your presence now is distracting him from Jane Moore, and forcing me to pay attention. From bad comes good.

A reluctant image of Madame Lu as a child comes to me. I push it away—I do not want it. What is one supposed to do with such memories? Is it because I do not want to deal with my own?

As a child I had many games with myself in the woods, the fields and along the strand. I would become a bush, a tree, or a tuft of grass. Sometimes it was a fox, maybe a hare or a starling. The child became an adult, and through the years learned to refine and change the game. You have to see the landscape around you with other eyes. At first glance, there is the visible part, and then there is that which shies from the eye, that which can be seen at second glance, and still the game of hide and seek continues. Most important is what the eyes can be trained to see. My first months in the city were spent re-learning how to see everything: the gray buildings, the carousels, the red marquise, and the striped sunshades. The skyline was different, as were the oceans of people, cars, bicycles and buses. It takes time to unveil and to determine how the artist has worked—the delicate touches of light and shade, and strokes of wizardry with his knife and brush.

I learned to be visible but completely forgettable, so forgettable that I was invisible. Who has not seen the timeless trick where the magician or trickster places a little ball under a cup? His crafty hands move the pieces around—you see it and then you don't. An average magician will trick you so that each time you choose the wrong cup. But a good magician will make the ball completely disappear and replace it with a dove. I learned to follow that ball until I knew what the magician was doing. His hand could not be quick enough to deceive me. I watched street magicians, saw them perform with ribbons and swords and understood that discipline, training and patience make the magic work. Living on the streets, and an empty stomach, pushed me to the edge; that was my school, my method of learning.

Now, it has become second nature to me. But to count only on the eye is to lose oneself. One must be able to catch the currents in the wind. You have to discern voice behind the voice, keep your nose in the air like a fox and catch the scent, taste the acid in the rain and feel the ground under your feet. Nature and its creatures were my first teachers. I would mimic the sounds, mime the movements, and float with the rhythms of what spun around me. It has served me well; all that learning has been used to survive, to live. But what use is all of that now? My own voice has been the most silent. If I were to speak to others or try to explain what I see and know, my voice and words would let me down and nobody would understand.

I have to go out and work. Do not lose sight of the ball under the moving tumblers. I look at my hands; the varnished nails cannot distract from the blue veins that betray so much about me. The face in the mirror is that of my mother. I put on the cheap plastic magnifiers that serve as glasses and study my eyes. Are they empty and vacant? Is there more there than I can see? As a child, I used to stare for hours into a cracked mirror that hung in the cottage and wonder if those eyes made me different from other children. People said I had mother's eyes—I still have her eyes.

I change my attire and go outside. Tourists file up and down the hill, carrying cameras, phones, bags... Two couples interest me enough to follow them; they laugh and joke together, happy to be in Paris. They have money and they intend to spend it. Oh, let them enjoy themselves!

There is another tourist; spiteful, stingy and thankless, enjoying nothing and thinking that everyone is trying to put one over on him. Maybe so, but why come here? Why go to all the trouble of coming to Paris if you are going to make everybody else miserable? It is in his back pocket— his life is in his back pocket. I shake my head, as many times before. How can he be so witless? The carelessness of the woman he is with is more forgivable. She is carrying a bag full of makeup and fluffy bits and pieces. The peevish parents who walk near them can be excused too, but they should have known Paris is no place for sniveling children; it seemed such a good idea to bring them at the time.

Arms entwined, young lovers go by, aware only of each

other. I have a lot of time for the carelessness of the youth, for they are young, but I have never had time for the mean and stingy.

Such things do not direct me, however; it is not that which guides me. That indeed would be stupid. I must never over think my actions; instead I listen to my instincts, the animal inside me.

Mister stingy will go into the church because it will cost him nothing, but still he complains. I overtake him and lighten his load.

But who am I to give lessons or to judge anyone? I am nobody. I look into my eyes and I see nothing; I look into my mind and know nothing.

I have a name: I am Nora Sheehy. I was like a sycamore seed that fell from a tree almost seventy years ago. It took root and grew, and though not a very strong tree, it stood in the shelter from the harsh Atlantic sea. My grandmother provided stability and strength until I could stand alone. But she let my mother cling to her—her own daughter would never be a tree or stand alone. A fungus sticks to whatever it can.

My grandmother would say that she herself was neither bright nor intelligent. But I believe Grandmother was bright enough to make it through this world and to help me onto my feet, and bright enough to let my mother hang on to her and not latch onto me. In her wisdom, my grandmother taught me a lot. I was not equipped to understand then and thought her cold and hardhearted at times. I suffered when she rejected my affection and pushed me away, wanting me gone as soon as possible. But I misunderstood her—that was not it at all. Grandmother had simply wanted her grandchild to grow stronger.

She knew that I would have to grow up quickly and that I could not count on anyone but myself. Grandmother knew that for me a life away from the cottage would be a better life, even if that meant being alone. She knew that staying there would force me to do my duty by Mother, and that would destroy me. If my mother had lived, I would have stayed.

But once my grandmother realized that her own days were numbered, she set about freeing me. I have often wondered if Grandmother put the idea in my mother's mind, and if she did it because it was the only way possible.

A vision comes to me: there are people standing by the old cottage gate. I see his face: he lived a good life and has left a son and three grandchildren. Of the three, Karen was the apple of his eye, and his love still surrounds her. If her brothers are like her, then he has indeed been blessed. But it is not for that that I was drawn; it is because she is linked to Jane. That is her destiny. However that link could end her life. While Karen is not the monster's target, she could end up protecting her friend and perhaps laying down her life for her.

Pierre wipes the sallow keys and plastic frame of the accordion with reverence. It looks no better after than before, worn, tarnished and stained. He has spoken about repairing the instrument or buying a new one. He will never replace it; that will be the only accordion that Pierre ever plays.

And there is that look of shame on his face—he was gone longer this time. His smell is too fresh, yet he is flaking away. If he had stayed with his whore and not returned, it would have eased my burden. I am not unfeeling, and only wish to save him more pain. But Pierre cannot stay away, for there is nowhere else to go. He has gone from one whore to another, but it brings him nothing anymore. An autumn leaf needs a place to furl and die. I never ask questions. Maybe I should have asked him to talk more of his past; maybe I should have been curious or jealous. Those emotions are foreign to me. Still there is something between us. I allowed myself to be in his dreams for a while, and it was nice being part of somebody else's dreams, especially when I had no dreams of my own. It brought me a sort of contentment, and I am grateful to him for that. I have thought of telling him but have held back because of his whore and his straying. And now my fear is that I have left it too late.

He pauses, stops polishing the keys, and finally looks at me. Our eyes meet for a second, and I return to sewing the silk shawl in my hand. My stitches are rough and approximate. The shawl is torn and I do not know how it happened.

If I look in his eyes for too long, I will see another cracked mirror—his broken dreams. They were his dreams, not mine, and I refuse to be part of them any longer.

I hear a note as his swollen fingers touch ivory, and Pierre begins to play just for me. It has been years since he played like that; his music was fashioned for Metro tunnels and carriages, coarse melodies to earn a coin. Pierre used to say it was our song, 'Le Temps des Cerises.' He is a bad liar. The accordion is slightly out of tune and one note is dead, but this time the melancholy sound touches something in me.

"Nar?"

Pierre always calls me 'Nar,' and never Nora. He is lonely, but does not know how to ask for what his heart wants. I am not without a heart of my own and turn to him. The accordion falls to the floor with a bang, and his face turns ghostly. It is time. I stand up and take his hand. Life is ebbing from him and he is at a loss. I help him stagger to the bed. He reaches for me and tries to make me lie with him. I shake my head. Does he not understand that it is the end, that he may not even make it through the night?

"Rest," I say. "Rest and I will get you something to moisten your lips."

A dog would understand better. Does he not realize that his life is being called to a close? I tell him to be calm, to be peaceful and I will bring a doctor. Pierre tries and fails to speak. I ask if he wants a holy person. He is frightened now—it terrifies him to hear those words—but he nods.

It does not take long to find the street and house. I have learned my grandmother's lesson and have often thought of what I should do when the day arrived. Over the years, I have gotten Pierre to write emergency cards. On the third ring, somebody opens the door. The Order of Dominican Brothers residing here can help. I show them the card that tells them I have trouble; it is their job to be merciful and their duty to come.

A Brother agrees to come with me. He is annoyed, but duty is duty. By the time we get back, I already know that it is too late. Pierre is no longer with me.

The file has been prepared; everything is in there. I give Brother Francois the file, together with an envelope and a lot of money. Pierre has written everything down—I made him do it a long time ago. There is more than enough money in the envelope and the Brothers will do the right thing.

Pierre Aimedieu will return to his home, the place he should never have left. He was from Provence and made for Provence. Paris was not the city for him. But now Pierre will be at peace.

I am unable to make out my own feelings. This has been coming for a long time. Every walk up that hill to fill my pockets has been with this in mind. The only offering I can give Pierre is a respectable end. I will not have the same. But it is more important for him than it is for me. Oh Pierre, Pierre, had you met someone else, it might have been better, it might have been worse. But you have left

me with very little time. They take your body away and I
will not go with you. Your people do not know me; those
of your family that remain would not be pleased to see me.
You never spoke of me to them; I am not in their
memories. To them I do not exist.

They take your belongings away. They can do as they wish
with them, for whatever they are worth, they are of little
value. The accordion wheezes a stray complaining note as
somebody knocks it accidentally against the door. Good
bye, Pierre, good bye. This is where we part.

I stand again at the window, sure that this place can no
longer be my home. It is time for me to make myself even
more invisible.

15

"*M*adame Moreau! Madame Moreau, what's the matter?"
Karen rushed to the side of the old woman slumped on
the ground.

"Oh...oh...oh," Chantal groaned. She was wide-eyed
and gasping slightly but managed to get up onto her knees.
She grasped Karen's arm to steady herself. "Help me,
please."

"Take my hands." Karen tried to support her as
Chantal struggled to her feet. She was surprisingly heavy
for such a feeble woman.

"Mon Dieu!" Chantal dusted herself down.

Karen was relieved to see that Chantal, although
ruffled, was apparently none the worse for wear. "What
happened? Did you slip on the cobbles and fall?"

"No, no, I was pushed."

"Pushed? By whom?"

"A man pushed me. I was at the recycling bin when
suddenly somebody shoved me."

"Did you see him?"

"His face was covered. But I saw his eyes; they were
savage and wild. For a moment, I thought he was going to

kill me. Oh, my God, maybe he has broken into my flat and is attacking Guillaume."

"Do you have your keys?"

Chantal shook her coat pocket and the clink signaled that they were there.

"Let's go upstairs and call the police. Then we'll call a doctor."

Chantal straightened her coat. "No, nothing is broken."

"Better not to take any risks," said Karen as she took out her phone. "I'm calling the police. I've had enough between letters and—"

"No!" Chantal tried to take the phone from her. "He ran away; don't bother anyone."

Karen stepped back. "I'm sorry, but I am calling the police."

Chantal looked around and whispered, "There are men in the building, very bad men."

Karen thought that Chantal was probably in shock and took her arm.

Chantal pulled away from her and walked ahead, but once at her apartment door, she just stood there.

"What's the matter?"

Chantal's hands hung at her sides. "I don't have my keys."

"They're in your pocket."

Chantal searched an inside pocket: "Oh," she said, finally producing a bunch of keys and opening the door.

"Where is your husband?"

"I will just see that he's okay." Chantal tottered off and left her in the corridor.

Karen heard her call his name and start to chatter. She waited as several minutes passed. Wasn't Chantal coming back? "Chantal!" she called out, but nobody answered. "Chantal!"

Finally there were footsteps and Chantal re-appeared, took off her glasses, and then put them back on and stared at Karen. "Oui?"

"I am calling the police?"

"Why?"

"To report the intruder..."

"No, no, go now, please," Chantal pushed her toward the door.

The woman was so frail that Karen was afraid to insist and was beginning to suspect that Chantal had made up the whole story about the intruder. It could have been to hide her embarrassment over her fall.

"Non, Non!" A roar came from downstairs.

"Oh my God," Chantal screamed, "he's back!"

"That's Frederic or Eric. I'm going down; you stay here."

Chantal had already banged the door closed.

A very angry looking Frederic strode up and down the hallway while mouthing information on his phone to the police.

Eric stood at the mailbox, letter in hand. There were tears running down his face.

"Is it another hate letter?" Karen asked.

He held it out for her to see. It was horrendous; spewing insults and curses. Not for the first time, an unwelcome thought passed through her mind, but it was better not to voice it unless sure.

Jane waved a page in the air. "I got this message from Madame Lune. Nothing's actually written on it, it's her business card—or should I say, her business piece of paper."

It had turned up in a little bag of jewelry samples that she carried in her purse. Jane felt it was no coincidence and planned to phone the medium. She had been busy and had also checked their little glass corner, discovering that it was not that expensive. In fact the agency had been trying to lease it for over two years. The small size made it difficult to rent as a shop. There was room for a counter and possibly a few wall shelves, and maybe space enough to receive two customers at the time.

"That's what we'd figured—a display case to accompany the online side."

"Exactly, but there is also a little room at the back, so if...well you know—"

"You mean, if I ever left Olivier, I could use it."

"Or something..."

Olivier was a problem that couldn't be ignored much longer; his behavior had changed since her outburst and he'd conveniently managed to be away on business most of the time. He'd found excuses to go to dinner parties and then end up spending the night on the sofa or not coming home at all. That was not the resolution she hoped for.

She opened her purse to pay for the coffee, "Let me, please. I have a load of change."

"No, it's my turn. What's the matter? What do you have there?" Jane leaned over the table. "Oh, Madame Lune's paper; you've got one too. Fancy that."

Karen had been dubious of Jane's story, but had no idea where this slip of paper had come from. She was sure she'd thrown the old paper away after the last visit. But her mind was made up to call the number and once and for all get to the bottom of Madame Lune and her dire warnings.

"Looks like we'll be together in front of the crystal ball..."

"I'm curious—you know Tony visited today."

"Is that so?" Karen didn't appreciate hearing that name. While on crutches, Tony had stayed well out of Jane's life. Suddenly, now that she was moving around better, he'd turned up. "What did he want?"

"He's stuck; the guy he hired to replace me left him high and dry."

"And he wants you to stand in for him?"

"Just for a few nights." Jane avoided Karen's eye. "That's alright, isn't it?"

Karen raised her eyebrows.

"The Tarot readings have made me some handy cash,

but I need to earn a bit more. I haven't done that many readings. It's tough, tougher than I imagined. I've come to the realization that I'm better at designing and making jewelry. Telling people's fortunes, as Madame Lune does, is really hard. I like intuition when it comes like that." Jane clicked her fingers. "When somebody asks you if you see or sense something, I can come up with ideas, but when they have a real question or when they want to know exactly what's going to happen, just as I did with Madame Lune, I can't make believe—it's not natural."

"At least you're clear in your mind about that. So you want to work at the pub some evenings with Tony for the money?"

"If I cover one week for him, then my debt is paid."

"You're debt?"

"I promised to help him until he found somebody, and I never really did, so just want to balance the scales."

"Are you sure you'll be able to say no afterward, because Tony comes running back to you every time he's stuck for somebody?"

"I told him one week, and that's all. I'm strong enough to say no, believe me."

"I do and—"

"Conard!"

An argument had broken out in front of the drycleaner's door. Madame Lu danced in temper, her fist in the air, while Monsieur Abu towered over her. Madame Dry came hurrying from the café. Those on the square looked on: Laurent folded his arms; Monsieur Martin leaned over his counter; the glasses rattled on the waiter's tray. Madame Dry's arrival calmed affairs, although Madame Lu managed to lob a few more insults before scooting away. Monsieur Abu roared and threw his arms in the air as he strode off.

"Nothing serious, I suppose," Karen commented.

"The usual," said Jane.

Karen was glad to get back to the flat. She sent Jane a few updates and then shut down her phone. She was restless and went to close the shutters and draw the curtains, sparing a glance at Madame Lune's window. It was dark inside the apartment, but the shutters weren't closed, nor were the curtains drawn.

And there was lots of movement on the street. Was that a man down there looking up at her window? No, that was nonsense. Another man wearing a hat leaned against a wall of the café and seemed to be scanning the entire street. For a second, he looked directly at her, threw down his cigarette, stamped it out and walked onward. Didn't Olivier and Jane say that a lot of action came onto the street at night, prostitutes and dealers and so on? She'd just never paid attention before. Rue Lepic seemed more unwelcoming, somehow.

A floor board creaked behind her; Karen jumped and turned. "Jesus! Olivier, I didn't hear you come in."

He stood looking at her through narrowed eyes. He'd lost weight and it made him appear more drawn and tired. His suit was wrinkled and there was a strong smell of cigarette smoke. Gone was the cheerful confident Olivier, and in its place, someone sadder and more unsure. He left his travel bag sitting in the entrance and went to close the other shutters.

"Olivier, are you alright?"

"Sure."

"We have to talk, but you're never here and..."

"Talk about what?"

"Us...this living together, only separately in the same apartment, is not working. It's time for me to move out."

He sat on the sofa and put his head in his hands. "I don't want you to leave; I want us to try to make it work. My traveling all the time is not fair to you. I have a chance for promotion, and if it works out, there will be much less travel."

"That's good, and I am happy for you, but it will not

change the fact that we're not matched. I've tried, but I can't pretend any longer."

"Karen, these past weeks have been hell for me, wanting you and at the same time afraid of hurting you. I need you more than ever."

Karen shook her head, "I can't, Olivier. Look, maybe I should just move into a hotel until I get a place sorted out." The glass corner shop wasn't ready yet, but in a few weeks, she would move into the back room.

There was a long silence.

"Do you understand, Olivier?"

"Yes." His voice was tight and low; his hands trembled and his face was damp from perspiration.

"Olivier, do you have a fever?"

"No, just lapsed into my bad habits, cigarettes and...that's all." He stood, put a hand on either side of her face then let them slide onto her neck. His fingers tightened slightly, exerting pressure, then he dropped his hands. "You want to go, I hear you. But promise me that you won't move out until you've found a place to stay. Don't go to a hotel. I want us to remain friends."

Karen nodded to his back as he disappeared into the bathroom. She waited until she heard the shower then hurried to prepare a bed on the sofa. It was as if a stone had been lifted from her shoulders; the relief was immense. There was guilt, but in the end, he'd accepted her decision—no arguments or fights—it had been easier than expected. Soon she would be free. Whatever else, her time with Olivier had made her grow up quickly, and that was something to be grateful for.

16

I am diverted by the voice of the busker that comes through the open window. A young girl is singing a very lonesome song, "Ma Plus Belle Histoire D'amour, C'est Vous." Her voice is sad, so sad. It reaches me like nothing else has these past days.

I have spent days and nights going through everything that Pierre had put on shelves, in cupboards—paper, more papers. They are a puzzle to me, but he had a good system arranged according to color, from the most important to the least.

There is a knock; I have been expecting it. I recognize the man standing at the door, although he has rarely engaged with me. Pierre knew him and that is why we came here. The landlord has heard about Pierre and commiserates. He is telling me things, giving me notice; we never had any real rights here. He is afraid that the old lady in front of him will not be able to pay. How poor is his judgement! It is the very same old lady who always paid. But the landlord is not without intelligence, and I am not without knowledge. I take him downstairs and onto the street and point to it. He has a room, a tiny space. It is all I need. His *chambre de bonne* has not been rented for years, for it is but a storeroom. It is cupboard size and lacks the basic facilities. I have lived in worse, have lived without. It is on Rue Lepic; it is important to me that the window looks onto this street. It means begging and stuttering my request to the landlord. It goes against nature to do that—begging is not my trade. He accepts because I am offering him money. He will be paid in advance for several months. The room is vital to me, to plan, to watch, to be left alone.

He has given me a week to move. A week is enough. The girls have received my messages and they will come. Madame Lune will see them one last time in the old flat. My words will be clear; I have practiced them. Both will be received together. Karen Moroney can do nothing if Jane Moore is not aware. It is clear to me that my message must frighten them. They must be made to leave Rue Lepic.

I look around me and feel grief. It is partly because Pierre is gone. I cannot allow myself to feel or think about that; it would be dangerous for me. There has been very little tying me to sanity and Pierre was one of those threads. He was my voice, and now it is gone; he is gone.

Visions come in my sleep. Many dreams go through my head. They take me to the past, rolling the years back and stirring dusty longings.

A cold sweat wakes me and the faces of Jane Moore and Karen Moroney are before me. If only I could escape, but something is calling me back to the old place; I would like to see it one more time. Panic surges inside me; it would mean getting a passport, going to the Embassy. That would bring me into direct contact with authorities and official people. I am not able to do that, to face such people. They would ask me to sign documents. I would once again be a dunce.

I get up, tread the floorboards and lie down again. My eyes are weak: sleep, oh but to sleep! When our senses shut down, we sleep forever. I do not want to believe that something else awaits us after death. I have spoken to wild spirits, heard voices and warnings, but I have not seen anyone who has woken up to a wonderful paradise. I have not seen people walking lovely meadows, caressed by the gentle breeze under blue skies. I have seen none of that. I have seen and heard only suffering souls—lost souls tangled in memories of their former lives. Paradise does not exist. Yet I would willingly let go of life if I could only be sure that our actions do not matter. I would not hesitate to wipe the monster off this earth and leave him to his filthy memories to suffer for eternity. There would be no more victims for him to take. Knowing that, I could close my eyes for evermore. Karen Moroney and Jane Moore would live their lives as they pleased.

What is holding me back? It is because something is telling me there is more connecting this life to whatever comes after. I have followed him from cemetery to cemetery and know where some of his victims lie. I have to know all, every one of them. Only then can he be cancelled from this earth. It must be done for the memory of the souls, and for the living. It must be done because maybe there are green meadows, gentle dales, purple mountains, saints and angels singing praises in the heavens. Maybe there are, maybe I have to give them a chance, listen to them, for they know better.

If I tie a rope to the rafters my life would end in less time than it would take me to explain it. A long time ago, I wished that. But I cannot. I believe that it is no longer for me to decide.

It came again to me last night. The image is always the same. There is a schoolroom; there are wooden desks and floorboards steeped in learning. There is a blackboard and chalk, pens and inkwells. There is a teacher and there are restless children. Nora Sheehy is one of them, raven hair and sallow skin, sitting second row from the front at that moment of realization when she knew that something was wrong with her, really wrong. They had told Grandmother that my speech handicap should not prevent me from going to school. I had ears, I had eyes, and I had a brain; I could learn.

The little girl could not get it, did not understand, though she tried and tried. Everything was swimming before her eyes on the board and on the page. Nora could make sense of nothing. Nora was...a dunce. They all could read and write, she could not. 'Dunce, Dunce, Dunce!' How could a girl be expected to read and write with the mother that she had and a nameless blackguard as a father. But Mother could read and write; Grandmother taught her. I saw my mother write her name and read story books. Though foolish in her mind, she could read the words, even if she was not able to understand them fully. Mother did not know what she was writing, but could write. Her daughter could not do that. No, but I could read nature and understand the words of the wild animals and creatures, and everything that was growing around us. I had learned to understand the movements of the sea and the clouds, and to map every rock and feature of the countryside. The other children were unable to do it, but I had no ability to express it because my speech was mangled. I could have lived with my stammer, but not without being able to read or write. I would have been better off if my mind had been taken like my mother's; ignorance would have been a blessing.

How simple minded you are, Nora Sheehy, to think that you had discarded those memories, left them in the old schoolroom. The people of my childhood were not nastier or meaner than any other. They just did not understand. The teachers tried for a long time before giving up. I would stare and stare at the words, looking at the lines and understanding nothing. All that despair turned inwards.

I became good at guessing and would invent meaning behind what was on the page. I would make big, ugly shapes on paper and pretend they were letters. Nobody was fooled. They did not know what to do with me: 'Teach her to sew, teach her to make things with her hands.' I was not as bad at making stitches as I was at making letters, but I was not very good. Nora Sheehy was useless, so they left me to cleaning. They sent me to scrub the floors and to clean the windows. A girl like me had no other use at the school. Later, I turned cleaning to thieving. But I still had not given up hope and would take Grandmother's newspaper and turn the pages, looking at the print until my eyes smarted and watered. I would take the fairy tales that mother read and just look at the pictures.

In time, I got better at guessing and more skilled at using my eyes and ears. If somebody spoke the word and wrote it, I would replace the letters with a picture in my mind. Each word had a shape and could be copied. So I eventually learned how to approximate words with pictures. It worked for some things. Grandmother did it with me; patiently helping me as best she could. Grandmother's way of speaking was unpolished, but she had beautiful writing. I learned several hundred words that way—pages of pictures. Nights were filled juggling those words in my head and using them to write sentences. What wonderful and grand sentences I produced with pictures. It did not work when it came to reading other people's handwriting, but I could manage something from those whose writing I saw over and over. It failed completely for the printed word; the typed word had perfect shapes—perfect circles, ovals, squares and rectangles—too perfect. Now everybody uses the printed word, and I can guess nothing at all.

In later years, Pierre showed me how to use symbols on the phone. I learned to do so very well. When we were separated on a train or a street, he knew how to send messages that were easy to understand. But we did not really need it for long because I read his mind and habits so well.

Oh Pierre! Where are you now? Who would have thought that I would miss you so? I came to Paris on the throw of a dice, put my money on a ticket and took the boat. It was not a bad thing to end up in a place where I understood nothing, where the language was foreign and where I had an excuse for not reading and writing and comprehending.

I learned to understand a new language. Strange words became familiar and I would listen to the radio in fascination, marveling in my discovery. I looked at people, studied how they dressed, moved and behaved. I became skilled at it. Nora Sheehy could be from a higher class or a lower class, could be an old woman or a young one. Disguising gave me freedom. People reacted to my disguises but not to me, not the real me.

It took hours of sitting on park benches and watching people. That is how my trade was learned. I would sit in Neuilly-Sur-Seine or Versailles town and learn to be Bourgeois; or trail the darker suburbs and learn more vulgar ways. Pierre played his accordion. My ear was attuned and receptive to the notes he made. There was some tenderness and affection at that time. He had potential and talent and I was prepared to pretend, even if it were not totally true. I had played before with people in my grandmother's cottage. My rhythm was good and my fingers nimble. I remember taking his accordion once and producing an air. His eyes flashed and I could see that it was not out of pride, but jealousy. I could play better than he could. That day, I put the instrument down and never took it up again. I had learned not to anger and frustrate people, never to be better than others, and above all, never to show it. It is wiser to be ignored.

Do not show yourself. Do not move to where you will stand out. Always fit in and be average. Average people are never seen.

The monster is the same, as chary as the evening shadow,

but to me he is not average. I notice every change and I can tell that today his energy is quieter than before. The air does not whirl around him. He has something to do and has to concentrate. It is annoying for him, but it has to be dealt with. It will not bring him pleasure, not even a shred of excitement. It will simply be an action to remove a problem. He knows that all things come to those who wait.

There she is, the woman who has not learned to be invisible. Discretion is not Madame Lu's brand. She knows a little, and a little is too much. She has been foolish and has already talked. When you have that kind of knowledge, you must mind it as a miser would covet a penny. You must be careful where you talk; close your lips and never whisper a word. Madame Lu cannot shut up. Her comfortable blue shoes should have been enough, but she will keep talking about the dress—the torn dress with blood stains. If Madame Lu has told one, she will tell more. She must be silenced. Yes, he must eliminate Madame Lu before ensnaring Jane Moore. Jane has once again gained time.

Madame Lu is thought by some to be a pest and by others to be useful. If only her tongue would stop wagging! The woman is the loud orange seam on a black background. Yet, standing out has helped her through life. Madame Lu is smart, but only smart enough to make her place. She has overstepped herself and is not smart enough to hide that.

Here she comes, ringing her bell and taking to the street at top speed. Everybody must know that I am coming, the tiny lady announces at each ring.

Different sets of eyes watch Madame Lu draw attention to herself, as a bright flower attracts the bees. She goes to the building where Karen Moroney lives to visit the woman whose mind is already elsewhere. Once they were poison together, but now they are just a burden to each other.

Glances crisscross the street. What's up? Something is up. The drycleaner's shop has been very busy today; business is good, very good. Who could imagine that cleaning rags could be so lucrative? The owner knows. She stands at the door, smoking idly. The drycleaner is not as idle as that. Oh, she is not given to manual work and does not like to make slow money; but she has a quick mind and uses it to suit her purpose. That woman is not the richest person on the street, but she knows how to make something from nothing, and to do it quickly; she's a scheming woman. She catches the newspaper man in her beam; she has taught him a thing or two. She gestures to the bin man and he comes immediately. Monsieur Abu has understood how to weave himself into street life. Unlike Madame Lu he knows how much to say, and how much not to say too. He knows his place.

The clock ticks. The flower man begins to dismantle his stands. He does not make an easy living. To do his job, one has to like it. He could be a farmer wed to his patch of ground. He jumps in surprise as a glass breaks in the café nearby. It is only the waiter. He is not a good waiter and should never have taken up such work. His shirt is never as fresh or crisp as it might be; his palms are always damp. He would like to be noticed and seen and wishes he had the ease to speak like the others. His impairment is shyness; it has been an obstacle in his life. People do not notice him, and that makes him feel belittled. He serves the customers, tends the tables, and they hardly know he exists. The older he grows, the worse it is. He is attracted to Jane and would like to draw her attention, but he cannot.

My nerves are aroused and I am uneasy. Night consumes the street. I do not like it; I like nothing of what I see. The sun will rise and it will not bring good things. There will be bad business soon on Rue Lepic. That is not an omen, it is a certainty.

17

The fortune teller hadn't just pulled a card showing them that Jane's life was in peril, but also that Karen's life was in danger. The sketch was of two ladies by a tombstone. She then took a postcard of Paris, pointed at them and drew an X across the picture.

Karen pitched her voice higher. "Madame, are you saying we should leave the city? You already told me some of that nonsense; I didn't believe you then and don't believe you now. I want proof, evidence and facts, please."

Madame Lune collected the cards and wrapped them in a silk cloth.

Karen glanced at her friend sitting stiffly on her chair. Jane had been so looking forward to coming. On previous occasions they had made appointments through Madame Lune's assistant. This time they had been given no choice, and following their leaving a message on the answer machine suggesting a day and time, had received a slip of paper in their letter boxes with a simple tick.

"Now look here," Karen tried again. "Stop with all those sketches and cards; talk to us!"

Madame Lune stood and readjusted the veil over her face.

"Is there not another way?" Jane insisted. "Can't you help us?"

Madame Lune pushed the postcard into Jane's hand and ushered them both unceremoniously out the door. Karen clenched her fists and shook them as it closed resolutely in their faces.

Jane put her hands to her head. "This is awful, terrible. What am I to do?"

Karen's voice cracked. "That woman is a gangster with an ulterior motive. I don't know what it is, but she can't play games like that and try to ruin your life."

"I think she's sincere; I really do," Jane defended.

"She's probably afraid that you'll take her business. And she must have heard that we are interested in renting that shop for our venture."

"But that doesn't make any sense."

"It makes perfect sense to me. We have to find out who Madame Lune really is; check her background and everything about her."

"I'm confused." Jane wiped her eyes. "I can't think straight."

"Has that woman managed to alarm you so much, Jane? Did she make you cry for words of doom that have been made up?"

"Don't mind me, you know I cry easily. I'm just...I don't know. And you, Karen, do you really not believe her?"

"I did not believe her the first time, and even less this time," Karen was lying a little for Jane's sake, but wasn't going to give into doubts.

"Why didn't you tell me that she had already warned you? If you thought there was nothing behind her warnings, then you should have said something to me sooner, but you didn't."

Karen shook her head.

"Well?"

"It was so outlandish that it was better to say nothing.

There was no point in passing on that sort of non-information."

Two creamy hot chocolates at Café Lepic helped to settle their thoughts and nerves.

Jane fiddled with her place mat. "We can't just forget it; we have to go back and see her again. We have to be more determined, force her to tell us. We must ask her if she's acting out of pure flashes of intuition or has a concrete reason for saying what she did."

"I'm all for that, but it's not easy to pin her down. She doesn't speak and is obsessed with her cards and drawings. If you raise your tone, you're out the door; ask a question, you're out the door anyway. As I said, we need to dig up more about this woman."

"I can begin by asking around if people know her," Jane suggested. "We can ask Laurent, or Monsieur Martin..."

"Exactly! We can inquire from Madame Lu and Monsieur Abu. If anybody knows what happens on this street, it's that pair."

"That's what we'll do; planning and taking action makes me feel better."

Karen watched Jane shred her napkin. "If you don't feel you can sleep in your room, you can stay with me?"

"No, no, no! You're in the middle of a break-up. Besides, I've got to stay alone."

"You don't need to be brave, and Olivier is hardly ever there."

"If I start getting cold feet now, I'll never do anything or go anywhere again. I ran away in the past because I had to. Running is over for me. I have a life here and am not abandoning it. I know it may not seem like much; just a little room, an idea for a business, a chance to create and work on my art, but that's my light, my future."

"I understand," Karen began then turned her attention. "Oh hi, Laurent."

"Don't move because of me." Laurent raised his hand in apology.

Jane pointed to a chair. "Feel free to join us."

He smiled. "You are too kind, angels; maybe if you're still here in five minutes." He sauntered inside.

Karen looked over her shoulder and saw that Monsieur Martin was standing just behind them. Had he been listening? She wasn't sure if he spoke English or not. On second thought, perhaps it wasn't a good idea to make inquiries about Madame Lune with people like him.

She lowered her voice: "Look, Jane, I can understand you wanting to go on with your life as usual, but if you're working at Tony's one of these nights, don't go home alone. Even without Madame Lune's warning I would have told you that. Get a taxi or call me. Will you promise to do that?"

Jane sighed. "I promise to be as careful as possible."

Laurent returned, pulled up a chair and from his top pocket produced a single flower for each of them. "One for each pretty angel."

There was a carnation for Jane and a red tulip for Karen. Jane laid hers on the table. Karen sniffed the tulip and could see Jane cringe.

"Monsieur Martin told me that you come from the countryside, Karen." Laurent stirred sugar into his coffee. "I envy you. Ireland must be a beautiful country."

"It is. I'm surprised that Monsieur Martin remembers. I only told him in passing."

Laurent picked up Jane's flower, twirled it and replaced it near her. "And you?"

"The city, mostly."

"You work at many things."

"We have an English expression, 'Jack of all trades'. I was and still am Jane of all trades."

Laurent laughed. "There is skill in being that; I've seen your beautiful jewelry."

"It's nice of you to say so. Once we get the shop open,

I hope you'll recommend us."

"I will, I will!" Laurent cupped his hands. "I'll shout it far and wide. What are you going to call it?"

"The Glass Corner seems appropriate as it is all windows and mirrors," Karen said.

"It's a good name," he said as his face grew serious. "It's a special corner—you see so much from there—you're just short of a 360° view."

"That's what we think too—eyes on the street!"

Laurent shook out a cigarette from a packet then bid them good evening. Lighting up as he returned to his stand, he shook hands with Monsieur Abu who had obligingly covered for him.

Karen and Jane tried to piece together everything they had about Madame Lune and came up with little more than what they already knew. They wouldn't even be able to identify her, having never seen her without her veil. There was nothing online or in the small ads advertising her business; even local shopkeepers had no knowledge of a fortune teller on Rue Lepic. They only had the slips of paper put directly in their bags to go by. Jane had tried ringing her number again, but the line had been disconnected. In the end, they decided to go directly to her place once more and get her to face them directly.

Karen pressed the doorbell.

Nothing.

Pressed again.

Still nothing.

She knocked.

Nobody opened.

"Let's try her neighbor." Jane knocked next door.

An old man peeped out. On seeing them, he was friendly enough. He explained that his neighbors had been discreet; but he was aware that the woman's companion had died recently and that she had moved to a *chamber de bonne* in a different building. He believed that it was two doors up the street.

They decided to follow up immediately. Luckily for them, there was no code due to renovation works in the main part of the building. The concierge confirmed that an elderly woman had moved in and gave them directions to the eighth floor.

After the ascent they were both panting hard. They knocked and listened, but their knock was met with silence. They tried several more times to no avail.

"She must be with family for a few days. Remember, she is in mourning," Karen said.

"That's probably true." Jane knocked one more time. "We'll come back each day until she turns up and opens the door."

"That's all we can do."

Karen dropped the remote control on the sofa, tired of zapping and not even looking at the screen. She then turned wearily to switch off her computer. After several days of checking the real estate agencies and individual sites for rentals, it was clear that finding something small, cheap and convenient wasn't going to be easy. A *chamber de bonne* might be the best option, and the only way to find that was by asking around. But in that case, it was just as well to wait to get The Glass Corner renovated and use the back room until something better turned up. That meant being stuck in Olivier's place a little longer.

Although Olivier had accepted her decision, it was still very awkward slipping around each other. It was tiring. When Olivier wasn't traveling, he tended to eat out and to come back very late. Karen would make sure to be sound asleep on the sofa, but that meant that he had to tiptoe around her. The mornings were even more uncomfortable, especially as he had no problem walking to and from the bathroom scantily dressed. Karen, on the other hand, made sure at all times to stay in a dressing gown and avoid any hint of provocation or misunderstanding.

She found herself curious and poking in corners, coming across odds and ends: photographs from Olivier's past with previous girlfriends and there had clearly been many. It wasn't right to look at his personal things, but these had been stuck in books, thrown into a box in the wardrobe. In the same wardrobe were a few bags of CDs and DVDs. She idly browsed through some; several were X-rated. That Olivier would have a few pornographic videos didn't surprise her, but it felt odd to be just noticing it now. Karen put them away; it wasn't fair to snoop through his things.

Something banged outside in the corridor. Karen went to the door and looked through the peephole and saw Chantal scurrying away. She opened the door, but Chantal had already gone downstairs. Since the changed status with Olivier, and everything else that was in flux, problems in the building had taken a back seat. In truth, Karen had avoided meeting people so as not to have to make polite small talk and answer superficial questions about Olivier.

She opened her eyes; he was leaning over the sofa staring at her. There was a strong smell of alcohol.

"Olivier, are you drunk?"

"I've been watching you sleep, you are lovely." He went on his knees beside her and pressed his lips to hers. His breath smeled sour, of garlic, wine and cigarettes.

Karen pushed him. "Go to bed, Olivier. You're drunk."

Olivier swayed back a little and slurred, "I still love you; don't you like me a little?"

Karen sat up, keeping the blanket around her. "We'll talk about it in the morning...what are you doing?"

Olivier managed to unzip his trousers. He held his sex toward her, his eyes rolling and a silly grin on his face. The entire scene was ridiculous.

"If you don't help me, I'll have to do it alone..." He rubbed vigorously.

"Stop it!" Karen dragged herself off the sofa and away

from him. Olivier groaned her name then muttered something and toppled into the bedroom. The bed springs creaked and then there was silence. A few minutes later loud snores came from the room.

Disgusted, she closed the bedroom door firmly and almost tripped over his jacket on the floor. Some papers had slipped out of a pocket. A receipt caught her attention: five hundred and fifty euros spent at 'Deux plus Deux,' dated the same day. Had Olivier spent all that this very night? Karen put it back. She had never heard of the place but knew that no ordinary night club could have cost that much. Who cared what he was doing. Now there was little hope of sleep. A quick get-away in the morning so as not to face him was the best plan.

Karen dozed only to be fully woken once more by Olivier pounding across the floor boards as he rushed to the toilet where he was violently sick. Feeling mean, she pulled the blanket fully over her head. It wasn't easy on him, what with having her in the apartment and no longer being together. But it wasn't easy on her either; the sooner she got out on her own the better. What a mistake it had been, and it was frightening to realize how blind she could be. Olivier seemed so different now.

18

I walk along Rue de Maistre toward the cemetery making sure that nobody is near. While Madame Lu rolls on those wheels, I have time. It was once a manhole but has been abandoned for as long as my time in Paris. When you live my sort of life, you learn quickly about the maze of tunnels. I discovered this one forty years ago. It has been useful to me on and off throughout that period. No cataphyll has ever been here, nobody has been here except me.

Age is without mercy. But although my legs are less steady and my limbs are shakier than they were for my first descent into this world, I am still fit enough to handle it. The torch is powerful though hardly necessary to someone who knows their way in the dark.

It is wise to go slowly, snail-like, turn right, left, left, and left again, and then right. It goes on and on, and in the end leads to an opening. I run my fingers across a stone ledge and take an oil lamp. It lights up a small bunker. It is reassuring to come back here and to know that apart from me, it is virgin territory. I unfold a sleeping bag and a heavy quilt. It is warm and comfortable enough.

This place has been useful at different times during my

life. It was useful when I found myself temporarily homeless, and when Pierre had disappeared, and my money too. It will be useful again. It would not be a bad place to finish my days. There are worse places to die. But it is not what I would choose. There are other catacombs that host millions of bones stacked layer upon layer. It is difficult to see them and to remain unaffected; those bones were once people who lived and died in misery before ending up in these caverns, and many were much more deserving than I am.

My heart is heavy. What is the emotion? Is it sadness? Is it for the past or what is to come? Pierre is in his resting place now, with his family. I am alone.

The girls are looking for me. Jane Moore should have left Rue Lepic by now, but unfortunately they did not heed my warning and will not move from the street. It may be too late, for the monster is alerted to her heightened awareness of danger and is more driven than before. It is I who has erred by assuming too much and telling them too little.

There is a mound of hard earth which serves as a seat. Food is the last thing on my mind, but the body must not be left unnourished. I take a tin from my bag, open it and put sardines on a piece of bread. I do not want it, but I force myself to eat. A mouthful of water from a plastic bottle helps the digestion a little.

After my simple meal, I take a shovel and move further along, where the ground is damper and the tunnel less welcoming. I make my toilet and cover the spot with some earth, just like a cat. I return to my bed. It is difficult to break down the meal. I feel discomfort in my gut; my stomach is sickly. I zip up the bag and try to sleep.

When my eyes open everything is blurred. Is it possible that for once I have slept longer than usual? It must have been for three hours. There is nothing to see around me, no window to look through, nothing to watch. That calms me. My eyelids shut and sleep returns. But I have eyes to see inside and dreams to trace back the years. I relive my time with Pierre and talk to him in my mind. I tell him things that could not be said when he was there, things that he would not have understood before, and might now...if there is a place for him beyond...if there is a beyond.

Boxes and squares—that is what it's all about out there in the world. What does anybody know about destiny and choice? Pierre was my choice because he would never force me to be someone else. I do not need anybody looking inside my head; it is mine, mine. Nora Sheehy is the only person who knows who she is.

I am mourning Pierre. It is my way because I miss him. A sort of depression has crept over me—my task is not finished, but it is important to feel things—the loss. I watch inside my mind, build stories and images. It is a long time since I took so much liberty to daydream. I smile to myself. What books I have concocted and written like that—hundreds and hundreds. It gives me freedom not to be shackled by incomprehensible words to create my own fantastic stories. 'That is right, Nora Sheehy, mock yourself. You are a spider, so weave your web where each thread is a tale. You did it as a child, do it now. You need people, just as a web needs a leaf, a branch, or a rafter to make its fragile way, just as a stone needs the earth to hold it and to embed in.'

Above all I needed to be solitary and would sit for hours in the fields, watching and learning. I discovered that everything has a purpose and that knowledge gave me comfort. Neighbors were afraid and said it was not normal to sit as I did like a stone and not move. I was moving though, but to them, no. Watching nature taught me about life and how to read the finest and most perfect book of all. How can one be lonely when they accept that they are part of nature?

I once asked Padraig to read a book for me. It was a

book I had coveted. The feel of the bound leather and the texture of the pages were beautiful against my fingertips. It had sat in Grandmother's cottage. He humored me—I had idolized him, the only boy who did not laugh at me, who seemed to listen to me. He read a chapter every day. But the book disappointed me. It was a romance story—so much promise and so little in the end. It did not speak to me as nature did, as the books in my mind did. Then Padraig would bring poetry books and I loved the rhythm of those verses. He also read some passages from a Bible and I found something more satisfying in those stories. The psalms spoke to me like sweet music. But in my desperate days what helped me most of all was to know that in nature there were a million books around me, and millions more to spare. I felt the lack less then, though I would have liked nonetheless to read and write. Oh, if I could write, truly write in a way that people could read, then I could say so much! But instead, I make sketchy pictures and approximate drawings learned at Grandmother's side.

Well-meaning people tried to persuade my grandmother to have me examined, to have doctors probe inside my head. Thank you, Grandmother, for never allowing that. Your beginnings were humble and working as a farm hand could not have been easy; it was hard to lose Grandfather so soon. You were married old and widowed early, but you were happy to tend the cottage and garden and help people when they called on you. You were a good teacher and taught me to stand on my own feet, to lean on myself, and above all, to trust nobody.

Two days have passed, maybe three. Down here, one loses a sense of time. But I must go outside...

It is snowing. Spring is tapping timidly at the door. I buy some bread; without bread one has not really eaten. Before going back down, I put out my tongue and let a snow flake rest there. It does not taste as it used to; it has the distinct taste of iron. It was different on the tongue of a child. Nora would try to eat the flakes, imagining them like ice lollies with a choice of flavors. Raspberry and strawberry were my favorites. Sometimes I did it for real; how marvelous to mash the snow with jam and eat it like a sorbet! It was heavenly on my tongue; how sweet to savor the cool velvet! But it was best in my imagination. I wonder if animals have imaginations? Is that what sets me apart from animals? My desire would be to become a fox. A fox goes out for food, warily. It is slow to trust and knows how to hunt and steal. A fox will only take a risk if very hungry. When we are starving, we have no choice.

It would be better to stay like the fox, on the margins. To do otherwise would open the door to emotions that would weaken me and hinder me from finishing the task that must be done. I return to my den where I take fitful but watchful sleeps.

There is the glade—a perfect circular opening in the middle of the grove. I am intoxicated by the most captivating and healing perfume of all, sweet woodbine...

It was here that my baby, Patrick, was conceived. It was here that Padraig and I shared our passion. My lover's eyes were never more vivid—his hands coarse, yet gentle, but I never mistook desire for more. That was enough for young Nora. She did not want flattery or gifts and sought neither promises nor commitments. How could Nora ask him to be tied to her ignorance, or to the burden of her mother? She only wanted to mold their shared passion and to experience what brought two bodies together.

I can still feel the soft earth under me and the pinch of pines as his weight pressed down on me. I hear the crunch of bracken and smell the perfume of the woodbine as it covers us like a fairy blanket. Our passion muffles all other sounds and thoughts.

I had been his first, and he mine.

He was desperate for me, consumed with need. We

met again and again. You cannot love like that without consequence. The consequences were all mine.

It could not turn out differently. For I had seen her in church, had seen the girl for him. She was beautiful and elegant, intelligent and kind, with background and education. He should never have been taken by the foolish notion of having me as wife. I was just a passing experience. That woman adored him and would make him happy in a way I could never do. I was not just poor and ignorant, but odd and strange. If he married me, then he would lose his family. I did not need to be told that. He was not a bad man, only young and careless, and I had allowed myself to fantasize for a frozen moment.

By then my grandmother was gone and my mother was gone, and I was free to go. So I chose freedom and took to the road.

My heart stops—I see the cottage. How empty it is! There are now gaping spaces where once there were windows. My grandmother is not there to fill it with life and gaiety. It is but a shack. Our beginnings were indeed humble. Briars twine their way around the garden and the scent of woodbine hangs over me like a new skin. But in my dream the cottage is still in one piece. I can look inside and the spirits are there, ghosts seated on the sugan chairs in front of the fire. Like an old traveler, I have come back to sit with them and wait for death to catch up with me. But it is not real.

I awake from my dream. It is not time to rise, so I close my eyes and go deeper into my search for peace. Images fight for space in my head.

—I see the face of a lecherous monster—it is him.

—I see myself in the schoolroom and my mother's face at the window. I hear the jeers of children.

—He is back again. He is standing, leering in the square. The screams of Jane Moore are all around him. Karen Moroney is on her knees in front of him, begging for mercy.

—It all washes through my dreams. My grandmother stands by my cold bed. She shakes her head in sorrow and whispers my name: "Nora..."

—There is blood dripping from his mouth; hot red fluid from his eyes. I try to fight him but he cannot be killed. Voices shout: "Kill him! Kill him!" But it is he who is pushing a knife into my ribcage, again and again and again. "She is mine!" he roars. "Jane Moore will be mine, and no stupid dunce will stop me."

—Mother is running like a fool between the school desks: "Where is Nora, where is my Nora?" Grandmother is running after her: "Get out of here, get home this minute! What curse was on our family?" I shut my ears to the derision. "Nora, my darling," says Mother, "I don't know where you came from. He came in between my legs, and lo and behold, out you came between the same legs!"

—Blood continues to spurt from his mouth. "Who do you think you are to try to stop me? Do you think you can prevent what is destined?"

—"What are we to do with you, Nora?" Grandmother's voice is sad. "School is no place for you. You must wash and scrub for a living—that is an honest way. Let the others go to school. Learning is over for you, my girl."

—"Nora, Nora, Nora!" Mother's cries rise from the sea as the waves pummel the cliffs. "Let her go; let your mother go," Grandmother tells me. "It is the only way..."

—The knife is over my head, his face is close to mine. His mouth is open and his gums are rotting. "I will skin you, old woman, and you will die slowly. You deserve to be punished. You cannot stop me. I will separate your limbs from your torso and crush your bones." The tombs shake and the dead laugh at me.

—"Be an honest girl," Grandmother warns. "Oh, Grandmother, I was not honest a day of my life..." The gates slam; the cottage is empty. There is nobody, nobody. I cry out, "What happened to you, Grandmother? You who could milk forty cows alone and carry any burden, no matter how heavy? Why do you go each day to the church to pray? The more often you pray, the lonelier I feel. You are wasting away, and look at me with these eyes of death. Do not go away, please, stay with me." The gates are banging and the cemetery walls are closing in on me. I have no voice. I have lost my ability to speak.

—He is once more before me: "You cannot speak properly, you cannot read or hardly write your name. Your place is scrubbing floors dunce!" I am running... Wailing rises out of the mausoleums. The voices of the dead grow louder and louder. They call out, "Jane Moore, come and join us!" He stands over her and prepares her body for his salacious assault. I try to reach Jane, but thousands of hands grab me...

I open my eyes—where am I? I am deep in the earth, buried underground. For a moment, there is hope: maybe I am dead and it is all over. But no, consciousness returns. Nora Sheehy is lying in a Paris catacomb and must face what is outside. I do not want to sleep anymore; I do not want the nightmares that sleep brings. If I have to stitch the lids to pin my eyes open and stop this persecution, I will.

How wise we become in our old age, how clearly we see, and how much we know... I only sought to see one hour through: hour by hour, day by day, that has been my life. It has been a poor life. And yet in my final days there have been many thoughts and visions. Knowledge has come pouring in. If my knowledge then were what it is today, I would have put my determined mind to work in other ways. It is too late to have regrets now.

I drink from the bottle of water. Everything is dark, but his face stares back at me through the darkness. He is outside on the street, walking and pacing. Tonight, he cannot sleep either. Winter is giving its final salute, and his patience has run out. But he too has memories; a mother and father and sisters. He taunted his sisters and would break their dolls and disfigure them. He loved to make his sisters cry and hear their screams of horror on finding their mutilated toys. Yet, he was born with the same light as they were. But each year he leaned more and more towards the shadows, shying away from the sunshine, cowering in the shade. He could not stand the flowers in his mother's garden, nor bear the flowery patterns and frills on his sisters' dresses. He tore everything in temper.

I rise from my bed that brought no rest. I have to face what is outside.

19

"Sunshine!" Jane applauded as she crossed the square. "I'm so glad that you opted for the café terrace. It's like a summer day in the middle of all the terrible weather we've been having."

"You can say that again." Karen looked inquiringly at her friend. "Still nobody?"

Jane dropped her bag on a chair and shook her head.

"Well, we just have to keep on going back there until Madame Lune shows up; she's bound to come home one of these days."

"Next time I'll slip a note under her door."

Monsieur Martin passed through for cigarettes and put a newspaper in front of Karen.

"*Merci*, Monsieur. I thought it hadn't come in this week. Let me pay for it."

"It came late yesterday evening. Take it with my compliments."

Karen gave him her broadest smile. "That's very nice of you. *Merci beacoup*."

He bowed slightly and went into the café.

Jane nudged her. "That was thoughtful."

"I don't know what's come over him."

"Maybe he sees us as future fellow merchants..."

"Competition?"

"Not exactly," Jane reasoned. "Our business won't do anyone on the street any harm, only add a pretty window. But maybe that makes us count somehow in his estimation."

"I was telling mum and dad about our plan. They're delighted for me. They told me that being in business runs in the family."

One could only admire Karen's industrious family, running a B&B and a farm. Her brothers also shared the entrepreneurial spirit and were planning on returning home permanently, both having traveled the world. Gerard was likely to take over the farm and Eamon had plans to start a restaurant. Jane thought it was a great idea; her mouth was still watering as she remembered Christmas dinner at the Moroney home. "Seems to me that you were born to be in business," she said to Karen.

"It was lovely growing up on a farm; it's still close to my heart." Karen didn't say anymore, thinking how ideal her childhood had been.

"Stop it."

"What?"

"Not sharing something because you think I can't take it. Be natural, totally natural. You have a warm, loving family, and though all of you have traveled, you are very close. Be proud of them. My childhood wasn't nearly so ideal, but I came out of it okay. Jane Moore is no a loser."

"Point taken. I would love to show you around Ireland; you must come again. My parents were sincere when they invited you back"

Jane took her hand, "And I would love to visit Ireland again, one day very soon."

"Consider the invitation open. They all loved you and they consider you as one of the family."

"Great!" Whizzzzzz... "That was close." Jane moved her foot quickly out of the way.

"ATTENTION!" somebody roared from the footpath.

"Very close," Karen said. "Madame Lu is on a tear again."

"I met her when I was coming home from Tony's last night."

"You went to Tony's?"

"I wasn't working late. He's got someone else that he's training, so one or two more shifts, and that's it."

"Good. What was Madame Lu up to last night?"

"Probably just helping some old lady in a room or flat somewhere around here. I suppose you were safely tucked in bed?"

"Yes... And on my own! But with the laptop on to work on our business plan."

"No change of mind?"

"It's over with Olivier; I'm counting the days until I can leave."

"You know, I sort of got asked out last night."

"Did you?" Karen was hoping it wasn't one of Tony's friends.

"Yes. He's come into the pub once or twice. His name is Cyrille and he's just moved from Lyons to Paris, taking a flat near Place Clichy. He's between jobs and on a break after working many years on the Stock Exchange. He's single and available."

"Family?"

"No children, but three sisters."

Ticking off the positives and negatives of his profile in her mind, Karen couldn't come up with an argument against it. A relationship might be good for Jane.

"He's not a user," Jane was eager to clarify. "I can tell. He's very comfortable financially, but he's one of those guys that needs to be doing something. He's not slick or phoney, just an average guy."

"Go for it."

"You should have seen Tony's face. He was jealous as hell."

"What's it to him? Tony never treated you well, so he can't have you on the rebound."

"No, I see Tony differently now. I had coffee with Cyrille mid-morning and it did me good. I produced six pairs of earrings afterward."

"So things are moving right along?"

Jane looked at Karen: "I'm not exaggerating when I say that this is the first time in my whole life that I've accepted an invitation from a guy who seems keen and where I didn't feel under pressure."

"Best news I've had all week. Somebody else is probably disappointed."

Jane looked toward the flower stands. "I gave Laurent the 'not available' signal, loud and clear."

Jane began sketching on a napkin. She told Karen about meeting Chantal Moreau on the street the night before, but the woman had not recognized her. Karen believed that Chantal was losing her memory and wanted to fill Jane in on her other suspicions about the woman.

"*Salut, les jollies filles!*" Laurent sat down at the table next to them.

Philippe came hurrying up, a damp cloth in one hand and a coffee in the other. He wiped the table clean and placed the coffee in front of Laurent.

Laurent seemed to have closed his eyes and drifted to sleep. But Karen saw that they were still half-open, and he was watching Monsieur Abu who was engaged in a conversation with Monsieur Martin. There was a hint of annoyance in his eyes. Karen looked farther down the street and the glint of silver from Madame Lu's skate-scooter reflected back from Madame Dry's door.

Jane rose from her seat and called Philippe for the bill. They said goodbye and left the correct change on the table.

Karen's phone flashed: she scrolled the screen rapidly then put it away.

"Olivier? "

"He's gotten into the habit of letting me know if he'll

be back to the apartment or not." Karen spotted Jane's napkin sticking out of her pocket. "Can I see what you drew?"

Jane handed it to her. "Only Monsieur Martin at the Kiosk."

"It's just hands."

"Yes, his are enormous. Haven't you ever noticed?"

"I've noticed his dirty nails. Not sure I like those hands."

"Me either. I think I'll work on them."

20

The wind scales my skin, paring it like tree bark, layer after layer. It would have been good to have stayed down in that tunnel forever, like an old fox that goes away to die, shrinks and shrivels and starves itself to death.

The monster does not leave the street directly this evening, but goes to the brasserie nearby. It is not often that he does that. He sits inside the window and watches. The light is on in the girls' shop; they call it The Glass Corner, it is a good name. They step outside to take a break from their work; they smile, joke and exchange banalities with others on the street. It makes me wonder what it would be like to talk like that, freely and easily.

He cuts his meat slowly and chews it slowly. He takes his time; he is deliberate with everything. But The Glass Corner never leaves his focus; his eyes are burning. The edge of the knife shines in his hand. He knows how to use knives. He is very hungry but his mind is not on the food. The meat is carved piece by piece.

My grandmother showed me how to kill a pig. She explained the proper way to slit the veins, cut the arteries, and drain the blood. She taught me how not to hear its squealing; you have to believe it can't feel—animals do not have human emotions. Killing the animal, butchering the meat and packing it for people was a job she often did. Grandmother was good at slaughtering.

It is not the same when we take up a gun and shoot. There is a definable distance separating us from the game. A hunter can be cold, without emotion. Grandmother could take a goose or a turkey, grasp its throbbing neck and snap it in two. It does not take much wit to do that. We have forests, seas and mountains, and we can think of nothing better but to kill our fellow creatures. The eyes of the turkey darted and the wails of the pig filled the countryside. I stood by her side but wished myself elsewhere. Do the creatures know, I wondered? They do, they know.

She never asked me to do it, but I had to watch. My eyes were open, but closed inside. It was a way of life. Grandmother did not tremble with excitement when the animal screeched; it was just a task, it was meat. The monster is not like that; not the same at all. He has other demons. The victims' screams feed his appetite and his entire being trembles at every cry.

If I have wit and foresight, I got it from my grandmother. Her rough exterior hid it well. If I have violence in me, I got it from elsewhere. I hope I have violence in me and that there is a savage beast in waiting. From my mother I brought the rest, and the rest has brought me nothing.

It takes intelligence to set up something for somebody else as my grandmother did. Long before she passed away, Grandmother started putting ideas in my head. She would say, "Go to Dublin when you can, go to the city; there's nothing for you here. There are a lot of things in Dublin; maybe they can help you with the reading and writing. If you stay here in the cottage, you'll grow old very quickly."

Grandmother would say things like that even when my mother was present. My mother never showed that she had understood; it is impossible to know if she had realized that my grandmother was preparing herself to die.

Grandmother's coffin was still in the church and nobody paid attention to what mother was doing or noticed that she was very quiet. I did. Who could have guessed what was in my mother's head, what she had decided? I had. But I am sure that Mother was not capable of planning it alone. I believe Grandmother also worked on her mind, just as she had done with me. She had told Mother when to do it and how to do it. That had been grandmother's way to cut me free.

I saw my mother and grandmother buried side by side, and watched the clods of earth fall on the coffins.

The 'Travellers' came to town. They were not the 'Traveller' families that people knew and welcomed; these were outsiders. People said that there was trouble in the pubs and on the roads. Each time they came to our area, they were spurned. Locals said that my father was there among those 'Travellers.' The word father is insulting to me; I have no father and refuse all thoughts of one.

By then I had fully understood the farce of my conception. There must have been a lot of pain and tears before my birth. They say that breeding breaks out. He was a 'Traveller' so what else was I to do except to take to the roads? Had my mother any idea of what was happening when he abused her? Did she have any choice? Was there pain in her impaired mind? Was there awareness that he had taken her virtue by force and then run off like the bastard that he was? If there was, my mother never spoke of it; she had wiped out of her memory what had really happened with the 'Traveller.'

There were comments about my dark eyes and sallow skin. There was talk that he was not a true 'Traveller.' Real 'Travellers' had dignity and purpose. He was a fighting drunkard. I was born in violence and lust, his violence and his lust. My grandmother prayed for forgiveness. What had she and my mother done to deserve this? I was a shame, born in shame, but I came. Whatever my grandmother felt before, it is certain that she felt differently afterward. She loved me very much.

After the funerals of Mother and Grandmother there were people, so many people; all of them deciding for me. No amount of looking at my face in the mirror of the cottage could change the fact that something was wrong with me. It was already too late—another life was growing inside me.

I ran from the people who thought they knew me. I ran with my grandmother's words drumming in my ears. People were gullible and believed that by sending me to work with the Sisters in a convent in Dublin that I would be taken care of for life. They put me on a train and I was met by a nun at Heuston Station. I stayed with The Sisters of Mercy for one month. While I worked a plan formed in my mind: it was simple; run away.

I got to Grafton Street and met Pierre. If destiny has a voice, then that was it. Only once in his whole life had Pierre left his precious France. It was a rugby match; Pierre was not interested in rugby and spent his time busking. We were drawn to each other, and from then on, entwined.

Nora Sheehy thieved and told fortunes. Stealing came easily. I had been training all my life, observing people and their behavior. A person could have gone anywhere with that skill. I had the finest set of senses, from my eyes and ears to my fingertips. But there was no ambition in me— money was needed and stealing was the way. It flowed like spring water—wallets of every size and texture, purses, pocketbooks and handbags, big and small. I learned to live according to need, and to need very little. Why own a big house, or any sort of house, when you *are* a house? Why do you eat two cakes when your stomach can manage on one?

Reading fortunes came later. I thought it lazy work— something to fall back on when tired, when Patrick was close to term. Now I know it is not slothful work; it is the hardest thing in the world. So much could be understood through observation. That skill also came naturally. Madame Lune does not read minds, she only interprets gestures and defines thoughts.

The most difficult thoughts to face are the distorted ones. I have a good ear and have come to understand many foreign languages; but I cannot do anything with bent, fragmented pieces that are connected to nothing comprehensible.

The monster haunts me. It is possible to understand violence driven by anger, frustration, and even hate. One can predict it and foresee the movements, as one would of an animal. But I can understand an animal better than him. Looking inside him is like looking at a poisonous substance, vile and heinous. It should not exist—he should not exist. What he is should have died in the womb, or never have entered the womb. Seeing what he is has taught me to accept that evil does exist. He comes from nothing natural. There is a reason for light and dark, good and bad. But there is no reason for pure evil. While standing in a crowded street it is possible to see many colors surrounding people, but his diabolic blackness corrodes and devours the others. When my eyes rested on it was the first time I knew terror and feared another.

His energy must not continue. But he will try to paste himself to something; he will seep into some unsuspecting creature or incubating human to give him a reincarnation. That is how he exists. Yet, it has come to me again and again that he was not conceived or borne without light. He had his chances, but did not take them. I have thought about that: why would one choose to remain in darkness where there is no peace?

Age makes me fear more, because there is little time and Jane Moore and Karen Moroney will not be strong enough. There are questions I should ask, but do not want to. You are afraid, Nora Sheehy.

He has now finished his meal and gone. How quickly he moves when he has purpose: one second here, the next far away. The girls leave The Glass Corner and lock the door. They look up at my building, wondering where I am. I am here, watching out for you.

Monsieur Abu and Madame Lu stand near the drycleaner's speaking together, friends for a few minutes. Soon, they will argue again. Madame Lu is looking pleased with herself; it has been a good day for her. Little woman, you are no more than a fly to be swatted away. The girls speak to her; her laughter is a cackle and I think of the goose in my grandmother's arms before her fingers tightened; I hear the pig squeal.

A lot of things happened on the street today—too many things—plotting and planning. Madame Lu rests her hand against the wall. But when she takes it away, her fingerprints remain on the brick and a glimmer of her dark future flashes before me. I can do nothing for Madame Lu, nothing. I do not know exactly how it will happen, but her time has come. Make the right decision, little trotter of a woman, for you will have a choice. We always have a choice.

21

Karen swung her bag over her shoulder and crossed Boulevard de Clichy. She closed her eyes against the sudden gust of wind that blew dust into her eyes. Where had that come from? It had been very calm until then. Was it her imagination or did the street seem quieter than usual? The wind had thrown things into sharper focus. Though still March, a new season was taking hold. A little nostalgia played with her heart. It was the middle of the week and she had to fight hard against the tendency to feel down. Spring was coming; everybody should be in a buoyant mood. It had been a particularly hard day at the office; but it helped knowing that her plans with Jane were progressing.

She hoped Jane's dinner had gone well. Her friend had been out on a real date with Cyrille. There had been exhibitions, movies, and lunches, but this had been the first proper dinner. Karen would have liked to have said, 'Call me when you get home,' however it was out of the question to fuss and make her anxious for nothing. Fortunately, Jane had been considerate enough to send a brief text saying that she was home and well. Karen was dying to know how the date had gone, but she was probably going to have to wait until later.

The whiff reached Karen as she braced herself to climb Rue Lepic hill—the street had its own particular odor, but it smelled stronger this evening. She sniffed: there was another odor in the air as well that commingled with the familiar ones. Had somebody been burning something?

Karen ran the rest of the way up the street. There really had been a fire, she kept thinking: The Glass Corner! But no...

Burned and gutted with blackened walls, the windows blown out and the smell of damp soot, Madame Dry's was no more. Some temporary boarding had been nailed across where the windows and door had been. A simple note with an email address and phone number had been posted for customers who might be looking for information about their clothing.

"Jane," Karen tried to block out traffic noise and pressed the phone to her ear, "have you seen? There was a fire, and the dry cleaner's shop is gone."

"What!" Jane shouted into the phone. "I was there this morning; I'm coming right away."

Karen stood looking at what had been Madame Dry's shop.

Jane arrived, breathless. "My God, I don't believe this. It must have happened sometime late in the afternoon. I was inside The Glass Corner until four."

"Come on, let's find out," Karen nodded toward the square.

They went directly to the flower stands: "Laurent, what happened?" Jane asked.

"Bad work..." Monsieur Martin joined them.

"Very bad work," Laurent said. "She didn't stand a chance. She walked inside and five minutes later, the place exploded. People say that the equipment was too old. The wiring was faulty and did not conform to standards, and there must have been a lot of chemical products in the back. The whole place blew up."

"Do you mean that Madame Dry was killed?" Jane looked from Monsieur Martin to Laurent.

"Jacqueline! No, it wasn't Jacqueline," Monsieur Martin said as he shook his head.

"No," Laurent confirmed, "we're talking about Madame Lu."

"Madame Lu is dead?" Karen had to hear it again to believe it.

"Yes." Laurent took a broom and swept the path around him. "We heard an explosion and it was all over. Jacques...Monsieur Martin was the first to call the *Pompiers*."

"I called them immediately."

"Jacqueline ran back from the café. Everybody was too late. The fire wreaked havoc in seconds."

Monsieur Martin bit on one of his nails. "She should not have been there; Jacqueline didn't ask her to stand in for her today."

Laurent leaned on the broom handle. "Jacqueline never asked, but Madame Lu went there anyway. She was talking with me only a few minutes before."

"It's too horrible to imagine..." Jane's voice broke.

"Unfortunate that she did not talk to Laurent for a few minutes more," Monsieur Martin murmured. Karen thought that he had a particularly devious air, but he had such shifty eyes because of a squint that it was hard to tell.

"A few minutes more and Madame Lu would still be alive," Laurent agreed. "I had no idea that she'd planned to go to Jacqueline's. That woman always had a mind of her own, and of course she had the keys to the place."

"She had the keys to many places," Monsieur Martin added.

They left the scene and sat at the cafe. Philippe was clumsier than usual. The fire was all the talk among the staff; many were thinking along the lines of arson for insurance.

The coffee was bitter in Karen's mouth.

"It's hard to take it in," Jane said. "We've been talking about threats and danger and all Madame Lune's warnings, and then this happens. It could have happened when a customer was there."

"Like one of us... Like you!"

"Or anybody."

"It's strange that Madame Dry had just shut it for a quarter of an hour and that it happened in that space of time," Karen aired what had been bothering her.

"Perfect timing," Jane acknowledged.

"Yes." Karen watched Monsieur Abu and Monsieur Martin deep in conversation. "Do you think it was an accident, Jane?"

"There is a lot of coincidence, but what do we know?"

"Oh, damn," Karen put down her cup.

"What is it?"

"Chantal is over there. I think she's totally lost her memory now. I'd better—"

Jane put a restraining hand on her arm, "Wait. She's going into the butcher shop There's nothing wrong with that. Watch when Chantal comes out to see if she's got her wits to go home."

"Good advice."

"I think I'll just slip down to get a newspaper." Jane got off her chair.

Karen sat up straight and scrutinized the street. It struck her that Laurent's flower stand, like the newspaper kiosk, afforded a fine view of Rue Lepic—a view every bit as good as the one from The Glass Corner. She stretched her shaking fingers and tried to steady herself. Madame Lu's death was probably a freak accident. Chantal came out of the butcher shop carrying a shopping bag; she'd aged a lot, become more haggard and bent. To Karen's relief, the old lady returned directly to her building. Though a little sorry for Chantal, that feeling was now mixed with dislike. She'd been hoping to sit Eric and Frederic down for a good long talk but hadn't gotten around even to telling Jane of her suspicions.

Karen turned her attention back to the fire. The drycleaner's was very old; places like that did go up in flames. The idea of a deliberate fire for insurance seemed plausible. Could Madame Dry have organized it? That would be one way to pay for renovations. It was probable that she hadn't expected Madame Lu to be there. Madame Lu had put her nose in where she shouldn't have and she had ended up as collateral damage.

What a stunner Jane was! Sitting back and watching her chat with Monsieur Martin and Monsieur Abu made her see it all the more. Her friend had long legs, a great figure, and an elegant ease when she moved.

"Why are you looking at me like that?" Jane returned to her chair.

"I was admiring your style. You could have been a top model, but you're far too good looking for that. You're turning every eye on the street."

"A model? No way! Anyway, those guys are too busy whispering and gossiping to notice me."

Karen sat up: "Look, I think that's her?"

"Chantal?"

"Madame Lune... That's her, I'm sure of it." Karen sprang from her chair and cut across the street. Too late. Madame Lune was gone, or had never been there.

Jane was paying for their coffees: "Was it her?"

"Don't know. Whoever I saw is gone, vanished into thin air."

Rather than waste the evening brooding, they felt the best thing was to dedicate a couple of hours to their shop. Karen returned to the apartment, shed her office clothes, threw on some overalls and went straight to The Glass Corner. It felt good to help Jane. They had decided to do as much of the renovation work as possible themselves, except those parts which needed real technical skills.

Karen took the cloth handed to her and helped to polish the tiles. "You didn't say anything about Cyrille."

Jane was very concentrated, bent over doing meticulous tiling work.

Karen tried to see her face, but Jane's expression was giving nothing away. "So, the night went okay?"

"It was a good night."

"Just good? Or more than that?"

Jane put down her grouting knife. "Well..."

"You didn't?"

"No, but we might as well..."

"What does that mean, exactly?"

Jane had gone to his place to chill out with champagne. They'd both been very turned on and she had wanted to sleep with him but had managed to put on the brakes before it went too far. She still needed more time to get to know him. Cyrille had not only respected her wishes but understood, and that had made her fall for him all the more.

"You must meet him; I'm going to arrange coffee together."

"So you keep telling me; I'd love to meet him."

"I would have introduced you sooner, but I have to learn to trust my own judgment and not depend on others."

"From what you've mentioned before, and now last night, he's won my approval."

"He can be a bit quiet, sometimes...goes into his own world. I think that's his untapped creative side. Cyrille is big into gardening; he's got pots everywhere—even a cat."

"He probably set it up to win you over...only joking."

"If he did, it's working. It's just...oh, nothing."

"What?"

"He doesn't reveal much about himself. But I guess that doesn't matter, because he seems more interested in asking questions about me."

"Is that difficult? I mean to talk about yourself?"

"It's too soon to tell all."

"Is your past a burden for you? I mean, it shouldn't, but..."

"I don't see it as a burden. In fact, it helps me to separate those who take me as I am from those who just want to use me."

"I think you're not going to wait long to finish what you didn't finish last night."

"I guess that makes you clairvoyant or something—just like Madame Lune!"

"Chantal, what are you doing standing there?" Karen looked at her watch: almost ten o'clock; Jane had wanted to finish the tiling and they had stuck it out longer than planned. She had been looking forward to a bath and hoping that Olivier would not turn up.

Chantal stood in the darkness of the courtyard. The odor from her was very bad; her coat was open and the dress underneath not properly buttoned. "They're coming for me."

"Who's coming for you? And what are you doing with all those bags?"

"I'm going away."

"Without your husband? Where are you going? Is Guillaume going with you?"

"Guillaume will be ready when they arrive."

"Chantal, I think you should go back to your apartment. I think you need help; you can't take care of Guillaume anymore. Let me call someone."

"No, they are coming."

"Are you talking about your relatives?" Karen had heard that Chantal's family had been informed of her condition and would be coming to Paris to manage the problem.

Chantal moved away from her. "Who are you? Another foreigner?"

"Yes. Is that a problem?"

"They are coming!" Chantal stumbled on the stairs.

Karen took her arm firmly. "Come with me; I'll take you upstairs to your apartment." There was something white poking out of Chantal's pocket. "Is that a letter?" Karen took the envelope: "Do you want me to post it?"

"No!" Chantal snapped it back from her hand and pressed it to her breast. But Karen had seen the names on the envelope: ERIC BOUZER/FREDERIC CHUL, written in bold print.

"Chantal, did you put those hate letters in the box of Eric and Frederic?"

The door banged. "Speaking of our neighbors, here come Eric and Frederic now," Karen said loudly. "Is that letter for them?" It was mean to prey on the woman's mental weakness, but she was beyond caring.

Chantal scrunched the envelope: "No."

"Why don't you give it to me?" Karen insisted. She saw from the guys' faces that they had put two and two together.

"Shall I call a doctor?" Eric suggested.

"I'll do it," said Frederic, taking out his phone.

Chantal scurried up the stairs, "I have to see to Guillaume."

Karen shook her head. "I'm sorry that you should have suffered because of her. I don't know how much is explained by her mental condition."

"Can't say it's news to us, but it doesn't matter anymore," Eric said. "Now we know, so we can put it behind us."

"Yes," Frederic said, "we had begun to suspect her, always hanging around the mail boxes and the yard. Her nasty letter writing days are over."

22

*I*t was stupid to have let down my guard. I allowed my mind to wander back to the cottage after more than fifty years away, and I was a stranger unto myself. Nora Sheehy had become an Irish woman on the street, and Karen Moroney recognized me.

I don't want to fight to stay ahead of the tide anymore. What is inside me is swelling. My skeleton is smaller and my weight less; all that can torment has built up and cannot be held inside much longer. The road ahead is short, the shortest one I will walk; but it is too long. If only I could leave it behind and get back to the by-way, I would take my stick and limp to the end.

Grandmother's face is always before me; her eyes are wise. Is it possible to love somebody our entire life, no matter how long gone, how young or old? Yes, just as I have loved Patrick, though he never became a boy and remained but a whispered promise. There is something else that ties all of us; within and beyond our horizons— farther than sun and rain, rocks and sea.

Karen Moroney looks at me with the eyes of someone I once knew. If anything were to happen to her, it would crush her family. But it is not for that reason that she must survive; it is for that whisper. Her friend Jane must live on too. I see so much of what I might have been in Jane.

They both must be protected; but that is impossible, for it would mean having heaven on earth.

Karen should not have recognized me. That was careless; I am still paddling in salty water. I must regain the rhythm that I have been living for most of my life. Nora Sheehy must become a watcher again, and above all, prepare.

Why did neither girl listen to me? Why did they not leave the street? They should have listened to me. Should I warn them once more? Would trying again make any difference?

Madame Lu is dead; she walked into the trap like a lamb to slaughter. He could not believe his luck. You went up in smoke, little woman, shoes and all. Now, the energy has changed, I have stood very close to the monster, and the waiting is over for him. Oh, for the love of God, or whoever put you here, Jane Moore, get off this street, save yourself. Get out of this city, and better still, leave this country. That is the only thing that will save you. But would it be enough? Would life throw you together again one day, in some forsaken place? Act, Nora Sheehy; act and try again to communicate with Jane Moore. Her life is at stake.

I have left three leaflets. Why is she ignoring them? Would it be too big a risk to go to her door?

I begin to put everything on paper, with pictures and diagrams. The only way open is to return to where the holy people are. I will find Brother Francois, who helped me before. It is a decision taken out of desperation.

The Brother agrees to meet with me. I ask him to try to put what is represented by my rough pictures into the normal written word. It is not working: he looks at me as if a lunatic sits before him. My tongue will not do my biding: 'Speak! Tell him everything you think he should know.'

'Sir, Father—Brother, there is a monstrous killer on my

street. I know where his victims lay and who his next victim will be. You have helped me before, you must help me again—if not for my sake, do it for the sake of the dead and for the young woman's life he is about to destroy.'

But my message is clear only in my head; it is not what he hears. Suspicion is written on his face. He has been tolerant with me before, but this time he really thinks I am out of my mind. My convoluted explanation is beyond him and my words unintelligible—what I am trying to say and how it sounds on my tongue are worlds apart; my expression is that of a blundering dunce. I cannot make my thoughts comprehensible to him. He is shaking his head and telling me, "You ask too much, too much, too much."

I scream inside.

I make a great effort to control the feelings and put my package in his hands.

The Brother looks at it in confusion but keeps it.

Inside are the pages Pierre had written. They explain about Nora Sheehy and her son Patrick. I have added my drawings and pictures which try to explain more, but it may not be enough. Brother Francois nods, pretending he understands; that is the best way to get rid of me.

I leave him; too much time has been lost over such things. I must not look back; I must not look ahead, except through the eyes of the monster. See the future as he sees it. Forget all else. Try to see into his world, control only that space and time. See only what I must see. I must take myself out of the picture, out of the foreground and background. I do not exist, I am not important, for I will not be there afterwards.

The colors of the municipal police building flash before my eyes. If Brother Francois, who is acquainted with me and with my difficulty, did not believe me, how could I expect the men in uniform to trust me? If I told them, they would not listen. If I walked in there and said I know a killer, they would not hear my words. They would ask questions about me and inquire from people on the street as to my sanity. The killer would be alerted and it would ruin it for all.

As I walk the street, he does not see me. Karen Moroney does not see me, and Jane Moore does not see me. Nobody on the street sees me. I feel reassured that my shell is intact and secure.

I go to Gare de Lyon, Gare de l'Est and Gare du Nord. I go to the Latin Quarter and the Marais. I need money, lots of money. Some of it is cash for my landlord; he has asked me for more and claims that there were many outstanding bills from the old flat. He came to the door and waved the papers before my eyes: water and electricity charges. I must take his word for it for I know Pierre was capable of deceiving me. I will not leave any duty undone; I will pay all and offer the landlord even more for the room. He will not say no to such a windfall. It is a risk: he could take my cash and throw me out. I will take the risk. In my case, it is a small risk. Money, money and more money is my only aim, for I will owe nothing to anybody, so I steal and steal and steal. I am no longer Nora Sheehy of the cottage, I tell myself, I am a thief; I was born a thief, lived my life as a thief and will finish my days as one.

In my hand is a leather bag full of paper; it is a decoy while I fill the lining of my coat and the inside pockets. It is Pierre's coat, his magic coat. The notes slide into creases and all the covert places; the discarded leather purses and wallets finish up in bins. I have become gluttonous—it is not greed that is driving me, but necessity and duty. The day is fruitful, though it is not enough; my work must continue into the evening. I am not a night worker by nature—darkness produces a different breed of criminal.

There are eyes everywhere. The eyes that bother me are those of another thief. I have been sighted by someone of my own nature—a solo thief. I have been a vulture and broken my own rules.

I have to outsmart him. The other thief is not aware that I have seen him watching me. He knows only that my coat is rich, and he wants it. I leave Notre Dame Cathedral and walk along the left bank to St. Germain des Prés, marching on and on. He is not far behind me. If he wants what I have, he will have to take the whole coat by bringing me down and fighting me. He cannot do that in the middle of a busy street.

Damn! We have both been spotted. One mistake after another—what is it with me? A policeman is on our tail. Will I, who has been so careful all my life, be caught on my very last outing? I am sweating heavily under the coat; my entire body is in water. If I am taken, both girls are lost. I must control myself, change nothing, and keep walking straight. The other thief has gone, disappeared. All the suspicion is on me. I am losing my touch. The policeman is behind me. Keep walking, keep walking; do not change pace.

Boulevard St. Michel spreads out before me. Still he tracks me. I stop at a café, go to the counter and point at an Espresso cup. He sits outside on a wall and waits. I take my time, drink the liquid slowly and allow the minutes to pass. An idea comes to me: I leave change on the counter and go out a different door. I cross the street, hail the first taxi, and I am gone.

I look behind me through the back window. He was not expecting that. Common thieves do not take taxis, but this one does.

"Clichy," I tell the driver.

He asks me to repeat and manages to grasp the word: "Place Clichy?"

I nod.

Place Clichy is close enough; nobody from my street must notice me getting out of a taxi. We arrive in silence. The taxi driver is surprised because I pay him twenty euros for a six euro trip. He was overcharging me by asking for fifteen, and yet is rewarded with more. I do not want change, especially his change. After paying, I look him straight in the eye: this driver must remember that I am no fool. I am limited, yes, but a fool I am not.

The round-about way to Rue Lepic is safer. There are crowds leaving the cinema and queues to enter; it is a cold night and the bars and restaurants glow from the inside out. The supermarkets have still not closed their doors and shoppers bustle by with bulging plastic bags and caddies. Jane Moore is walking against me—a beautiful black, American woman. A bolt goes through me like a heart attack. The light is all around her. The glare blinds me— the shock of truth, her fate.

She is a jewelry maker, an artist. She has made wonderful pieces and designs. The tear in her glass rose will bring more sorrow than a crown of thorns. She cannot hear them, but I do; there are voices all around shouting at her, 'Go, go, run! Jane Moore, run away from here, it is your only chance.' Did you fight your way out of the gutters? Did you battle to see the lights of Paris only for it to end mercilessly and brutally? Was it just for those thousands of designs that you came this far? Are they your gift to the world? Indeed, they will move and reach millions. One day, your creations will be applauded, but will you not see that day? Or is it just for Karen Moroney, a girl you didn't know until you settled on this street? Did destiny bring you here simply that she may live longer? Have you been her shield? If you were not here, would she have been next on his list? Is that what I must understand? Have you, in your short life, already fulfilled your purpose? You have surely experienced more in a few years than many could in a lifetime. You are beautiful in the same way that my baby was beautiful; a vibrant spirit. You could have been narrow and mean, but you are none of those. You chose generosity and compassion. Why should you have to suffer more? Is your brightness meant to counteract his darkness? I walk close to you for a while, watch you climb the street and enter your building. You are safe in your room now. You will live one more night. If I can change fate, you will live many more.

I fool myself into believing that the wind can be directed, but my wishes cannot change what will befall Jane Moore. Can things of this world only be explained by this world? Is there a higher power, somebody who can help?

Go on then, Almighty God, the all-powerful, let thunder and lightning raze this street! I know you won't because you are not there. I have seen ghosts and spirits rising from memories, but none of that proves that there is One Greater, that all our human lives go on to serve a higher cause. Where is the thunder? Where are the flashes?

I shake my fist. I will not be mocked by joyful images of heaven, I curse heaven. There is no heaven, no place of eternal peace and happiness.

Why should Jane Moore run the circle of pain twice? Why should she be born in pain and to a childhood of pain? Is it because she could take the hurt of others, absolve and heal it? Why should she be forced to live it again? Has she not suffered enough? Is it because sorrow should greet sorrow?

I am looking for someone to blame. It is easier that way; it lifts guilt and responsibility from my shoulders. And that is why Jane Moore will run the circle of pain again. Put a rat on a treadmill and it will run and run and run; jumping off the wheel means falling through the abyss, so it will keep running until it eventually falls off and dies of exhaustion.

It would have been easier if the world were flat. It would have been easier because we could have jumped off. There are so many ways: we can take sleeping pills and never wake up; we can put a gun to our head; hang ourselves, or jump off a cliff to our death. My mother did it: she jumped from the cliffs and I did not stop her. I see her face, but I no longer see it through the eyes of a girl, but through my eyes, an old woman's eyes. Her face is serene. Is that my mother? I did not understand her burden and knew only my own. Now I understand what she bore. But if there is no God, and no afterlife, then why does Mother come to me now? If there is no justice, then why can I not turn my back and walk away? Why should it matter to me? If there is no more to people's lives than rats running on a wheel, why care?

I take a narrow lane and something flies at me. I fall to the ground. Somebody is upon me and trying to tear my bag away from my shoulder. Again I have allowed my mind to wander, my senses to dim, and have been caught by my own arrogance. It is a boy thief, and he wants my bag. The lane is damp and dark; it would be easier not to fight him, but to let him have the bag. It contains only balled-up papers. But then I remember that the postcards I stole from Karen Moroney are there too, along with some sketches I have made of graves and bodies. They are useless to the boy, but I will battle for them. He does not give up and the bag rips open; the papers spill out. He jumps on the contents, rooting through them, but very soon it dawns on him that he has been duped; he has met his own kind. I struggle to my feet, out of breath, and ignoring the boy, go to collect the scattered contents. I turn, expecting him to have gone, but he is still standing there, his eyes glistening, about to cry. He is just a child. My vision clears and I recall having seen the same boy thieving in the Metro tunnels. I flap my arms as I might with annoying pigeons, "Get away! Get out of here!" He doesn't run, so I ignore him and leave the lane for the brighter street. He is still following and I swing around at him, holding out the valueless bag, but his eyes are on me. A dog abandoned and mistreated by humans will continue to put its faith in people because it still needs them to survive. There is some pity left in my heart. I stop and wait for him to approach. When close enough, I take his dirty hand and open it. He does not try to run. I close his palm, and when he reopens it, his eyes widen in amazement: a fifty-euro note is pressed there. I used to play the trick with Padraig and a Sycamore leaf. That is magic, the only trick I know. I push him away and wait until I'm sure that he is gone.

I watch the sun rise over Paris. Jane Moore is at her window; she has risen to work and is in high spirits. Her smiling face makes the morning bow. Many things pass through her mind; they are all good thoughts. Jane cried for the little woman on her skate scooter and prayed for her, thinking that she took the blow for all. Jane believes that the danger I spoke of might have been mistakenly meant for Madame Lu. Mediums can get their visions mixed up.

When working in her room, her thoughts are joyful and good. This is a new day, she thinks, and I am happy to live it! She is young and light, full of hope and dreams, and a little in love. My dear Jane, love is not for you.

To know that we are happy is a gift. She received that gift this morning as the rising sun greeted her in her city of dreams. I must go to her and explain everything. There is no other way.

I do not understand myself any longer; my world is strange to me. I cannot keep moving like this from pain and sorrow to incomprehension. I fooled myself into believing that my shell had been rebuilt, that Nora Sheehy was the same watcher as before. She is not the same, nothing is the same. She has changed. I have changed. I see differently and feel differently. I suffer, but it is a different kind of suffering because I will never again be humiliated for my ignorance. I must now do my duty, do what I came into this world to do. Face the darkness and let hell burn to a cinder.

23

Karen checked the mailbox, then reached hurriedly for a handkerchief to stifle a bout of sneezing. Jane had warned her not to put her nose inside The Glass Corner until she was over her cold. It was too damp there and it would be stupid to risk her health. Of course it would be nicer to be in the shop working with her friend, but Jane was right.

She clapped her mailbox shut and turned around abruptly into Eric's path. "Sorry, you startled me. Am I in your way?"

"No, if you'll excuse me."

The frostiness of his answer made Karen glance at him a second time and was surprised to see a stiff face.

"Is something wrong?"

"No, nothing," he pretended to be busy with his door keys.

"Eric?"

"I was just wondering how your party went last weekend?"

A party? Olivier must have been up to something. Karen realized that Eric was miffed that a party had taken place and no invitation extended to the neighbors. "I wasn't here last weekend, and Olivier told me nothing about a party. I took Friday off work and went with Jane to take part in an exhibition north of Paris, at Ville Pinte. It's all about start-ups and the arts and crafts business. We stayed in a hotel nearby and I came home very late Sunday night."

"Are you sure?" Eric rubbed a finger across his trimmed brows.

"Of course I'm sure, I know where I was. Ask Jane if you don't believe me."

"Then Olivier—"

"I guess he was on his own."

"Oh, we thought we heard...never mind."

"You mean Olivier wasn't alone?"

"I don't know. Well, have to be going." Eric coughed.

"Hey, Eric, don't be like that. It's not impossible that somebody did visit Olivier. He probably invited people, you know, friends."

"Maybe that was it," Eric said. "I just thought I saw you, or somebody like you, on the stairs."

"Me? You must be hallucinating. When?"

"Friday night, and again on Saturday."

"He has a sister who looks a bit like me, especially from the back; it could have been her."

"Yes, of course."

"Look, Eric; it's finished between Olivier and me, so he does his thing and I do mine. As soon as The Glass Corner is ready, I'll move in there until I find a better place."

Eric looked around, at a loss for words, and was saved by the sound of footsteps.

Chantal scurried by, deliberately pushing her way between them and knocking against Eric before darting up the stairs as quickly as her unsteady legs would take her.

"We have to do something about our troublesome neighbor."

"Yes, I know," Eric said. "She's all over the place. Frederic had to bring her off the street yesterday."

"Excuse me."

They looked up to see a shabbily dressed Chantal standing on the balcony above them. "Could you please keep the noise down?"

Chantal gave Eric an icy look and climbed up the next flight of stairs. They heard her keys jangling, and then she shouted an insult and slammed the door.

Karen thought that for everybody's sake, somebody authorized would have to intervene, quickly. It was apparently easier said than done. Inquiries had already been made into Chantal's situation and that of her husband, Guillaume. But those left in their direct families were too old to take charge of the problem. Fortunately, there were nephews and nieces; however some lived abroad and it was taking time to sort everything out.

Chantal's screaming reached their ears.

"My God!" Eric paled.

"It's okay, Eric. I'll go and see what's happening."

It was now quiet in Chantal's apartment. Karen knocked.

The door opened just a crack, but enough for the strong stink to reach her nose. The smell was nauseating.

"Chantal!" she called. "Chantal, are you okay? Has the cleaning lady been here to help you recently? Or the nurse? When did the nurse come? Is Guillaume there?"

"They killed her," Chantal hissed.

"Killed whom?"

"Madame Lu; they killed her. Now she can't come to help me."

"It was an accident, a fire. Madame Lu wasn't really your cleaning lady, was she?"

Chantal didn't reply.

"Chantal, you're ill; let me help."

Chantal peered at her. "She told me things, she knew a lot."

"What things?"

"Madame Lu knew what they were doing and saw

inside his place. That's why she died."

"What are you talking about? Tell me exactly." Karen tried to make sense of her gibberish.

"Oh, go away." Chantal prodded her shoulder then looked hard at her, "Who are you?"

"You need help, Chantal," Karen raised her voice.

"They killed her!" Chantal shouted. "Those unnatural people..." The door banged.

Karen walked the floor, up and down, up and down. She took aspirin for her fever and tried to be sensible. She knew she should go directly to bed. A key turned in the door.

"Olivier?" She went to the hallway, but there was nobody there. Her nerves were unsettled after the exchange with Chantal. Eric had spoken about a party, seeing a woman on the stairs. It was Olivier's business what he did in his apartment, but it was not comfortable knowing that the moment she wasn't there, he was inviting people—women.

Karen jumped up: 'What time is it?' She reached for her phone automatically and squinted at the screen. It was a quarter to one. Go back to sleep, she told herself. At least her cold seemed to be better. She touched her forehead: only a slight fever.

Her thoughts turned to Jane. Was Jane out tonight? Hadn't there been talk about owing Tony a few more shifts. Maybe Jane was with the mysterious Cyrille. There had been a promise to introduce him, but Karen was still waiting for her friend to keep that promise.

Karen fluffed the pillow. Feeling thirsty, she got up, poured a glass of water but hardly touched it and then went back to the sofa-bed. The sheets smelled fresh; it was the dry cleaner's fragrance. But sleep did not come—a cloud of sadness fell over her. An image of Madame Lu at her perky and energetic best, speeding off on her skate scooter, came to her. Karen turned her head into the pillow to stop the tears. It was natural to cry over her death; whether a good or bad person, nobody deserved to die that way. What had Chantal been talking about? Nonsense, probably...

Jane's name kept coming into Karen's head, prompting her to send a text: *Can't sleep. Are you awake?*

There was neither reply nor acknowledgement of reception. Maybe Jane had come home late and had switched all systems off before sleeping. But Jane never did that. Was it possible that she was still in the pub and with all the noise did not hear it ring. But why switch off her phone? In the end, Karen couldn't resist and rang Jane directly, but she was transferred to the answering machine. Maybe the battery was dead.

Karen stumbled onto the floor and put on a pair of jeans and a pullover. It was silly and crazy to go out at this time of night, but it was either that or wonder sleeplessly until dawn.

Karen zipped her coat. It wasn't really cold; autumn had been smooth so far. Goose bumps broke out across her skin. *What am I doing standing in the street like a fool? Jane can take care of herself.*

Rue Lepic was practically devoid of people. That was an impression, she was sure that a closer look would show the street in another light. Karen didn't care for that closer look.

As she walked she let everything pale into the background: car engines on the distant boulevards and the hum of Paris. Only the sound of her footsteps was audible. Who was that woman in a heavy coat? Madame Lune? No. The figure disappeared again.

The burned-out, ground floor of Madame Dry's was more ominous in the dark. In her ears, the skate of Madame Lu's scooter resounded, together with her chirpy 'Good morning;' her high-pitched arguments with Monsieur Abu echoed in her ears; ghosts of her own making.

At Jane's building Karen rang her phone again: no luck. Who is that now, she questioned silently? The dark-coated figure loomed in front of her again.

Karen stayed in the shadows then back-tracked as far as The Glass Corner. Though all fingers and thumbs, she eventually selected the right key and unlocked the door. It felt safer inside. The heavy-coated figure went to one of the benches in the square and sat staring at Jane's building. Karen went back out on the street to try to see more clearly.

Her phone lit up: "Jane?"

"Karen!"

"Jane, is that you?"

"Who else? Why were you looking for me?"

"I was...you know."

There was a long pause. "Darn it, Karen."

"Where are you?"

"At the bottom of Rue Lepic."

"Were you at Fintan's?"

"Maybe. Where the hell are you?" Jane asked.

"At The Glass Corner."

"What are you doing out on the streets at this hour?"

"I didn't know where you were," Karen whispered, "and there's someone sitting on a bench watching your room—that's not normal." She glanced toward the bench to confirm her facts. Damn it, the person had gone. He must have heard her speaking on the phone.

Her friend came through the mist.

"Jane, I'm sorry; I had to know that you were okay."

Jane was resigned. "Now you see that I'm okay. Where's this person on a bench?"

"I wasn't making it up."

"I believe you, but—"

"Sorry, I'm worse than Mother Goose with her chicks."

"People do sit on benches, you know. Look, Karen, we have to live our lives as usual and forget about premonitions; you are going to have to put Madame Lune and what she said behind you. That medium told us things completely off the wall and we were worse for believing her."

"I know, I know, but about Madame Lu—"

"It was tragic, but it was an accident."

"You're probably right."

"I know I am—there's no probably about it. So let's get some sleep, you especially. You'll be getting up in less than four hours. We'll talk about this again tomorrow, okay?"

"Okay," Karen said in a small voice.

Jane opened her arms. "Come on, a hug."

Karen hugged her like a naughty child: "Tomorrow then."

Jane laughed. "Yes, tomorrow. Now get your beauty sleep!"

They separated, but Karen couldn't help turning around just once in time to see Jane enter her building. Jane turned at the same time and waved.

Karen lay on top of her bed until it got too cold and then snuggled under the blankets. But now she was thirsty once more and needed water: up again to refill a glass. It was an excuse to return to the window; it drew her like a magnet. Her eyes traveled the street; it was a bit voyeuristic, but fascinating. A man was propositioning a prostitute. He looked like Olivier—he was Olivier! She threw open the window, stuck her head out and strained her eyes. No. No, it wasn't. But for just a moment she could have sworn...

24

There is now only one solution left to me: I must approach Jane Moore directly. It would be dangerous to try to leave another piece of paper in her bag or pocket. There is no time to lose. It is decided; I will go to her room.

It is not easy for me, it has never been easy. I practice what to tell her and how. But I have to be convincing, very convincing. I go over the words in my head, speak them out loud again and again until ready.

Jane opens the door warily to my knock, so much more cautious with me than on other occasions. I have frightened both of them and she is no longer fascinated by the powers of the medium. I have my fortune teller paper in my hand; I remove my veil and stand under her gaze feeling naked without a disguise. She says nothing, but makes a sign for me enter. I am struck by her room. The most captivating sketches, pictures, and designs surround me; they are everywhere. She is working on one; it is a mass of gray and in the middle are lovely flowers condemned to live with the dead. I have never thought of it that way before: flowers among graves bring life to the consecrated ground. She was preparing to go out; her coat is on, her sketching bag at arm's length.

"Tell me the truth," she says. Her eyes are shaded with unease.

I show her some drawings that I have prepared. The first card is of a man and a dead woman; so is the second, and the third. I have done ten, all showing the same image.

"Madame Lune," she pleads, "please leave me and my friend alone. Stop harassing me with your warnings. Why do you do it?"

I put my hand to my heart.

She waits.

I open my arms helplessly.

Anger and disbelief battle inside her.

I try to control my stammer and to make my sentences coherent, but her face is closing. What is it? Is it something on my tongue? Is it something within me? Will no one believe me?

Her eyes never leave mine. "Then give me his name, tell me who he is..."

I knew it would come to this. Trust is hard to give. Will Jane believe me?

"Do I know him? If he is on this street, then I know him. Tell me who he is!" She hands me a sketching pad and pencil, her look unwavering.

So I draw a picture and include the details that expose the identity of the killer.

Jane shakes her head and draws closer trying to discern truth or lies in my face, "Why haven't you gone to the police?"

I cover my mouth and see that Jane Moore is beginning to understand.

"If you know of some of his victims, and know where they are, show me what you know, all of what you know, and I will go to the Police. Maybe they will listen to me."

She is sincere and her suggestion reasonable. But I wonder how Jane would react if taken from tomb to tomb and shown where the bodies lie. Do we have enough time? No, we have no time.

"Show me, please," she demands. "It is the best way."

I do not think it is the best way but in the end I nod. I do it because I cannot find another answer, and she will not act without proof.

"When?" she asks.

I raise four fingers and point east.

"Four in the morning? I'll be ready," she gives her word.

I have been understood. I weep inside; Jane Moore understands me.

I awake determined to tell her more, to show her more, to show her everything. She is not like the others...

I go to the window and look outside and my heart ceases to beat. My lungs stop breathing. No, no, no! the words scream in my head. It is not possible, it cannot be possible. Is it too late? Has it all been in vain? I will not speak to Jane Moore ever again, for she is no longer alive. The knowledge is so profound in me that I cannot be wrong. I search the bottom of my soul. Is it my fault? I should never have given her his name, never have weakened and given in to her request. Clever though Jane was, and a fighter born and bred, he knew. He knew that she had uncovered his secret. What did she do after I left her yesterday? She must have gone back outside to paint, to finish her work, and on the way crossed his path.

My actions are robotic and my eyes watch numbly as the morning street traders and shopkeepers busy themselves with their duties...and I see him. I know it is too late—it happened just before nightfall. Was he so daring? Yes, Jane stayed too long, got lost in her work; she did not even feel the cold. What a fateful evening. There was probably not another sole in the cemetery. The monster did not enter through the gate, for he knows another way inside. Oh, I cry, I cannot believe that I would fail her!

I can hardly move; my arms and legs are stiff and wooden, my heart is empty. I take the long way to Montmartre cemetery keeping far away from where he might see me. It is too early and the gates are still locked but there is a place where one can enter. I go directly to the mausoleum where I saw him preparing the death bed for Jane. I sense nothing; it did not happen here. Her body is not in this tomb—it was a ruse, he never intended to use this place. But there are thousands and thousands of mausoleums, stones and slabs. I cannot check every single one of them.

I close my eyes and concentrate: pain engulfs me from the memory of Jane Moore. What happened? Did he creep up on her, catch her at dusk, imprison her in one of his underground vaults and come back later to torment his victim? Did he try to lure her first without realizing that Jane knew? He wasn't expecting that and would have had to kill her instantly. The monster's rage is pounding my brain. It rises and fumes around him. He is beyond reason because gratification slipped from his grasp.

Images and voices come hurtling at me. My head is exploding—I am bent to the ground under the weight of it. Jane would not normally have gone to the cemetery, but instead waited for Karen at their Glass Corner. Yesterday, she did not wait because Karen did not go to The Glass Corner after work. Their plans had changed.

So the monster struck in the dying light. Jane knew too much and he had to act quickly. And now, he will have to kill her friend, for they were like sisters, sharing experiences and knowledge and love.

Now the visions are coming more strongly and I fall on my knees. He is as fast as lightning. A terrifying violence erupts out of me directed against him. It is not good; I must control my emotions, must suppress them. They have not served me well and have helped nobody. I am powerless.

Yet I get up and follow the spiral of pain. For a moment, there is a faint hope: perhaps Jane is still alive, locked up somewhere. No, no, it is too late. I must face reality: I will find her, but I will find her dead. But I must find her, for without her remains, and without knowing where she lays, I cannot help her friend. Only then can I unleash my anger on him. There will be nothing left to do but cut him down and rid the world of his putrid soul.

Of course he will be too fast for me, so I will have to be prepared to deliver the first blow. I will have one chance to stand before him and finish him forever.

I close my eyes tightly and hear the sea—waves crash off the rocks and the shrieking cries of the gulls pierce my eardrums. Jane Moore's voice calls out, but I still do not know where her body rests. Her spirit is beyond, but I do not know about the beyond: nobody knows. I let the sea rinse my thoughts and cleanse my intentions.

I stagger ahead, around marble and stone. I walk through centuries of souls. What are people but ash and bone? The essence of her memory must be here. But it is not easy to find, because he has tried to possess it.

You are dead, Jane Moore, but you are here, I see a stone, a tomb, but not like the other ones; this one has something, some*one* I am looking for. I once saw a diviner looking for the source of life, a spring. He walked the land until the current bent the hazel rod he held. He said, 'Sink your well here.' Divining death is not the same, for when I look around the cemetery my eyes fail to find the place. It is impossible to match the picture in my mind to the right place. If Jane's body is here, and I know it is, he will come back. I will have to be patient but he will lead me there and show me exactly where the body is. It is better that way. So leave this place. I know enough. I must now rebuild my defences and strengthen my resolve, and I will return when ready...

I refuse to hear the voice of Jane calling to me from Montmartre cemetery. I refuse it for now, but it will whisper to me in my sleep and in all the waking hours I have left in my miserable life.

I will go to where he lives. It will take but five minutes. I have avoided doing so until now, but I must try. The building is constructed like mine. He has two rooms: a downstairs storage space looking out onto the yard, and a seventh floor room where he watches the street and rarely sleeps.

It is a building that also serves the practices of several doctors and dentists. There is no code on the door during the day. I walk in, but there is a second door. The concierge has opened it; he is cleaning the glass panes. I walk past, as if with a purpose. His storage room is at the opposite end of the court yard. The windows are smeared and difficult to see through. I cannot be caught snooping around here. If there is something to find, it will be upstairs in his room.

The stairs lead me there and it is easy to find the corridor. I learned how to open doors and can open some easily. This one is not an ordinary lock, there are several bolts and they cannot be opened by simple skills. It would take too long. I go back downstairs and hesitate to return to his storage room in the courtyard. I take the risk and return to the grubby windows. I catch a smell that I once thought fresh and innocent. Now it sickens me. I leave the building, defeated.

There is no choice left to me except a vigil. I will watch him on this street and watch the cemetery. Karen Moroney will eventually go to that cemetery. She will be led there when drawn to retrace the steps of her friend. It may take her a day, or several days, or even weeks, but it will come to her. He knows that.

The monster waltzes from foot to foot. He is not used to being out of control, to having to change his plans. If

Jane Moore suspected him, then others might also. There can be no rest for him until he is sure of what clues or signs Jane might have left behind. It is too risky to go to her room; there is too much to lose; and Jane will have left many things with Karen Moroney. He fears what evidence might be there. Ire blazes from his eyes. The monster has killed her and has not had his exultation. He will not be able to live in the memory of his act, for she resisted to the end. There can be no rejoicing in remembering how she submitted to him, for Jane did not submit. No voice crying for mercy rings in his ears. It was a combat to the end and Jane almost overcame him. His work was hasty and sloppy. There are signs everywhere, but rain is coming and soon everything will be washed away.

I walk by the police building many times, but no longer wonder. It is not the solution. The responsibility is mine. I must watch Karen Moroney and try to understand her future. She will go to Ireland, for a few days, perhaps more. But Karen will return and will not give up until Jane has been found.

The monster walks freely. On the outside, he is so normal and calm; no different than anybody else on this street, in this city. How is that possible? I wish that he did not look so normal. But the skin, body and bones do not tell us as much of the mind as we would expect. We think that an ugly mind should be housed in an ugly body. But no; it is random, it is always random.

Jane Moore had intuition and instincts; life taught her to have them. She knew that all was not right with him, that something was not as it should be. But her knowledge was not enough; too little, too vague and too late. It did not save her, and I did not save her.

The sea crashes once more on the rocks of my thoughts. Karen Moroney will soon be back in our shared homeland, and in great sorrow. She will run to her family for comfort. They will have the right words and will help her. I see her already standing by the cottage walls. One day, Karen will return to Ireland for good. Her place is at her parents' side. She has more to learn from them and they still have much to teach her.

It is impossible to accept the death of a friend, for few people have real friends like Jane Moore. She was unique, and Karen will not fill that vacuum. It is worse to accept death in circumstances of violence and murder. There are no words to describe how hard and cruel it is. But it is not the first time, and it surely will not be the last.

Second after second, I sense his brutality. A fury rises in me again. I want to walk across that street, to take a knife and stick it in him a thousand times. Would it not be the best solution? They would lock me up, but what difference would it make? My life is over. Jane Moore was only at the start, and Karen Moroney must go on living.

I hear the crows on the branches of a silver birch; its trunk is rising up through cement and concrete. I look up at the sky and pray to the creatures of nature, asking for calm. I must keep a vigil; if I am not calm, I cannot help.

And what is the lesson of old age if not patience? If I succeed, then he will pay for what he has done, and Karen Moroney will live and preserve the memory of Jane Moore. And through Karen, Jane will live on. Thousands of sketches and designs, great and small, will be her legacy. Karen Moroney will take on her work. Jane's life will not have been in vain; her courage and beauty will live on.

25

"Olivier, I am not stupid, tell me the truth. You've not been faithful to me, have you? All your talk about marrying and wanting children was insincere."

Olivier stared at her but did not reply.

Karen had not expected anything to come from this confrontation, but it was important to her to cut through the pretense. Eric's words had sparked a string of dormant suspicions in her mind and she'd begun to doubt everything.

"How many were there while we were together, two, three, more? Prostitutes?" She hadn't intended to say that, but the way his eyes looked away said it all. "Damn it, Olivier, did you even think about the risks you exposed me to?"

"I took no risks..."

"You used protection: is that what you're trying to say?"

"Believe me, Karen, I never take risks?"

"What is wrong with you? How could you talk marriage and know all along that it was a sham?"

"But it wasn't!" Olivier gripped her arms: "You are

normal, solid; you would never have...I thought you would save me."

"Save you from what?"

Olivier dropped his hands and walked to the window. "From myself! I have needs, cravings... I didn't want you involved in all that. I have impulses, urges—you can't understand. There are clubs, places...many places."

Finally, Karen was beginning to understand. She listened as he recounted his addiction, the double life he led, the constant fear of not being able to control his wild urges and of being found out placed him in situations where he could have it all: group sex, libertine nights... He pretended to travel to cover his tracks...and to protect her.

"You put me at risk."

"No, no, I never—"

"There is always a risk." Karen could only shake her head, "You need help, Olivier. I'll move out in the morning; I should have done it weeks ago."

"I swear to you, I stopped all of that when we were together; I felt you had freed me. Then it all went wrong; you rejected me."

Karen couldn't look at him: "Just leave me alone now."

At five o'clock, Karen got up from the sofa and collected some essentials, deciding to come back during the day when Olivier had gone to work. Jane's foresight about the utility of the back room in The Glass Corner was about to be confirmed.

Damn, he was up: she would have preferred not to see his face. Olivier stood at the bedroom door. "Let me know what I owe you for the month's rent or whatever."

"Karen, can we..." He moved to stand in her way.

Stepping around him, she said, "I'll be back for the rest of my clothes. The next time you return, I'll have my stuff cleared out."

She grabbed her suitcase, straightened her back and strode past him.

Karen felt self-conscious walking up the street with her suitcase. Fortunately, none of the regulars were out and about yet. She flung the case into the back room of The Glass Corner; it was cold there. Jane had stored a sleeping bag and some blankets, useful for a cat nap, or if one just got chilly. The place smelled mustier than usual. Hadn't Jane been in there yesterday? She bundled herself in the bag and blanket and feeling sorry for herself, nodded off.

When Karen awoke, it was after seven. It was still too early to phone her friend and probably easier to wait for her to get to The Glass Corner. There were several messages from Olivier to which Karen replied with one text: 'Stop texting me.' She wasn't even mad at him anymore, only frustrated with herself for not acting sooner.

By eight o'clock, Karen was dying to text Jane. By nine, the text was ready after several re-writes. It was short and simple: 'Just to let you know that it's not a burglar when you get to The Glass Corner, it's me; living here now, left Olivier.' Again, there was no acknowledgement of receipt. She hated that but would be patient this time.

Patience was not her strong point; the next hour was spent pacing, watching the street come alive, pacing more and making tea. She decided she would go back to the flat, shower, and clear out her things. She did not want the kitchen equipment—she didn't want anything except her music and books. She felt horrible, down. She needed to talk to someone. She needed Jane.

Not being one to hoard, there wasn't much to collect. Most of the equipment was Olivier's. One suitcase and a large rucksack did the job.

Why wasn't Jane checking her phone? Perhaps a late night that she was sleeping off, or maybe she was taking a long weekend with the mysterious Cyrille. But wouldn't Jane have told her if that were the case?

"Chantal?" Just what she needed; her neighbor stood in

a state of undress on the landing. Karen put down the suitcase and removed the rucksack; this was going to take time. Chantal Moreau looked like she was sleep-walking.

"You aren't dressed; go back inside your flat."

Chantal shook her head. "I can't."

Karen left her bags and linked arms with Chantal. "I'll take you."

"No, no," Chantal resisted. She reeked of sweat and other unpleasant odors.

Chantal freed her arm abruptly and ran down the corridor of her flat and into a room. Karen followed. "Oh, my God!" She put a hand to her mouth to stop herself from screaming and forced her eyes to look at the corpse propped upon the chair. "Your husband, Chantal, that's your husband, Guillaume. How long has he been dead? Why didn't you get help...or call someone?"

Chantal shouted, "They killed him!"

"No, Chantal, he was ill. Why didn't the nurse come?" Karen suddenly felt like she was going to be sick and moved to leave. It was too late. She raced to the kitchen and managed to lurch over a filthy sink to vomit.

Chantal started blubbering a mixture of fact and nonsense: "I sent a letter to tell the social security to stop the nurse from coming because she was a thief. Madame Lu was supposed to come, but they killed her, and now they have killed Guillaume."

"Stop talking about killing, Chantal," Karen shouted over the noise of the running tap. Her stomach was turning again.

Her command was effective. Chantal ran into her arms, crying hysterically.

"We'll sort it out," Karen said as she put a handkerchief to her mouth.

Chantal prattled on: "I was there, among the dead. He was there."

"Who was there? A foreigner?" Karen asked. Humoring her was best, otherwise Chantal might become aggressive and try to run off.

"No, not a foreigner. He was there and she was there."

"Who are you talking about? Where did this happen?"

"Madame Lu told me to be careful, that there was blood on his clothes, and strange things in his bins..."

What was Chantal on about? "What do you mean by blood?"

"He killed her!"

"CHANTAL!" Karen yelled.

Chantal Moreau shut up immediately and fixed her with saucer eyes, then burst out crying. "I don't know. Where am I?"

Karen extracted herself from Chantal's spidery arms and went outside, preferring to wait on the landing and make some emergency calls. Chantal's husband must have been dead at least two days. For some reason, or confusion of communication, the nurse had stopped visiting. Chantal probably did tell her to stop coming. It was awful—Jesus, she was going to puke her guts again...

Karen left Olivier's apartment building; the authorities had taken over—gendarmes, firemen, ambulance and a host of curious neighbors had gathered—enough was enough. She'd phoned Eric and Frederic at their salon to explain the situation and likewise had contacted Oliver to give him the same details. Now she just wanted to get out, leave the place and never return.

The best cure was to throw herself into work at The Glass Corner. By early afternoon, Karen was fed up and kept having nausea attacks and tried phoning Jane again, but to no avail. Her phone was still switched off. She wanted to talk with her friend and decided to go to her room. Taking the spare set of keys to the *chambre de bonne*, she reasoned that Jane would understand and forgive her.

Karen saluted Monsieur Martin and Laurent, nodded to Monsieur Abu and other familiar faces. The news had spread about the Moreaus and she wasn't up to giving the gory details. It wasn't easy to look casual and cool, instead of someone who had not only walked out on her cheating boyfriend, but had discovered a dead body.

Mounting the stairs to Jane's room, Karen suppressed a queasy sensation. She put her ear to the door—not a sound. Was Jane still sleeping? This wasn't normal; Jane never slept that late. She turned the key slowly and opened the door. All of Jane's things were there, her bed was neatly made, but there was no Jane. Karen didn't want to rummage—it wouldn't be right to look through Jane's private things. Her friend had probably spent the night with Cyrille. A quick look around told her that Jane's art bag and rain coat were gone. There were lots of sketches and pictures stacked—she'd clearly been working hard. Karen left not feeling reassured.

Evening brought little comfort and no answers. She had received a number of calls, all of them about Chantal, but not one from Jane. Each of her own calls to Jane was intercepted by her answering machine. It seemed strange: the same voice; the same Jane, but far away.

Weakness and worry had made her give in and phone Olivier. He had been kind and understanding, wanting to do whatever he could to please her. *Of course he'd help her; if Jane didn't get back to her, call him again and he'd do something. But it was wise to wait; going to the police was premature.* He'd told her that he missed her, that his apartment was open to her; suggested that she was in shock over finding Chantal's husband, and that it would be a good idea to speak to a professional to help her come to terms with that. She had barely registered what Olivier said; it was Jane who was on her mind.

Night had fallen and Karen couldn't stop looking at her phone hoping that a text had come in, or that maybe there had been a missed call.

She'd gone to Fintan's, but once again, no Jane. Tony hadn't seen her in a few days. Tony pretended to have no knowledge of Cyrille and said that he'd never heard of such a person.

Karen left the pub puzzled and racking her brains concerning Cyrille, having little to go on in terms of either a physical description or personal details. There wasn't even a family name. The only information was what Jane had given her, that he'd been working in Lyons and had suffered some kind of burn-out in his work, had come to Paris to make a new start in life and was well off, or so it seemed. He apparently lived somewhere in Place Clichy.

Karen tossed and turned. Closing her eyes meant opening her mind to anguish. Everything was mixed up in her nightmares; Chantal was bawling, Olivier was clinging to her, Eric and Frederic were smiling with Dracula teeth, and Jane was screaming for help. No, those were Chantal's screams; Jane was weeping...

The only relief that Saturday brought was a break from work and the possibility of devoting more time to her friend's disappearance. She went back to Jane's room: it was exactly as it had been the last time she visited. That's it, Karen thought, I'm going directly to the police.

The station was quiet. One young policeman received her in a small room. Karen explained the situation. The policeman was calm and listened patiently then asked her questions and typed the details painstakingly with two fingers. He told her that they'd received no information of any accident or incident associated with the name Jane Moore, or anyone corresponding to her description. If he or his colleagues did, they would contact her. However, the police were not in a position to launch a search given that Jane was a responsible adult and it was too soon to declare her a missing person. There was no evidence of violence or anything suspicious.

"Don't worry, Madame, I have your number, and if there is any news of this woman, I will contact you."

"Thank you, sir."

There was nothing more to be done so she went to Eric and Frederic's salon. They were working their way through a full appointment book. The salon was noisy and happy—too happy for her mood.

"I'm really sorry about everything," Frederic said.

"And so am I," Eric joined him. "Your time in our building has been terribly unlucky; between our trouble, your break up and...you know."

"Don't concern yourselves about it; I'm more worried about Jane right now." It was true, Karen would remember that day as the day that Jane had disappeared and not the day she'd left Olivier or found Guillaume Moreau's corpse.

"I cannot imagine where Jane is," Eric said as he blow-dried the hair of a client, "but we've been run into the ground here, arriving early and getting home late, so we haven't had time to see or meet anyone."

Frederic shook out a towel. "My advice is to go to the police."

"Been there," Karen said. "For the moment, they can do nothing."

"Isn't that just typical?" Eric said as he switched off the dryer. "*Now* is the time to do something; before it's...the police are always slow."

"I'll tell you what," Frederic said, "we'll ask around and post photos of Jane here."

"Would you?" Karen was grateful. "That's kind of you."

Eric dismissed, "That's the least we can do. We like you, and we like Jane too. You were there for us when nasty Chantal was harassing us with notes and her obnoxious insults and threats."

"Chantal frightened me," Karen said. "Imagine, a little old lady with such nastiness. Is her flat completely empty now?"

"Yes," Frederic grimaced. "I hope somebody nice will come to stay there."

"I never want to see that woman again," Eric raised his fist. "Chantal Moreau brought us so much pain." He scratched his head, "But hey—I seem to remember that her nephew mentioned that she'd been talking a lot about a woman."

"Really?" Karen felt her heart flutter.

"Chantal Moreau is not totally out of her mind; she still has very lucid moments, or so we understand."

"Come to think of it," Frederic seemed to be remembering more, "Chantal Moreau said something to me also; something about a dark woman, but I didn't understand her at the time."

Karen jumped up. "When was that? What did she say?"

"It was nonsense; something like the black foreigner is flirting with every man on the street. Chantal talked a lot; she called everyone with dark skin, a foreigner. It's difficult to say when. I think it was around two weeks ago. Chantal seemed to have forgotten her hate for us and wandered up to me when I was in the hallway. She'd just come in and was muttering about the American girl. She spoke as well about Monsieur Abu and how some people had set Madame Dry's shop on fire."

"Did she say more? Was there anything more precise?"

"No. She suddenly seemed to remember her hatred for gays and ran away from me. You'd better not lose time on Chantal Moreau's ravings," Frederic said. "Do you know what I think you should do? I think you should hire a detective to find Jane."

"Yes, you should do that," Eric encouraged. "We have names of agencies, and we'll give you someone that we were thinking of contacting; however, in the end, we didn't have to."

The idea of hiring a detective seemed drastic. Karen was not ready for that yet. For now she would just keep asking around. Monsieur Abu was at the newspaper kiosk talking to Monsieur Martin, and Laurent was making bouquets. It was pointless inquiring once more if they'd seen or heard anything, but it made her feel useful. Monsieur Abu strode away before she'd reached them. He'd been cagey since Madame Lu's death.

Monsieur Martin shook his head and suggested that it might be something to do with immigration. Then he shrugged and turned to serve another client.

Why blame him? How could one pretend to be sincerely concerned about someone he didn't know well? Madame Lu had been on the street for much longer, been motoring about on her skate-scooter for several years. Now it was as if the Vietnamese woman had never existed. Jane had been less than two years on the street and people had other things on their mind.

Karen walked on to Laurent's flower stand without much hope.

"Any news?" he asked.

"Nothing, but I'm thinking of hiring a detective."

Laurent finished tying the stems of a bouquet he was making. "A detective?"

"Yes."

"You are very anxious then?"

"Jane has been missing several days; I'm worried sick."

"You are a good friend; of course you must do everything you can. I have been going over the past days and weeks in my mind, over and over, trying to remember something. But all I have is that memory of the last time I saw her sitting at Café Lepic."

At least he cares, she thought.

Laurent began tying a second bouquet.

"I like that plant," Karen said pointing to a small fragile group of stems with tiny orange flowers peaking out of a few buds."

"This one?" Laurent picked it up.

"Yes, I'll buy it." Karen didn't know why she saw it as a little candle, a flame of hope.

Laurent put it delicately in a colorful paper bag. "No,

no, please don't pay me for it. I am not sure it's going to live. Let me offer it to you; I want you to have it."

Karen put the plant on the counter inside The Glass Corner. Laurent had told her that it liked light; she felt that somehow it linked her to Jane. Nighttime fed her with negative thoughts which inevitably led to nightmares. Music didn't help, it just triggered tears. A talk radio station was better as background sound. But after awhile, it got on her nerves. She got into the sleeping bag and sat with eyes fixed on her phone; jumping on it at the first ring. It was only Olivier checking on her.

The days went by, still no Jane, no Jane. Karen struggled to concentrate at the office. If Jane had run off, then fine; but Karen needed to know that her friend was alive and well. Then at least she could get on with her life. A medium or a clairvoyant might be more useful than the detective, but there wasn't a trace of Madame Lune either. Karen resorted to faith. She prayed and prayed that the horrible feeling in the pit of her stomach wasn't an omen.

Karen returned to Jane's room and this time had no misgivings about poking around. The first cupboard she opened was full. That Jane had produced a lot of paintings and drawings wasn't a surprise, but there were stacks and stacks of them, and sacks full of crystal jewelry too. She identified what seemed to be the more recent sketches. There were several drawings of what at first looked like a garden. Was it a garden? There were floral arrangements against a gray background.

A few loose pages fell from between some sketches. There was Paris looking magical, a photo of Paris on glossy paper lit up in all its beauty. Those were the photographs that had become Jane's dream. That's what had brought her to Paris. Karen put them on the little table then rolled up the most recent sketches and took them with her. There was something strange about those flowers that Jane had been painting. She loved wild flowers, but those painted in the picture were withered and scattered over the ground. In another scene there were flowers covered in yellowed plastic, some potted plants, and farther off, shrubs or flowers that looked very cultivated.

Karen returned with the sketches to The Glass Corner and stared and stared until her eyes watered. Tell me, Jane, if there is something I need to know in what you were sketching! Tell me!

26

She is trying to find me, but that cannot happen. I told her friend Jane Moore, and now I sit here in a tunnel in failure. Telling Jane was the wrong decision. Even if Karen Moroney knows and has time to go to the police, he will get her. Karen will never find me again.

I have been thinking of my baby, Patrick, and what sort of man he would have made. It was God's will. (Yes, I am having conversations with a God in whom I do not believe. I have taken to arguing with Him. It does me good.) And so, on the same day that I think of my baby in a way I have never done before, I see Dimitri. This God is very clever. That drunk is no less and no greater than my precious Patrick. For a drunken body does not make for a drunken soul. I put a roll of money in his hand—for Pierre's sake. He will drink it, all of it. Before I turned to go, he looked at the money and then at me. He recognizes me, of course, the woman that his father spent years with, but he has never had any wish to know me. Dimitri neither likes nor dislikes me; he is indifferent. His fist closed over the money. Spend it well, for there will be no more.

I have made few decisions, but each has been

important. I made love to someone I could not love, and who did not love me. I left my home and my country. I brought into the world a baby, a boy called Patrick, who never grew. I stayed with Pierre and that was my fault. I made my living as a thief. That I stole was wrong. It goes against social order; if you go against a better way of living, it hurts people. In the beginning, I stole out of need and ignorance. However, although still in need, but no longer ignorant, I continued to steal. It cannot all be laid at the door of my handicaps.

I have seen what can be seen and what should not. I made a decision to help Jane Moore and I failed, failed horribly. What arrogance it was to imagine that it could be done, how useless my efforts. I believe that there is only one decision left to me and it has been taken. It is clear in my mind. If there are any other decisions to take, they will be instantaneous acts. Jane Moore is gone and her murderer must not go on.

I will sit in the cemetery, day-in and day-out. Soon he will return to Jane, to where she lies: today, tomorrow or next week, no matter, I will watch. But I will do it as a hunter—watch and wait. And when the time is right, I will kill him.

It is five o'clock in the morning. I smuggle myself into Montmartre cemetery and walk without real direction to a grave of cold stone. Jane Moore does not talk to me; her voice does not come today. Her cries are lost. He has tried to possess them and to dominate her soul. But the monster is not all-powerful and cannot control everything. His shadow does not succeed in shrouding her totally. He understood a lot about her, but he had not realized that she was a street survivor and tough as nails. She was never going to be his victim. The final pleasure of his victory was stolen from him. He lacks the taste of it. Victory was hers, and now he is ravenous and even more treacherous than before.

It is Karen Moroney she will reach out to. Jane will accompany her night and day; reach for her through her dreams and sorrows. Karen: you are too soft, your upbringing was gentle. He will avenge his defeat on you; it is the only way known to him. You must return to the sea for good and do so very soon. Your adventure is over; Paris has nothing more to teach you. Return and spend cherished moments with your family. Your own people have things to teach you; listen to them. Take Jane's work with you. Let the waves and sand speak to you; watch the sea, and from that light will grow inspiration. What you and Jane have started together will inspire many.

I know why he has not yet returned to the body of Jane, but the monster will have to return. He will have to cleanse his dirty work. It may not be visible to the average eye, but it is to someone who is paying special attention. It is difficult for him to return because it reminds him of his defeat, that he did not possess her as he would have liked. What he ravaged afterward was a mockery, and coming here will force him to face that. But he will return, for if nothing else, he is thorough.

If I have one half hour of sleep, then the tunnel will serve me better. It is a place where noise is filtered out. It will make me stronger, sharper.

Then it comes to me that the very tunnel that holds me can lead me underground to the cemetery. Every night I take the torch and crawl; each time trying a different way until finally I find what I am looking for: a cavern, a crypt, old and untouched for years. My preparations are simple: take the tunnel many times until it has been learned by heart and without the torch light; keep practicing until the way is in my head and the journey can be made with my eyes closed. The next step is to find the entrance from the outside. That is easy, for as sure as Nora Sheehy knows the lines and tributaries underground, she is able to weave the same patterns above ground.

I go back to the cemetery, find the place and work for hours until I am able to lift the slab and get to the crypt from above ground. I cover it again carefully and hide my traces. That is my way, my entrance and my exit.

It must be close to half past midnight. Measuring time is easy, there are many signs. The night is bright, the stars and moon are my companions. A cat slinks by a tomb.

The monster has arrived, though he is still invisible. He did not enter over railing or wall but rose from underground: he too has another way into the cemetery. I pin my eyes to him; nothing else moves in my body except my eyes. He is visible now and moves forward in edgy motion. My heart tightens; he is going to Jane. How easy it is to find her when he shows me where she rests! Is that where you are, Jane? I might have uncovered that place in a few seconds, a few minutes or never. He goes inside.

I count the hours he is there; one, two; then he reappears. A fire of hate rages around him. He storms off to conduct ordinary business, like an ordinary man, and will not be back for some time.

I go to where he has been and walk in his footsteps, trying to close my senses and not feel too much. It looks old and undisturbed, as if nobody has been here. I stand by the mausoleum that protects the tomb and stretch my hands toward it. A bolt shoots up my arms, paralyzing me on the spot. It hurts so much that I am prostrate in front of the tomb. This is the well of suffering and sorrow.

Time passes. Finally, I lift my body from the stone—that cold, cold marble. It is beginning to rain: large heavy drops of acid water turning to ice hit the ground. I stagger away.

But a few seconds later I return; I must see it all. So I push the rusted gate of the mausoleum and lift the stone that opens the way to the crypt—I have to be sure that it is Jane who is in there—and find a mangled body. I, too, am gutted and flee. It is too much, too much, I have seen enough, I cannot face more. I put the stone back as it was. The rain is coming tonight, there will be a storm, and it will wipe away my scent.

I take flight to my tunnel and find a pen and paper to draw a map of Jane's grave, then a second and a third. I can draw perfect maps. My job is slow because I am slow. Where are the old envelopes and the stolen postcards where the name and address is written? I copy the addresses as one would a picture: every line and curve of what is printed. There will be three envelopes for three different addresses. Maybe I will send one to Brother Francois. I have to pick the right time to send them because once posted the clock will start ticking. If time is on my side, I will have done my deadly act before anybody receives them.

My pen and paper task is not over. The way to every one of his victims must be transferred from my mind and from my rough sketches onto maps. It is long and laborious work. Over and over, I take pains to make each map. Those too will be sent, but they will go a day later. If they were to be posted together with the map of Jane Moore's tomb, confusion would ensue.

Karen Moroney knows something; the knowledge is all around her. She has information, but not the name of the killer. She cannot know his name for she is chatting to him with the ease of someone who does not suspect. But he has sensed her changed disposition. I spit in temper—once again I am too late to do it my way. I can read her mind as he must surely read it: Karen knows, or thinks she knows, where Jane is.

She makes her way up the street and out of sight. But I know where Karen is going. The loyal friend is looking for signs that will lead her to Jane. He watches her go and would like to follow, but he cannot—not now, not yet. I must not take my eyes off him.

Karen is away for a long time. It is three hours later that I see her back on the street. She has found a clue; it is evident from her gestures. She has not found Jane, not yet, but suspects the truth and will return to the mausoleum later, in the dead of night, to open the crypt. Karen Moroney, you are oblivious to his stare; you have only one thing on your mind. It is not your safety you care about, but the truth. You want to know and you will sacrifice your life to know, because you don't care anymore for yourself. You are in pain. You loved Jane.

Night comes and I go outside to stand on the hill at Sacre Coeur, the hill of martyrs. Paris is at my feet. It is a handsome city and it has been my home for many years. Far off on the horizon are the woodlands of Boulogne—nature in the city and the city in nature. In late mornings and languid afternoons it comes alive with families walking, resting and playing. Prams and buggies, wheels of every sort have passed me by. The city is alight below—millions of lights! Do we really need so much light? Are we so afraid of the dark?

I stand in the cemetery and continue to wait. Is this what the end of my life has to offer? I stand among slabs and stones, monuments to sticks and bones.

Something has happened to my mind. My flashes are becoming more and more permanent—spectres of another world floating side by side. I am flesh and bone, blood and skin. I must beware of what I see and hear, of what my human senses are doing, and the games they play on my mind. When I stand in front of a mirror and no longer see myself, am I going insane? The fit has taken me several times. In the somber light of a single lamp, and the hint of street lights streaming through the window, I saw that Nora Sheehy was not there. I walked past my cracked mirror and saw nothing. If I cannot see myself, can others see me? I tried to touch the glass and felt nothing. I could not find myself. Was it an illusion? I moved invisible fingers and legs and saw flesh peeling away. Was Nora Sheehy so ripped from the world that finally her roots and props had gone?

It was easier to be calm when convinced that there was no afterlife. Yet, I had a sight that saw more and a gift to see something beyond. How could I have had that and tell myself that there was nothing else? I never cared for God, never warmed to the God of my upbringing. The God of churches and religion is weak and selfish.

That place beyond had always mocked me; the idea that there is something pure and simple, a love greater than love. Should it exist, it is not the place of memories, the parallel existence of the dead, or what I experienced in Versailles. That world exists, but it settles around us, only to sneer at our arrogance, our science and logic. Yet when I open myself to it, there is something inside, something that lives without the body. I have seen that flame—I see it now, guiding me. I hang on to it, for that is who I am. That flame will be with me always.

I stood at my grandmother's bedside as she died. She took my hand and her eyes held no fear. There was something different in her that I was not able to explain. It was not death, nor the presence of a priest. She had no need of a priest, nor did she need her beads. I saw that flame in her. It was just a second, but for that second she was no longer the grandmother of my childhood, that loud, rough woman who had managed life with simple ideas, sweat and toil, was no more. I saw a lady filled with assurance and wisdom. In that instant, she had found herself again. That is the afterlife I would like to find.

27

The dream was very intense and she woke up to the plaintive calls of her name: "Karen! Karen!" She scrambled off the ground mattress, swayed on her feet and tried to find her balance. The bedside lamp flickered weakly. The place spoke to her of Jane. The motifs on the tiles showed her tasteful attention to detail. The Glass Corner was to have been their partnership and it was nearly impossible to accept that her friend was gone.

Karen pulled on jeans and a knit top and threw a coat over her shoulders. The cold never left her even though it was a mild autumn. Maybe she should have taken Olivier up on his offer to stay in his apartment longer. But that wouldn't have made her feel better; something in her kept hoping that Jane would try to contact her or come back to The Glass Corner.

There it was again, a slight creaking noise. Was it in her head? It must be. Every night the same noise disturbed her, and each night she went through to the shop to find nothing out of the ordinary.

Karen stood in the pristine space surrounded by glass, mirrors, a display counter, neat cupboards, and the lovely tiling. There were a few pieces of jewelry in drawers. She opened one, took out a pendant and began to stroke the stone, trying to feel something, to extract its energy. Clairvoyance had never been for her, despite having done it for fun. What she wouldn't do now to see into the stone pendant and to know where Jane was. Her eyes adjusted to the street light coming though the shop window until it was easier to see shadows and objects in relief.

She laid her head against the wall and closed her eyes for a moment. Weariness overcame her and it became impossible to even take the few steps back to the mattress. She was too tired to move from the stool and too tired to sleep.

She rubbed her eyes, took the stone pendant again and let it swing. It reflected different colors and led her to a place of peace. A pink light glowed and soothed her. A vision came to her. Jane had pulled up the second stool and was sitting beside her.

"Jane, you've come back!"

The moment the words were out, Karen knew that it couldn't be true. Her bleary eyes had created a vapor image of Jane. Yet it was there, a face, Jane's face.

"What happened, Jane?"

Suddenly the smoky image grew agitated.

"Are you hurt? Did someone harm you?"

The image darkened and the eyes grew thunderous with emotion.

"Jane?"

The colors changed, and it was no longer possible to see the face very well. But words came into her mind. It was Jane's voice: "I'm not hurting now, but look outside." The image appeared to be pointing across the street.

"What are you pointing at? Is it that building, Madame Lune's place? Can Madame Lune help me? Is the medium responsible? What is it? Tell me, Jane!" The words choked in Karen's throat.

All the while, Jane was shaking her head.

"What are you trying to show me?"

In the vision, Jane's sad eyes never left Karen's, and her arms were out stretched. Karen blinked several times. Had she dreamed the entire encounter? Was it fatigue, or the many nights without closing an eye, that had led her to conjure the vision of Jane?

She got off the stool and went to the door, unlocked it and stood on the street. A deep longing for the countryside grew inside her. On Rue Lepic, there were city sounds and noises everywhere. Her entire being craved the sea in the background and the wind through the branches of the trees. These gray dusty streets were suffocating her.

I have to go to her room to see if Jane is there, she thought. I must know if she has returned.

Karen walked up the hill. It was self-torture, but it had become her nightly procession.

Stop this craziness, she told herself, but she didn't listen to her inner voice. Instead she keyed in the code, crept inside and up the stairs. Stop doing this, she warned herself, it's destroying you.

Jane's room was empty and sad. But someone was coming up the stairs. Karen closed the door to within an inch and waited. It could be a tenant coming back to his room. But whoever it was appeared to be going stealthily, like her. The footsteps followed along the same corridor. Karen closed Jane's door fully, turned the key and bolted the inside as noiselessly as possible. It wasn't Jane; that wasn't the sound of her steps, nor her scent. Who was it? Was all this in her head? No, there was an odor of sweat. It was a man. She was certain of it.

Karen pressed her ear to the wooden panel. Someone was definitely out there. She moved back from the door and sat on the edge of Jane's bed and switched off her torch. The handle turned and there was a scraping noise.

The scraping stopped, the handle was turned again, and then...nothing. Karen drew a breath. The intruder knew someone was inside. To her relief, the footsteps moved away and back down the stairs.

It was better to remain in the room. The window afforded a view of the street, but the visibility was poor. The intruder stuck close to the walls and was impossible to see. To have followed him would have been stupid, but going back to The Glass Corner right away wasn't a good idea either. It would be better to wait until the light of the morning. After another half hour of turning round the little room, Karen gave into exhaustion and lay on Jane's bed. She closed her eyes; tears came and finally with them, sleep.

Karen had taken her parents' advice and gone home to Ireland. It had done her good to be away from Rue Lepic as well as a relief to let her parents spoil her and keep her busy. Her brothers constantly came and went—taken with dozens of projects, their energy lifted her. The entire family encouraged her to chip in and run errands. But it was the time with her father that had helped her most. Though always close to her mother, Karen had felt a new connection with her father since her grandfather's death. Like her grandfather, he didn't talk a lot, but when he did, it was to say something that might be treasured as a piece of wisdom. He'd sensed in her the pain of loss, and of not knowing. She'd stood with her father near the cottage where in the old days laborers who had worked on the farm had lived. Nobody had been there for years. There were many family stories that originated there.

Her father advised her, "Go back to Paris, Karen." Go back and try to understand what has become of your friend. Then come home. This is your place, this is where you belong."

"I will, Dad. I will." She hadn't really thought about her promise but had felt that he was right. There was something to do in that quiet part of the countryside. Karen didn't know yet what it was, but she knew it would be here.

Returning to Paris was hard: crowds, stress, aggressive commuters. There was a notice on the dry cleaner's door stating that it would re-open in a month. Renovations were almost finished and Madame Dry would resume her business. Life went on.

Karen walked up the hill to Sacre Coeur. Preferring smaller more intimate churches, humble and simple places, the basilica was a place that had never really attracted her. But Jane had liked it. Her friend would sit and sketch the stained glass windows for hours.

Karen returned to the shop, sat down and took up a few of Jane's last sketches. She poured over them hoping for clues, ideas, anything that would provide her with a notion of what had happened to Jane.

Seeing a new detail, Karen took one of the sketches to the window to look at it more closely. Of course, of course! Why didn't I see that before? It wasn't obvious when she'd first looked at the picture, but for some reason it was as clear as daylight now. The gray in the sketch was in fact tombstone gray, and the flowers were cemetery flowers. Jane had been painting in Montmartre cemetery. There was even the faint outline of a name. It was difficult to make out but she squinted to see the lettering: 'Latevy the third'; at least that's what it looked like. It must be a family name, she thought. Internet maps of the cemetery didn't help much; the name was not notated.

Karen hurried outside and up the street. People must think her nuts—even worse than Chantal Moreau had been—as she ran in and out, up and down without an apparent sense of direction. But there was a direction. She walked toward the outskirts of the quarter, in the direction of Montmartre cemetery. She was certain that Jane had come here; that's what was in those sketches.

Karen had only visited the cemetery once before. There were similarities with the other cemeteries in Paris, but it was not as large as Montparnasse or Pére Lachaise. Many mausoleums went back to the 1830s. Some were in a state of abandon and the government was waiting to possess them to give them to someone else. There were cats everywhere, and the cawing of crows was the dominant sound in the cemetery grounds.

The autumn sun was setting. She went toward the waning rays. Light sparkled on sandstone, and pebble dash glittered back. Information on the Internet explained that this former quarry had served as a mass grave for some of the thousands killed during the 1798 Revolution. It was eerie to see a tomb with a recumbent sculpture and effigy; the name inscribed was Godeffroy Cavaignac, 1801—1845. Nearby was a modern photograph of a middle-aged man; the photo looked out at her from behind the glass plaque. The contrast between the historic and recent past was disturbing.

In the distance, one tomb seemed to stand out. Karen thought it must be at least fifteen feet high with its elaborate spires. Another tomb bore the name Emile Zola. It was strange because although the tomb still stood, it was empty: documents had said that his body had been removed to the Panthéon in 1904, just a few years after he'd been laid in Montmartre. His place was here, Karen thought. The tomb with the large upright statue under an arch and golden rays around its head was unmistakable. The legendry singer, Dalida, almost reached to the sky and seemed surrounded by a mountain of flowers. Karen read the dates out loud: 1933-1987. The singer had died by suicide. Her final words had been, "Life has been unbearable for me. Forgive me." Karen turned away.

Those words, as well as the landscape she now beheld, were both familiar and ironic. Wasn't that the background in the last dozen pictures that Jane had sketched? Those trees, the light and wall: this was the spot where Jane had sat painting her scenes. But she couldn't be sure.

Karen's heart beat faster: Keep going, don't stop now, you have to find it. Go to the end of your intuition; good or bad, no matter if it brings sorrow and pain, you have to know!

Weaving over and around the graves, it seemed that while a few stood out, so many looked alike. They were practically sitting on top of each other. Jane could have painted from anywhere and it would have looked the same. How could one find the exact spot where Jane had sat? The options were to try to find it by going from tomb to tomb, mausoleum to mausoleum, like an archaeologist following a grid and systematically uncovering every square, or to simply follow her intuition. She decided to veer away from the central, neatly cared-for cobbled paths and go with her original instinct of walking toward where the last flush of the setting sun lingered. The rays were fading now and darkness was falling. A drizzle was coming down. Panic rose within her.

One particular tomb in the 3rd division, chemin Halévy, more secluded than the others, caught her attention. That was where Jane had sat—she knew it! There was no proof other than the angle Jane had captured in her drawings. Jane's writing had been difficult to read, stylized, but it was now obvious that it was *Halévy*, not *Latevy*, and the number referred to the section, *troisieme* division, chemin Halévy. She would have to come back with the sketches to confirm it. Jane had done several still life pictures here; including part of the tree, pots with decaying plants, some knocked over, and had added in some flowers, probably for contrast. She'd started painting in those she'd seen growing nearby, almost wild, but not quite. The scene was imprinted upon Karen's mind, but she would double-check against the sketches to be sure.

She tried to peep through the window of a mausoleum but it was too dusty and impossible to see clearly. The door bolt was rusted, but not locked: an old broken chain hung from it.

"Were you here, Jane?" Karen spoke aloud.

A tiny fleck glinted at her. Was that an earring? A band

tightened around Karen's heart as she fell to the ground and picked it up with shaking fingers. It was just a shaving, shiny and luminous; but it was a piece of Jane's earring. That piece of earring was the sign she'd been looking for and would prefer not to have found. She went back on her knees. Dark stains shone on the stone, which looked as if it could be easily lifted with the right tool. She put her finger on one of the stains and broke out in a cold sweat.

Karen wiped sweat from her brow and shivered. It was late: better to go home and think carefully about what she had found. She could come back before dawn, this time more prepared, with torch and tools.

But now it was dark. Where was the way out? She looked for the railing to follow it. Her eyes were beginning to adapt to the twilight, helping her to reach a boundary wall. But in the dark the wall seemed endless. Losing patience, Karen tried to climb over the stone and railing before abandoning the effort as ridiculous; it was too high.

Follow the wall, follow the wall... It brought her to an overhead bridge, which was easier to climb. She heaved herself up slowly but surely. Keep trying, keep trying... Finally, with the help of good shoes and perseverance, she managed to climb up, cutting and bruising her fingers on the rough concrete. She remained poised for a second before half-jumping, half-sliding down, landing clumsily on the road.

She returned to Rue Lepic. Some businesses were now shutting down for the evening. Laurent was brushing his part of the pavement. He was wearing headphones and didn't notice her.

Karen waved at him.

He removed the headset: "Karen, what's the matter? You're bleeding!"

"I got locked inside Montmartre cemetery and climbed over a wall to get out."

"Let me get a bandage for you," he offered.

"That's alright, I'm as good as home, I'll dress it as soon

as I get back."

"Are you sure?"

"Yes."

"Well, take care now. And good evening."

"Good evening, Laurent."

"Karen!" he called."

"Yes?"

"Why were you walking around the cemetery after dark?"

"Just wandering, thinking and praying."

Laurent smiled sadly. "You suffer for Jane, don't you?"

"Yes, I do."

"I am sorry, really sorry."

"I know, I know."

Karen bought a small cake and took one bite; she'd didn't really feel like eating, but she knew she had to try. The street had lost its shine for her. Madame Dry's was freshly painted in cream and gold, and the owner talked with Monsieur Martin near his kiosk. They were both laughing.

Karen tossed the paper from her cake into a bin. Laurent had finished his clean-up, exchanged some words with Philippe at the café, then slammed his van door shut, blew the horn and drove off. He was so much a fixture on the street, yet he also seemed able to keep a restrained distance, an insider turned outsider.

Karen stepped back, "Monsieur Abu, you startled me!" For a big man, he moved very silently. "She has not come back?" His words seemed flat and dull.

"You mean, Jane? No."

"Gone, like Madame Lu..." He sounded sad and his eyes were wet with tears. Was it possible that he missed Madame Lu? Although they'd fought, they had much in common too.

Karen made an effort to reply but could only sigh.

Jumping at the first ring of her phone, Karen exclaimed,

"My bag, my bag, there it is!" She rooted inside: "Quick, quick—my phone!"

It was a blind number.

"Yes...yes, this is Karen. Cyrille! I have been looking for you. I didn't have your full name or telephone number."

But Cyrille wasn't ringing her to tell her that Jane was safe; he too had been trying to contact her.

"I don't know where she went...what happened," she told him. Her heart was leaden; she had been hoping against hope that he would know more than she did.

"I got your number from Tony. I was wondering if we might meet?"

"Sure, Cyrille," she promised, "I'll meet you tomorrow. Do you know Café Lepic? Let's meet there." Maybe meeting him might help. But that was tomorrow. Tonight she would go alone to the cemetery and try to discover if what had been burning in the pit of her stomach all day was more than just a feeling.

Karen woke up from another nightmare. Her phone alarm had been set to one o' clock, but it wasn't yet midnight. The idea was to get a little sleep to rebuild energy for her return to the cemetery. Her sleep was sporadic at best. Rested or not, it was safer to examine the mausoleum at night when she was sure that nobody was around. It would be nice to confide in someone, even Olivier, but she resisted, and instead thought of Jane's drawings and her jewelry. Her friend had been insistent on taking out a licence for her work and had put it in both of their names. Had Jane understood something instinctively, intuitively? Had something inside her been preparing for danger since Madame Lune's warnings?

Karen gave into temptation and telephoned Olivier. It was a mistake; he wasn't his usual receptive self.

"Olivier, I'm sure that Jane is dead."

"What are you talking about, Karen?"

"Jane is dead."

"We've talked about this before; your feelings can be wrong and do not constitute proof."

"It goes against Jane's character to have run away. She just wouldn't leave everything and walk out."

"Karen, what do you really know about Jane?"

"Nothing, really, I suppose."

"Listen, Karen..."

"Yes?"

"Chantal Moreau died yesterday."

"Then may God go with her and forgive her."

Karen tried once again to sleep, but Chantal's mumbling invaded her slumber. She talked incessantly about killers, about Jane. With trembling hands she took out one of Jane's drawings. They were unusual sketches. Jane had often played tricks in her sketches. One picture had several aspects and meanings. Depending on how you looked at them, you saw something different. At first glance, it was a small bush growing in the corner of a garden. Another examination revealed a few more flowers in a tiny patch of garden; and when one looked at it again, they saw it was a gravestone with overturned potted plants. Added in were flowers. Her mouth went dry: that wasn't a bunch of flowers, it was a wreath that had been bleached and yellowed by the seasons.

It was time. Karen put a powerful torch, along with a pick, a hammer and other tools that might help into a small backpack. The shop didn't lack tools because of the renovation work that Jane had been doing. 'Damn!' The plant that Laurent had given her had tumbled off the counter. She must have knocked it over when putting on her coat. Karen cupped the earth back into the pot. She would fix it properly later. She put a hand to her heart; it was thumping hard. It seemed ridiculous indeed to be going to a cemetery in the middle of the night, intent upon entering a Mausoleum, and...

28

She arrives, her torch is powerful—on and off and on again—checking. Too obvious, too obvious—not thinking of her own safety. So much grief. Any doubts Karen Moroney might have had are gone and are replaced by the certainty of finding her friend's body. There is more. She knows who he is; Karen knows Jane's killer...

Fifty yards between us—her steps draw nearer and pass me by. I follow. She goes a few more yards, stops, hesitates, and then enters the mausoleum. Her torch is on again, pointing toward the stone slab on the ground. I do not need to approach or look inside to see her struggling to move the stone. I would help, but that would be helping no one. Karen knows the killer but does not realize that she has entered his burrow.

Karen is taking the steps underground, trying to go into the crypt. She has not descended very far, just to the first level. It is far enough.

A sound, a rabbit in a snare...her cry.

"Don't cry," I say. "Jane is free and is not suffering anymore. If she has sorrow, it is for you, Karen, it is for you. Jane Moore fought to the death and is still fighting for you. He possesses nothing of Jane, for her soul was far away when he assailed her. He tried to finish his deed—an animal would not try to possess the remains of a dead body—an animal kills to eat or in self-defence. I am sorry you had to see your friend like that. You will need strong faith to understand that she is beautiful now, more beautiful than when you knew her. Jane is not what you see before you. It will take time for you, Karen Moroney, to accept this end for Jane. For beauty lives in memory, and your memory of her is in shards. It is what he would want, but he cannot and will not control your memories. Does time heal? I do not know if it does. It does what we permit it to do. I think that it helps us to change things, but pain is always pain in different guises. For if time really did heal, why in the winter of our lives do those early memories grow as vivid as if it happened yesterday? The more years we gather, the more powerful is our recollection of youth. We grow backwards, back and back and back to the beginning of our journey. We return to the origin, the soul of our existence.

You, Karen, will remember Jane in so many ways and it will shape you to the end of your days. Make that shape pretty, make it unique, have the most special life you can. It will be your choice; it will be what you make of it.

What is that? Who is that? Is it he? The monster has risen out of the ground from his hidden catacomb.

'Are you prepared, Madame Lune? Will Karen Moroney have a memory to keep and protect?

I put my hand to my heart to calm it and I become a tomb among tombs. Oh, he is sure of himself. Only the scurrying insects know him: he creeps, he crawls, and he slithers toward me. The monster has become a demon. The last of what made him human has fled and shelters in horror in the shade. Should I try to take him now? Should I wait? I stop thinking and let pure instinct take over.

I listen for every blade of grass that sticks to his soles, every grain of dust that disintegrates under his step. A robin would make more noise than he makes.

Run, Karen Moroney, run now, while you still have a chance to escape. Leave this battleground to me and him, let me do my work. But you cannot hear my thoughts. Should I shout out? Is this the moment for me to move? Or should I wait? If I act too soon, I may fail. I am not young and swift; but I can be still and invisible and can jump from this mold of stillness and catch him. But when? When he tries to take her? I will have to take the risk that he will not kill her immediately, that he will want to draw out his pleasure. I do not know how Karen will react. Will she try to run? Will something alert her? Will he take her down? It all passes through my mind in a second. I give myself over to instinct, totally and fully, stop trying to think, to guess and to predict. I have one more asset and it is the most important: I want to kill. At this moment, I want his life more than he wants hers. He wants her soul, her memory and her memories of Jane Moore. For he chose Jane, not Karen, and wants revenge for what Jane robbed him of. Death will just be a consequence. For me, death, his death, is my primary purpose. I have come here to kill him, intentionally kill him, to wipe his smear from the place, clear him off this earth. I refuse to think of anything else. I do not want to hear of God, or forgiveness, or of the world after. How can I ask God to aid me? I am planning to take a life. The true path to salvation does not allow that. God, tell me, what you would do. Would you let him continue to take lives? If that is your purpose, I cannot understand it. If that is the way others have to learn in the contorted plan of your universe, then that is not a religion or belief that I can adhere to. If that is your plan, then failure will be mine tonight, for God is all-powerful and I am nothing. But my universe and that of such a God are different. Mine is that of animals and nature. They are closer to the freedom of the spirit. I am seeking that spirit. That is my God, and where I want to return to—what I had before being trapped inside this body and this mind. If that is the true God, then I have a fair chance tonight. If I succeed, it will bring no joy, but it will bring no guilt either. Madame Lune's destiny is in her own hands.

The eyes of nature and its creatures watch the tomb. I am one of them, at one with them. I do not move a hand, but I am conscious of my coat, Pierre's magic coat. I cannot afford to make a mistake.

Karen has come back above ground, needing air and to make sense of what she has seen. Aware of nothing else except Jane's mutilated body, that image will stay with her for life. But it is no image; it is real, it is death. I cannot explain to her that it is not Jane Moore she sees—it is what *was* Jane Moore, a girl that brightened this world. But Jane is in a different place and is something more, so much more.

A light has dimmed inside you, Karen Moroney, like a fading star that winks no more. It is extinguished forever. For some, a lifetime could not do that. You will never find that star again—not in this life. I am sorry for that, for that loss of innocence and hope. Nobody deserves to have that taken from them. You do not know what to do. Should you call someone? Should you run? Or should you wait until the light of morning tells you what you already know? That Jane is dead, as dead as one can ever be—Jane is dead.

You will do none of those things, for he is behind you. It is too late to run or to hide. All you can do is fight.

Can you fight too, Karen? Can you fight as your friend did? Turn, turn, he is coming.

She turns, but it is too late. No time to scream, only to choke a muffled whimper. Just as I feared, he is fast, faster than I could have imagined. She cannot escape now. I am poised; I am ready...

But Karen has hidden strength and struggles. Maybe Jane is with her. This time she screams: it is not loud, but it is a scream. He is furious and tightens his hands around her neck, clamping her to him. She jerks away and he strikes her once, twice, three times. She falls. Her head hits stone and she fights no more.

He stands over her, stiff and tense. Has he done too much? He puts his hand on her neck to check, then relaxes; she lives and will live long enough for his revenge. With ease, he carries her limp body into the crypt of the mausoleum.

I draw closer. He uses no light, does not need a torch. I cannot see, but I know what he is doing. There are ropes and cords to bind her like a mummy. This one will not escape him; he will have his revenge and he will kill her slowly. He wants to hear her beg for her life. He must hear her cry...

But Karen is still unconscious so he must wait. His lungs rasp; the struggle has cost him, but not enough. His veins are filled with something other than blood: anticipation; excitement. It is for these moments that the monster lives. This is the sustenance from which he draws life.

He has decided to leave her there...for a while. How long? He pulls back the stone and flashes his lamp just once round the tomb. There is time, sweet time. He can come back later—even tomorrow—to take slow pleasure in every agonizing second of her end. He will glory in that. If it were to be that way, then I could leave this earth without the stain of murder on my hands. If that were his choice, I would have time to save her. But I know that he cannot go home tonight because tomorrow will be too late. He picks up her tools and wraps them in a cloth. He stoops again and grabs a bundle. He has found sketches in her bag. He looks at them, tears them up and piles everything into a plastic bag. His mind has changed...

The monster comes outside. I am layered against the side wall. His rancor grows and grows because his preferred plan is ruined. Those pictures brought her here, and they could bring someone else here. He doesn't know what Karen has told others, or in whom she has confided. But he is now sure that before dawn he must take her.

He goes back into the mausoleum and prepares to descend into the crypt.

It is now or never. My hand moves carefully until the weapon is in my palm.

I spring! I have the power of the sea and waves behind me. The blade flashes. The waiting is over.

As he turns, I go for his heart.

But he is too fast and jerks aside as the blade goes into his shoulder. It is the wrong place, not hard or deep enough. I push harder and he roars like a wild beast and swings back on me, throwing me outside the gate. He punches with his fist and makes contact with my left cheek. His other hand follows it to my chin.

I am slammed against the wall and stunned; the knife slips from my hand. A beast comes into me. It fills my body with hate, and that hate gives me strength. The monster goes for the knife on the ground.

I do not try to retrieve it, but pull another knife from my coat pocket and throw my body at him with all my force. The blade catches him on the hand, but something pierces my skin. I feel the tip of steel as he stabs at my stomach. The pain does not last long, I am beyond feeling.

It will be a battle between a giant and a mouse, for he has ten, twenty, a hundred times my strength. But he is injured; I have hurt him badly. It makes his blood boil, though it has also weakened him and his movements are more sluggish. His face is outlined by the light of the torch that has been cast aside. He kicks the torch violently and the light goes out. Darkness will be our witness.

But night is my friend too. He has no idea about me, but I know everything about him. I know he is incensed, and that inhibits his judgment. I go for him again. He sees the knife in my right hand and brings my own knife down on me. The edge lances my thigh.

My hand holds another dagger. I go for his eyes and he

bellows, howls, bawls, then lunges at me. This is my chance to jump on him while his vision is blurred by the blood flowing down his face. My thoughts have become wicked and foul: Kill him! Kill him! Do it now!

My legs feel like they are being ripped from my body, shredded and stinging from the wounds the knife has inflicted. All pain is to be refused, ignored, even if his dagger peels every scale off my old skin. Skinned alive, I will continue to fight and will keep fighting until his life is mine.

We are both on the ground; knives are everywhere. But there are two more in my hands, drawn from my coat. Again and again and again those blades plunge into him and as often, my own flesh is gauged. All caution has left me. He must be sliced to the ground if it is with the last of my strength and the last drop of my blood. He comes back at me like a fiend; evil has many lives and many ways to survive. My brain is sludge and consciousness is slipping away. My lungs are outside my body. Do I have one more blow in me?

He rises again and I try to reach for what is left inside me. But nothing responds; my limbs will not obey, my veins empty...

He charges toward me: my fingers, hands and arms are lifeless and refuse to reach for the last dagger. Is all lost?

Suddenly, something skids between the monster and me. Pebbles shower us, we are not alone. A creature shuttles past with a shriek as more pebbles and stones rain down, but most fall upon the monster. He curses as a larger stone hits his head.

It is enough; my fingers finally respond and find their way inside a pocket. They curl around the handle of the last dagger.

The creature that saved me flees; the boy-thief has been my savior, and what happens now is in the hands of fate. I let the dagger fly, and with it the last chance.

It sails through the air...

The monster has regained his focus and is coming, coming, coming...

The knife is carried by a mighty energy that is not mine and lands in his chest. This time his body falls, wrenching in spasms. I watch until it twitches no more.

What remains of me wants to turn over and die here. But that is not my will. This is not where Madame Lune will be found; and Nora Sheehy will never be found.

I use the wall as a lever but cannot stand; there is no more strength, and nothing more to be done. I can only hope that it is enough, that Karen Moroney is alive in the crypt and that my letters will do the rest. I hope too that the monster is dead in body, mind and spirit. God, I ask you: If you have been by my side, for I believe that that last dagger was guided by your hand, then let Karen Moroney wake in the morning, and let the picture here be what I see now: that the monster no longer lives!

They will read my poor maps, try to understand my incoherent messages. Be merciful, please; do not judge the hand that could not write, the eyes that could not read, and the tongue that stammered. Understand that I did my best.

Get up, get up, you cannot stay here. Hurry, Nora! You have to be in time for the tide.

I let my body roll and slide—there is no other way to go forward. My fingers tear at the earth—a serpent going through grass, over gravel and stones. I have killed and do not regret it. I would do it again and again to him or to others like him. I must get back to my tomb—the one that has been chosen. Like a cuckoo, I have borrowed another's nest. Pain consumes me and my blood is spouting freely. My wish is that they will never look for me, and if they do, that they will never find me.

I do not know how long I have been crawling; consciousness has left me several times. Something moves; it is the stirring of a bird on the branch of a tree. There is a stiff breeze—it wakes me. My body is bloodless; my limbs are torn from me. A thunderstorm is coming; I have to keep going.

It is too hard. I cannot make it; time to give up. The rain pelts down on me forcing my eye lids shut. I let everything go and trust in Something Greater.

There is the cottage by the sea. I always thought that here is where my days would end, that I would go back one more time, that my tongue would taste the rain and it would be different, that it would be as it tasted in my happiest moments, when playing amidst nature. It would be winter and the waves would crash off the rocks, and the sea spray would climb so high that it would caress the wings of the soaring birds. The foam would be softer than the bed of suds that glistened on the calloused skin of my grandmother's hands as she washed and scrubbed. I would be far from the crowded streets of Paris, an Irish girl with an Irish future before her. And my grandmother would be there. She would call to me and I would go willingly and gently, as I believe my mother did. We would meet at that moment, that split second when the tide turns.

And Mother, what would you have become if given half a chance? You would have done well, very well. You would have been a good person with a good mind. Even in your simple state, you rose above and never made an angry gesture. Your eyes never showed a hateful thought. I smell the pages of that old Bible you loved. You looked at the pictures and saw something that your child could never see. If I could go back again, Mother, it would be to tell you but one thing, that I loved you. I did not know it then, but I know it now. It is not the mother in you that I loved, for you could never have been a mother; but I loved that in that feeble mind you were given, you could not bear to see others suffer; I loved the kindness of your spirit.

Is this it then, my cold grave? It is a lonely place. I grasp at grit and roots, scrape at marble, but cannot find home. I have been a watcher all my life. Is there somebody out there to watch over me?

A creature breathes on my neck. Is it a cat, drawn by the scent of death? It is a bird that has come to feed on my blood. It takes my hand; my boy-thief has not deserted me.

He supports me; it is not difficult to carry a feather. He does not speak but listens as I try to tell him where to take me—across the cemetery.

Somehow we reach my tomb. He helps me to lie down on the stone slab. I direct him to open my coat and to take out the bundle of notes hidden inside. That is a poor gift, but money is money, and a boy has to eat. I speak to him but do not know if he understands: "Spend it wisely," I whisper, "and find a way to steal no more."

He bends over me and touches my face. My blood is on his fingertips. He looks at it and at me, and then turns and runs.

The last steps are mine to take alone. I let the stone slab fall into place, leaving me in darkness. My body rolls and rolls along the burrow underground until no further effort is needed.

My eyes are open, but I am elsewhere, in a place where a little girl is running away from the tide. She runs and runs, faster and faster. It has been a game all my life. The tide has never caught me, yet. But this time is different; the girl stops running and turns to wait for the sea.

Ebb and flow, ebb and flow
Body and soul are ready to go
I bow to greater—to he who is my creator
Ebb and flow, ebb and flow
The moon has risen—my time's been given
Ebb and flow, ebb and flow
Now the tide is coming, but I'm not running
For I shall run no more

Look at the sky overhead. Watch the seabird swoop and glide, plummeting into the foam. This is the day I have longed for, the day I have been waiting for. I will leave behind unfinished work, but work nevertheless. There are those that are better than I to finish it.

I am tired of watching, and weary of what my eyes have seen. I will watch no more. I smile as I feel the water at my feet; it ebbs and flows. It rises and makes me dizzy. It is to my ankles, my knees, and my waist. I am floating. Everything is light and the moon beams caress my face. The tide has turned; it is carrying me out, and I am not alone.

EPILOGUE

Karen stood back to admire the stonework on the cottage that her father and brothers had helped to restore. The cottage was rustic on the outside, and though modern and practical inside, they had managed to retain the simplicity and character of the original. It had been very therapeutic work; she loved the feel of the material under her hands. She rested her palm on one of the gray stones and felt a strange tingling sensation on her arm; the old walls, steeped in memories of the people who had gone before, had a special energy. She had learned bits and pieces from her father, but the laboring family that had lived there was long gone by the time he was born. Her grandfather had not spoken much about them except to say that they were good people.

In Karen's vision, this cottage would be the cornerstone of what she and Jane had started together: The Glass Corner. The idea was to have an arts and crafts center and workshop that would allow local artists to showcase their works; on the other hand, it would operate as a shop selling and marketing both directly and online. The first step would be to expose Jane's work. The seaside village of Ballybunion and surrounding communities were very excited about it. It was a simple idea, but the early signs were good.

Still, Ballybunion was a long way from Paris and Rue Lepic. It wouldn't be easy to shut out the terror of coming face to face with Jane's killer and the two days spent in the underground crypt in Montmartre Cemetery. Jane had never been totally at ease with him. If only... No, there was no point wishing; things were always clearer with hindsight. The media had been full of the gruesome details. She had avoided reading and hearing most of them. But some headlines stayed with her:

LOCAL FLOWER SELLER TURNED SERIAL KILLER

She didn't want to think about what had driven Laurent Lebois to carry out such horrendous deeds.

Karen turned to look toward the trees and glimpsed the foam of the waves beyond. Her life would be here, at least for a while. Olivier had informed her that he'd rented a flat in the Versailles district. Good luck to him. She didn't imagine they would have much reason to stay in contact in the future; there was little binding them together. He'd told her that the entire street was in shock. She'd received dozens of cards and...flowers.

The police had been unable to trace the person that had killed Laurent Lebois. Karen had thought a lot about that and the mysterious individual that had sent the strange sketches and maps leading to the different addresses where the flower seller's victims lay. With those maps they had uncovered all his victims. She'd wondered about Madame Lune and where she had gone, and if the medium had been behind the letters. However, the police had been unable to link the letters to anyone, and thus far had not discovered the identity of the other person in the cemetery. There had been a storm that night and it had poured rain for days afterwards making forensic investigation even more difficult. Perhaps one day they would learn the truth. But the medium had tried to warn them several times and they hadn't listened. How had she known? Had she really foreseen it? Why hadn't they believed her? And yet Jane had had a sense of her own morality; it had probably come from her childhood and upbringing. Her wishes had been clearly spelled out in her will. Some of her ashes were to be kept in Paris, her city of dreams. Jane had loved Montmartre and Sacre Coeur, and that had been her place of choice. Karen was grateful to Olivier and his parents for wielding their influence to gain permission for Jane's ashes to be put in a special place in the cemetery. She had requested that the rest of her ashes be tossed into the Atlantic near Karen's family home. And that's what Karen had done, respecting her instructions to do so without ceremony.

Was that the end of Jane, ashes in the earth and in the sea? She had never given much thought to what happened after death, and only paid lip service to the rituals of her Catholic upbringing; but now she would give anything to know if Jane had found peace. She had imagined seeing her inside the Glass Corner on Rue Lepic. The crystal earrings, Jane's gift to her, were warm against her cheeks. Maybe Jane had reached out to her and was close now. Maybe there was a life beyond.

Karen closed the cottage gate and made her way through the grove of trees toward the cliffs. She paused in a glade which formed a nearly perfect circle and inhaled the lovely scent of woodbine, and thought how lucky she was to be alive. One could meditate here; the aroma was so powerful that it almost sedated. The horror of what had happened had changed her in many ways, but since returning to Ireland, she now saw things with new eyes. Her senses were more alive to the sights, sounds and smells of nature. She took a cutting of the fragrant pink vine and decided it would make the perfect climber for the cottage gable.

She walked on until the sea was laid out before her. Standing at the edge of the cliff, she watched birds swoop and glide and plummet. The sky turned red as the sun sank toward the aquatic horizon Somebody was on the beach. Karen squinted to see—yes, it was possible to make out a child running across the sand. Laughter reached her ears. She looked around for an adult; surely the child wasn't alone. With the tide coming in it would not be safe. She found a rough pathway that led down to that part of the beach.

Once on the sand, she went to where she had seen the child. A little girl was paddling in the shallow water. Karen ran toward her, but the girl seemed to melt into the sea foam. Karen drew a startled breath.

"Behind you," a voice spoke in her head.

At first Karen saw nothing; but then her attention was drawn to crescent outlines in the sand. She heard laughter once more and saw the little girl again, this time further immersed in the incoming water.

"The tide is coming in!" Karen shouted. "Let me take you home."

"I am home," the voice reassured, "and Jane is home, too."

"Jane? Is she happy?"

"Happy and free..."

"How can this be happening?"

"The gift is within each of us," the voice confirmed.

Karen laughed uncontrollably as she scrambled up the path to retreat from the incoming tide. She laughed as a final release, expelling fear and doubt and grief, and sanctifying her ancestral home and her newfound insight. She screeched like a banshee and crooned like a lunatic. She knew that if she ever told anyone of this experience they would not only disbelieve her, but probably think her mad. But if this feeling was madness, then the entire world was inside out.

She removed one of the earrings that Jane had given her and watched it sparkle in the last rays of the twilight. Her ears tuned again to the water lapping against the rocks. The fluid motion soothed her spirit as it had never before been soothed; it was a rhythm which, she now knew, would remain with her for eternity.

AUTHOR'S NOTE

I am lucky to have very special people in my life who have shaped me as a person and writer.

A warm thank you to David A. Ross, Editor and Publisher, for taking a chance on me and for skillfully steering the boat.

An equally warm thanks to Kelly Huddleston for providing excellent support on all fronts.

Sometimes words just don't measure up. Huguette Jarrosson has been a well of wisdom, tirelessly guiding me; an inspirational role model of immense courage and intelligence. Time is precious and what you have given will always be treasured.

Aileen has egged me on with unconditional love; one of the first to grapple with everything I've written and ever willing to offer thoughtful critiques. To have a sister who is also a friend is fortunate—having someone just like you is priceless.

I would like to express gratitude to all my family and relatives, especially my brother, Willie Joe, his wife, Eileen, and my nieces, Christina, Lisa, and Katie. The paths we have walked together have been rich in experience.

Majella has been a loyal and steadfast friend, uncomplainingly clocking up the hours, tidying my fledgling clumsy efforts. In her quiet and unassuming way, she has been a rock.

There is a particular set of friends who have been around me forever. Their generosity, humor, and folie have shored me up in good times and bad. I could fill pages with accolades, but alas must restrict my eulogy to names: Eilis, Joan, Breda, Timmy, Mary K., Kevin and Anne, Mary F., Maggie, Ségolène, Eddie and Triona.

Teaching has opened doors to many lives and experiences.

Merci mille fois, François Mauduit for sharing your culture and sagesse. It has meant a lot to have someone with an outsider's eye read my labors, listen and hearten.

Sincere thanks to Marie-Paule Le Corvec for your constant encouragement.

There are others no less important in lending an ear and giving a hand: Agnes, Carmela, Sylvie, Christine L., Christèle, Inès...

But I must return to my beginnings and acknowledge the two people to whom I owe everything. Although both have passed on, my father and mother have never left my side. They were my first teachers and story book—and the best. From my parents I learnt what has been the driving force behind all my dreams: be yourself—try—stay yourself—and try again.

42612731R00155

Made in the USA
Charleston, SC
02 June 2015